JAVANNA

Big Sky Montana 1

Robert Vaughan

Javanna
Robert Vaughan
Paperback Edition

CKN Christian Publishing
An Imprint of Wolfpack Publishing
6032 Wheat Penny Avenue
Las Vegas, NV 89122

Copyright © 2020

Paperback ISBN: 978-1-64734-230-2
Ebook ISBN: 978-1-64734-229-6
Library of Congress Control Number: 2020949646

JAVANNA

JAVANNA

Dear Reader,

Those of you who are familiar with my work know that I primarily write Westerns, war stories and adventure books. But I'm putting on a different hat for this book. I have teamed up with Sara Luck, a writer who has been a close friend of mine for over 45 years.

In this year of turmoil, many of us have turned back to our faith. *Javanna* is an inspirational contemporary family saga that shines a light on the anxieties we have faced in this tumultuous year.

I hope you enjoy meeting Javanna and Luke as they return to Crooked Creek Ranch near White Sulphur Springs, Montana.

Thank you,
Robert Vaughan

Chapter One

Javanna Caldwell had taken her dog on a longer walk than normal this evening, because she had a lot on her mind. Usually, she and her neighbor had a standing "date" to walk their dogs together at ten o'clock, but she went out earlier tonight. She was worried. Worried about a lot of things.

The number one thing that concerned her was her job. She was an account manager for Chicago Digital Media Incorporated, but the problem was she had concentrated on one sector for the advertising agency, and that was up scaled restaurants all over the city. It had been her segment that had suffered the most in the COVID 19 pandemic. Of the thirty-five accounts that Javanna serviced, twenty-seven had suspended their advertising campaigns. While she had a comfortable base salary, it was her commissions that provided the bulk of her income.

Three years ago, following the death of her husband, Javanna had sold their condo in Lincoln Square, and moved into an apartment in the Gold

Coast area. She loved living in her building on Oak Street. It was a little more than a mile to her office in the Prudential building and it had unlimited restaurants, shopping boutiques, and places to walk Riley. Her neighbor, Jay Butler, worked in the AON building, and the two of them walked to work together every morning, even in the coldest weather.

Javanna and Riley had walked over to the 875 North Michigan Avenue Building, the name change the product of some advertising guru, Javanna was sure. This building had been the Hancock Building since its construction in the sixties, and for most Chicagoans, it was still the Hancock Building. It had been a good walk for both her and her dog.

When she reached her street on the way back, she stopped. There was a disturbance ahead, and though she had never been afraid to walk in her neighborhood, she was rattled to see so many people congregating. She had been watching television and she was aware that there were demonstrations, or riots, as some people were calling them, in cities such as Minneapolis, Seattle, Atlanta, New York, and who knew how many other cities. But the downtown area of Chicago had not been a target.

She moved as cautiously as she could, trying to avoid the crowd, but she couldn't; they were between her and her apartment. At first she couldn't understand what they were chanting, but as she came closer, she heard:

"NO JUSTICE, NO PEACE! NO JUSTICE, NO PEACE! SAY HIS NAME!"

She heard the crash of glass, and knew that the front window of a nearby store, the Baroness Lucile Boutique, had been stormed.

"WE GOIN' SHOPPIN'!" somebody shouted.

It wasn't until then, when she looked down Michigan Avenue, that she saw two cars burning. The cars were stopped in the middle of the street.

Where were the police?

She wasn't sure how many people were running, but she would guess there were more than a hundred.

She heard another crashing window.

"SHOE SALE!" someone shouted.

This was the Elite Feet.

Javanna was frightened, but at the same time, she couldn't stop watching the mayhem that was taking place right in front of her. Riley, sensing something unusual, started to bark. When she did, she drew attention to Javanna, and two people advanced toward her.

"Hey, you, where you think you goin'?" someone shouted.

Javanna didn't answer. She continued to walk ahead, avoiding making any eye contact.

"Give us the dog," someone shouted at her. "Give us that barkin' dog." They added expletives that Javanna had heard before, but those words were certainly not ones that she, or the people she associated with, used. She was surprised when she noticed that the most aggressive people were female, although there was certainly a mix of both genders and races.

Fortunately for Riley and Javanna, the approaching crowd turned their attention to a fire, not fifteen feet in front of her. It was with horror that she realized an American flag had been set ablaze.

A young girl, who looked to be in her teens, was doing a dance around the burning flag. She had a bullhorn and she was leading several others in a chant, "Death to America."

At that moment, Javanna saw the lights and heard the sirens of four approaching police cars. Two cars stopped right in front of her. There were two policemen in each car, and wearing helmets and flak jackets they got out and moved toward the flag burners.

From somewhere, frozen water bottles were thrown toward the police, one coming so close to Javanna that she had to duck. She picked up Riley and cradled her in her arms as the dog began to tremble.

One of the policemen looked over and saw Javanna standing there, with the little dog in her arms.

"Miss, are you part of this," the policeman called.

"No, sir, I had taken my dog out, and I was coming home when I saw..." she paused for a moment, then took in the scene with a wave of her hand.

"Where do you live?" the policeman asked.

"There," Javanna said, pointing. "That burning flag is right in front of my building."

The policeman who had been talking to Javanna, looked at the cop next to him. "Mack, let's get this lady home."

With one policeman on either side of her, Javanna was escorted toward her building.

"Lookie here, there's a woman, two pigs, and a dog," someone shouted, and those within earshot laughed.

One of the protesters came toward them, with

his right arm stretched toward her, as if he was going to grab either Riley, or her.

"Come on, Lady, you don't wanna be with no cops now, do ya?"

"Back off," Mack warned.

"And what are you gonna do to me if I don't?" the protestor challenged. "Shoot me?"

"Back off!" Mack warned again, and as the protestor continued toward them, Mack brought his nightstick down, sharply on the man's hand.

The man shouted a string of profanities and then, "Did anybody get that? Police brutality!"

Javanna and the two policemen with her were then surrounded by at least two dozen people as they made their way to her building.

"Is this it?" the policeman said when they reached the double glass doors of Forty East Oak.

The doorman, seeing the two policemen, and recognizing Javanna, hurried to unlock the door.

"Javanna, what are you doing out on a night like this? Get in here, quick," he said anxiously

Javanna took a deep breath when she stepped through the door. "You don't know how glad I am to be here, George," and turning to the two policemen who had escorted her, she continued. "I can't thank you enough for coming to my rescue. I sincerely believe you were a lifesaver, and I mean that literally."

"I have a word of advice for you," the policeman said. "Don't take your dog out again—at least not while all this is going on."

"Sir, you don't have to worry about that." Javanna chuckled but to her own ears, it was the sound of a frightened child.

"And as for you, I believe she called you George, do you have any reinforcements for these doors? When these thugs get wound up, nothing is safe."

"Yes, sir, officer," the doorman said. "I'll put in a call to our security this very minute. How long do you think this will go on?"

"Your guess is as good as mine," the policeman said as he turned to go. "Look at Seattle. They've had a bloody encampment set up right in front of a police precinct."

Javanna and George watched through the door until the two men were reunited with the other policemen.

"You couldn't pay me enough to be a cop right now," George said. "Pray that those men get home to their families this night."

Not commenting, Javanna let Riley down, and moved toward the elevator. "What are we going to do now, old girl?"

"If I were you, I'd take her up on the sunroof for a few days," George said. "Housekeeping won't like it, but I wouldn't risk going out in this for awhile."

"Thanks, George," Javanna said as she stepped into the elevator, and pushed the button for the tenth floor.

She could see and hear the protestors who were still shouting out front. As the door closed, there was blessed silence. Not until then, did she take off her mask and put her cocker spaniel on the floor.

Once she was safety inside her apartment, Javanna turned on the local tv broadcast to see if there was any coverage of what was going on outside her building.

"There is a disturbing trend to all of this," the

commentator said. "The peaceful protestors are being invaded by, what some are calling anarchists. They have no boundaries, as evidenced by what is happening on the streets of Chicago at this very moment. So far, it seems to be contained to a rather limited area centering in the lower reaches of the Gold Coast."

"Let us hope that the police can hold these rioters, to that very limited area," the guest said. "At this point, there is only one answer. We must turn to God."

"Turn to God? There is no God," Javanna said. "If there really was a benevolent God, do you think He would allow bad things to happen?"

Javanna pressed the remote and ended the broadcast. She didn't need to be told what was happening in "a rather limited area" as the broadcaster had said. She had seen what was happening on the streets. There was no way the police were going to be able to contain this riot. She dreaded waking up in the morning.

Javanna realized she hadn't eaten, and going to the refrigerator, she searched for something to eat. She found a half-eaten box of sweet and sour pork that she had ordered a couple days ago.

"Baby dog," she said. "I think I may have made a mistake by not stocking up on more groceries, but you know what I was trying to do?" She talked to the little blond dog just like she was a person. "You know I was just doing my part—if any restaurant had takeout, I was determined to give them my business. You know they might want to advertise some day."

She walked over to the sofa and brought her legs up under her, while she expertly used chopsticks to eat the last little grain of rice that was left in the box.

Riley made a little whining sound, then barked as he pawed the leash Javanna had left on the coffee table.

"What is it with you, dog? Didn't you hear the policeman say we can't go out again?"

The dog began to bark more incessantly.

"All right, all right. You're not going to like this, but it's up to the sundeck with you, and you know you're going to have to share that little spot of grass with every dog in this building."

Javanna connected the leash and walked to the elevator, this time going up.

When the elevator opened onto the sundeck, it was just as George had suggested. At least a dozen other residents with their dogs were gathered on the roof. Javanna saw Jay Butler and she moved toward him.

"Javanna," Jay said, "I thought you'd be up here sooner or later. I guess we missed our date tonight." He was holding his Maltese dog named Lucky.

"You missed our date. Riley and I kept it."

"You don't mean to tell me you went out in this?"

"I did."

"Well you may be the biggest fool I've ever met. Have you seen what's happening?"

"I was in it, Jay, that's what I'm telling you." She joined him by the half wall that surrounded the roof.

"I'll bet it wasn't this bad," he said.

What Javanna saw was unbelievable. Looking

down Michigan Avenue, it was like a war zone. There were several cars on fire, and people were running in and out of some of the most iconic stores on the Magnificent Mile. Gucci's was breached, as was Bloomingdale's, Coach, Macy's, Nieman Marcus, Foot Locker, even the Potbelly Sandwich Shop, and those were the only ones she knew for sure.

"It looks like Armageddon," Jay said. "How is all this going to end?"

Far into the night, Javanna, Jay and several of the other residents, stood mesmerized by what they were watching. Finally the dogs began to get restless, and Jay suggested Javanna come to his place for a late, late night snack.

"What have you got?" Javanna asked, her stomach reminding her of her scant dinner that she had eaten, now some four or five hours ago.

"Let's just see," Jay said. "I think I can rustle up some Chinese food."

Javanna laughed. "Left over takeout, right?"

"Yes, but I make it better. I turn it into refried rice."

"Sounds good, to me. What time?"

"How about half an hour," he said, as he withdrew a small bag and picked up a little pile Lucky had deposited.

Jay was a very pleasant young man, and young was the operative word. He was twelve years younger than Javanna, and because they saw one another twice a day, when they walked to work together and when they walked the dogs, she felt very comfortable with him.

Javanna's work had kept her from making friends except for the people she worked with, and they were business associates, more than friends. Jay was her friend. Perhaps because of the age difference, she looked at him as a younger brother, and she was sure he looked at her as an older sister. The relationship worked well for both of them.

Half an hour later, Javanna knocked on Jay's door, and he opened it immediately.

"Oh, I can smell it," she said. "It smells so good."

"Yes, I make vedy, vedy good flied lice," Jay said, with what he thought would be a Chinese accent.

Javanna saw the table set.

"What kind of Chinese Restaurant is this, with no chopsticks?" she teased.

"For the lady," Jay said, presenting a set of chopsticks.

Chapter Two

Natchitoches, Louisiana:

Luke Bryant stepped out onto the balcony of the condo he had rented for the duration of the filming of *But for the Grace of God*. He ran his hand through his hair, as he looked up and down Main Street, taking in the Cane River that in reality was an oxbow lake. This setting was perfect. So why were there so many obstacles?

More than most locations where LTN Productions had filmed, the city of Natchitoches knew what to expect from a film crew. The town, established in 1819, had been the setting for close to twenty film productions over the last fifty years, the most famous being *Steel Magnolias*, but for him one permit after another had been pulled. LTN which stood for Love Thy Neighbor was not feeling much love about now.

And he could only blame himself for the problems. He had been too absorbed in his own personal problems, and he had delegated too much responsibility to Yancy Drum, his entertainment lawyer.

Since moving to Louisiana in 2002, Luke had been involved in fifteen films, nine while he worked with River Arts, and six for his own company. Every novice producer knew the first order of business was to form an LLC for each individual film. But Yancy had failed to file the proper paperwork. Now Luke was embroiled in a potential lawsuit with the city over damages, they were saying his crew had caused. It seemed that just about every conceivable site he had selected was part of the National Historic Landmark District, and if one little thing was disturbed, that was a problem.

"Meat pies are here," Maya Broussard called as she came into the condo. "You can't believe how many cars were waiting at Lasyone's. I was in line for at least forty-five minutes."

"That's what happens when you have a good product," Luke said as he came in off the porch. "Did you happen to run into Evan anywhere? Did he get permission to go back out to the Melrose Plantation?"

"I think he went to city hall," Maya said. "I did go by the post office, and you got something I think you will enjoy reading." She tossed Luke a copy of Variety Magazine. "Look on page seventeen."

Luke grabbed a meat pie off the counter and took a seat around the table. He flipped open the magazine and read the announcement that LTN Incorporated, a New Orleans based company, had started principal photography, on *But for the Grace of God*. The last paragraph of the article caused Luke to smile.

The films produced by LTN skillfully weave the faith content into strong story lines, portrayed by excellent actors, are written and produced so well that one can be entertained as well as inspired. Kudos to Luke Bryant.

"Well, that was nice," he said.

"You might want to thumb through the pages," his administrative assistant said. "There's another tidbit you might find interesting."

It didn't take long to find what Maya was referencing. There was a story about the latest release of the Magnum Pictures' production of The Long Journey. One part of the story, in particular, caught Luke's attention.

Sultry, sensuous Tia Brown doesn't just portray the troubled lead character, Madeleine King, she lives the part. A beautiful woman, Miss Brown, no doubt, generates fantasies in men from sixteen to sixty.

Luke made no comment, as Maya watched his reaction.

"I'm sorry, Luke, I shouldn't have told you."

"That's all right, Maya. You think I wouldn't have seen it anyway?"

"I know, but with all the problems we're having with this shoot, I can't help but wonder if everything would be better if Tia was here."

Luke laughed. "The one I really wished would have still been involved would be her dad. If Elgin was still our lawyer, we'd never be in the mess we're in now."

Tia and Luke had met when he was still at River Arts. She had a bit part in one of the productions where he had worked up to being an assistant director. They began dating, and over time, Tia took him home to meet her parents, Elgin and Virginia Brown. Elgin was a prominent lawyer in New Orleans, but as they say in the South, he came from "old money".

After a month or two, Elgin contacted Luke and asked him to come to his office.

"Do you think Tia has talent?" he had asked.

"She does, sir. She is a beautiful woman, but beyond that she has the potential to be a big star. She can act."

"Then how about setting you up with a company of your own?"

Luke remembered that conversation as if it had happened yesterday, but it was twelve years ago.

Love Thy Neighbor, or LTN, was incorporated, with Elgin Brown providing the lion's share of the financing behind the production company. Luke had wanted him to be his full partner, but to Elgin's credit, he had declined. He had said he didn't think his name on a faith based outfit would lend much credibility.

Luke began putting his company together and within a year, he was in production of a picture, with Tia as his star.

Before the picture was released, Tia and Luke were married in a very quiet ceremony, much to the dismay of Tia's mother.

The first picture made a substantial amount of money, and when Luke tried to pay back the money Elgin had invested, he said he didn't want it. He wanted his little girl to be happy.

And so she was. They bought a house in the Garden District in New Orleans, and the next four films, Luke produced all starred Tia Brown. In fact, he referred to her as "the franchise".

One film, The Angel of Bourbon Street, proved to be too successful. It won the coveted Inspired Faith Award and was played in theaters and other major outlets like Amazon Prime and Netflix.

But the movie that had been the highlight of Luke's career was the cause of a lowlight in Luke's personal life. As a result of her role in the award winning movie, Tia's acting ability had come to the attention of a major Hollywood production company and Tia was approached to come to Hollywood. She had been told that on the screen she emitted a magnetism that drew all eyes to her. Because of her beauty and talent, one could only say she had charisma.

At first Tia had hesitated, but as Magnum Pictures kept upping the ante, there came a time when she felt she couldn't refuse the offer.

"What do you want, Tia?"

"I think I have to take this opportunity. It's what I've wanted my whole life."

"And what about LTN? What do we do with it?"

"It's yours, Luke. I don't want any part of it."

"What do you mean, you don't want any part of it? LTN is a success because of you. You can't just walk away from what we've built together. If you stay in New Orleans, you can go anywhere and work. Look at Sandra Bullock. She lives within three blocks of us, and being in New Orleans certainly hasn't affected her career."

"Luke, I need to be in Hollywood...and I need to be alone."

For the next few weeks, nothing changed, and Luke had thought Tia had changed her mind. They did the things they always had done together and there was no more talk of going to Hollywood.

Luke had been away for a couple of days scouting out locations for a new project.

"Tia, I've found the place," he called. "It's in Natchitoches, you know where Steel Magnolias was filmed, and you're going to love it."

He got no reply.

"Tia?" he called again, still without a response.

As Luke wandered around the house, he suddenly got a feeling of emptiness. Then, opening the closet, he saw that all of Tia's clothes were gone. That was when he saw the note on the dresser.

Dear Luke,

This is the hardest note I've ever written in my life. I told you that I want to go to Hollywood. I would never dream of asking you to give up what you have, just to satisfy me. I know also, that I owe my career to you and I will always be grateful. But Luke, if we are honest with one another, we both have to admit that we have been drifting apart. I think it best that I have Daddy arrange a divorce for us.

I will always love you.

Reluctantly, sadly, Luke had granted her the divorce without contesting it.

Luke tossed the magazine aside, and shook his head to clear it.

"Where's the script?" Luke asked. "I need to see what we'll be doing for tomorrow—that is if we get to shoot anything."

Maya brought Luke the script and a cup of coffee, setting both down on the table.

"Thanks," Luke said. "I don't think I'll be needing you for a while. Why don't you go sit down by the water? Just listen to the people and see if you can pick up any dialect they may have—any unique colloquialism that we might be able to add to the dialog."

"I'll go sit by the river, but I doubt that they'll be anybody I can listen to. Everybody I've seen is taking this pandemic seriously," Maya said. "Just once I'd like to see somebody smile at me."

Luke had an exaggerated smile on his face. "Okay, now you've seen a smile. Now get your mask on and get out of here. I need to concentrate."

He picked up the script and turned to the Post-it Note that marked the page he would need.

SOUND: MUSIC
EXT. CAMERA LONG SHOT OF STREET
AND RIVER,
MOVE TO BRIDGE
CAMERA MOVES IN
TWO SHOT OF DAVID AND ANNA.
END MUSIC

David
I believe that God has a purpose for me. I can't believe that I survived—all that, only to be a high school football coach. There must be something more.

Anna
But David, how many lives have you touched? There are young men now who were once your players, your students, and they've become lawyers and doctors, business owners and...
ONE SHOT
ECU ON DAVID

David (interrupting)
Alcoholics, jailbirds, men who contribute nothing to society. I tell you the truth, Anna, I don't know whether I have failed God, or He has failed me.

Luke put the script down thinking about the line that he had just read. He bowed his head and began to pray.

Dear Lord, why am I having so much trouble getting this picture made? I need Your help. I think I'm serving You with the pictures I make, but have I failed You? Am I making these films for Your glory, or am I making them for my glory? Lord, I need Your help in discerning the difference.

His prayer was interrupted by a knock on the

door.

"Come in," Luke called.

Sherman Morris, a smaller than average man with thinning hair and wire-rim glasses answered Luke's invitation. Sherman was the business manager for the film.

"Sherman, you don't have to knock, just come in—at least during working hours."

"Well, this time I wish I didn't have to see you," Sherman said.

"It didn't go well, did it?"

Sherman shook his head.

"All right, let me hear the verdict. Are they going to sue us over the African House? Did you tell them we can repair the cypress slabs."

"Luke, if only that was our worst problem."

"You mean there's more? Let me have it. What else have we done?"

Sherman lowered his head. "We can't get around this one. There's another spike in COVID19 cases. Everyone must wear a mask, and there are no exceptions."

"What?" Luke yelled. "How can you make a movie when nobody can see a face?"

"I tried to argue that with them, but there's no getting around it. I think the mayor understands our problem, but it seems this is an edict from the governor. The city isn't willing to risk getting a fine or worse, if they make an exception. Maybe we can just go on back to New Orleans and wait it out," Sherman said.

Luke shook his head. "I'm afraid that's not possible. The delays we've been having with all this paperwork mess, has put us way behind."

"Then what do we do?"

"We halt production."

"You mean for just a little while," Sherman said.

"No, I mean we terminate. This project has been doomed from the beginning. The investment money was based on the expectation that Tia would be the star, and then...we know where that went."

Sherman looked away, not making a comment.

"As I understand it, according to the contract if shooting is halted, I have to return any investor's money," Luke said.

"That's right, and don't forget the kill fee. That's $30,000 a day." Sherman paused for a moment and then continued. "If it's any consolation, the good thing is, most of the money came from your own pocket—the bad thing is, most of the money came from your own pocket."

"Thanks," Luke said, "that's just what I wanted to be reminded of. It makes you wonder why anyone would ever try to make it in this business, doesn't it?"

"Well, when it's good, it's very, very good..." Sherman said.

"How do you think the cast and crew will take this?"

"They're all troopers, and they've known things haven't been as smooth as they were on the other shoots," Sherman said, "but they'll go however the wind blows."

"If we shut down, do you know right off hand what the bailout fees for the cast will be?"

"It'll be between a hundred-fifty to two-hundred thousand dollars."

"All right. Get the cast together and I'll tell them

what's up. Will you get in touch with the investors?" Luke asked.

"I can do that," Sherman said. "They've made a lot of money in the past off LTN. Maybe they'll take that into consideration and let some of their money ride."

"Thanks, Sherman. Do whatever it takes to salvage as much equity in the company as we can. We may be down, but we're not out."

Chapter Three

Javanna left Jay's apartment at around one a.m. She took Riley up to the sunroof for one last bathroom stop, and when she did she looked out over the city. There seemed to be destruction everywhere as police cars were converging on every conceivable intersection, then immediately rushing on to something that was more pressing.

It was with much trepidation that Javanna returned to her apartment. After having been outside the night before, and now seeing that the riots were still in progress, she decided to change into something she would consider to be get-away clothes. But what would that be?

Going to her dresser, she pulled out one of her oldest pairs of jeans, a soft plaid shirt, and she found her cowgirl boots that were in the far corner of her closet. As she started to undress, she thought about the ludicrousness of what she was thinking of doing. "Bug-out" bags were not in the general preparedness scenarios for most Chicago residents. That was a middle-of-the-country thought process—not for someone who lived on the tenth floor of the heretofore most safe area of Chicago. If someone got to her, the whole city would be doomed.

She did undress, but she put on her pajamas and she gathered Riley in her arms as she climbed into bed. The last time she looked at the clock, it said 3:15, but she must have gone to sleep because the next thing she knew, Riley was making little sounds indicating she had been in bed long enough. It was now, just past nine.

She grabbed a robe, and thinking she wouldn't see anyone, she went up to the sundeck, yet again.

"Good morning, sleepyhead," Jay said when she stepped out of the elevator. He was dressed as she was—still in his sleep shorts, and Lucky was running free.

Javanna let Riley off the leash and the two dogs ran and played together, as if nothing was different in their lives.

"I haven't turned on the news yet this morning," Javanna said. "Do we know what all took place last night?"

"It's bad. Take a look at this." Jay handed Javanna a copy of the Chicago Tribune. "I picked this up downstairs."

Javanna began to read: *On Monday August 10, 2020, looting began at 12:15. Caravans of vehicles entered downtown Chicago, all the while their horns blaring. One hundred looters were arrested according to Chicago police, while thirteen police officers were injured.*

"It was earlier than 12:15," Javanna said. "Riley and I were coming home about ten."

"Did you see the list of businesses that were hit?" Jay asked. "There were the ones we saw last night, but add to that list the Apple Store, Nike, Walgreens, the 7-ELEVEN and a whole bunch more. It says even the Urban Grocers was hit. My question is what's left?"

"I don't know," Javanna said, "but I intend to go see for myself."

Jay looked at her incredulously. "I said last night you were a fool to take the dog out, and now you're going out again."

Javanna smiled. "This time I'll leave Riley at home. If I don't come back, will you adopt her?"

Jay shook his head. "You're the most hard-headed woman I've ever known. I suppose you're going to go check on your precious job."

"That's right."

When Javanna got back to her apartment, she sent a quick text to her boss.

Devin will u be at office this am

In just a few seconds, she got a return message.

Here now. What's up?

I'm coming in see u in about an hour

U know u don't have to do that

Coming anyway

O K be careful

Javanna dressed quickly. She thought about putting on her jeans, plaid shirt, and cowgirl boots, but she thought better of it. If there were any rioters still lurking about, that may be like waving a red flag in front of them. What could be more white privileged than a Montana cowgirl?

When Javanna stepped outside her building, and started down Michigan Avenue, she was not prepared for the devastation that had befallen the Gold Coast, even though she had just seen the paper. Everywhere she looked there was broken glass, burned out cars, and graffiti on just about every flat surface.

Some were obvious:

DEFUND THE POLICE
FTP
BURN THE FLAG
RICH WILL PAY
DEATH TO AMERICA

But then there were letters that she didn't know and these four letters were written somewhere on every block that she passed.

ACAB

She'd have to ask someone what those letters stood for.

Most of the people she saw on the street were either sweeping up glass or covering windows with plywood.

"Ma'am, if I were you, I wouldn't be out here," one man said. "Who knows when all this will start up again?"

"Aw, she ain't in any danger in the middle of the mornin'. That's when workin' people are out," another man said as he sawed a piece of plywood.

"I hope you're right," Javanna said. "I'm thinking they all have to sleep sometime."

"Let's hope they don't come back again tonight.

They just about hit every business in the Loop."

Javanna moved on toward the Prudential Building where she worked. She passed many workers, and she noticed that only about one out of five was wearing the dreaded mask. How she wanted to yank the thing off her own face.

When Javanna reached the offices of CDMI, she went into the break room and looked through the drawer at the K cups. Usually she was a straight black coffee drinker, but this morning, she wanted comfort. She chose the Dunkin Caramel Coffee Cake blend and dropped it in the Keurig. Immediately the scent permeated the little room and it lifted her spirits.

Reaching her own office, taking off her mask, she collapsed behind the desk. She needed to make a decision before she talked to Devin Myers. Last night, or rather early this morning, her choice had been clear, but now sitting here in the nicest office CDMI had in the whole suite, except for Devin's of course, her options weighed upon her.

"Javanna, I thought I heard someone in the break room," Carrie Cox said as she popped her head in the door.

"Yeah, I just couldn't stay away," Javanna said as she took a sip of coffee. "Are you the only one here?"

"Well, except for Devin, yes. I must say, the phones are really busy this morning."

"Cancelations?"

"I'm afraid so," Carrie said. "Riots don't seem to be something most people want to advertise."

"What about my accounts?"

"You're down to three—Crystal Palace, Steak and Ale, and Mama Maria are still with you."

"Oh, that hurts."

Carried laughed. "You know why these are the last three."

Javanna rolled her eyes. "Don't say it, Carrie. You know I never fraternize with my clients."

"Oh? How many times has old Giorgio called about his account, and how many times did I have to set up a luncheon meeting for you two? You tell me, Mrs. Caldwell."

Javanna laughed. "You know, Giorgio Moretti is the main reason I changed the spelling of my name. When he saw Giovanna, he was sure I was a nice little Italian girl, just waiting to help out in Mama Maria's kitchen."

"No matter, what the reason was, Mr. Moretti certainly poured in the money to CDMI."

"He did, but look at what it got him? How many restaurants does he have now? I believe it is eleven, and who does he credit with his increase in business? I believe it is moi."

"All right, all right," Carrie said as she turned to go.

"Wait, is Devin in his office?"

"As far as I know he is," Carrie said, "unless he's jumped out the window."

"Don't even think that," Javanna said. "If my numbers are any indication of what's going on companywide, he has to be hemorrhaging money."

"I know, it's bad. After all, I'm the one who gets to tell him when everyone wants to drop their campaigns. Funny, it used to be that they all just skipped over the little lady who answered the phone, but now they're only too happy to have me deliver the news."

Javanna took a deep breath. "He's not going to like what I have to say, either."

Javanna started toward Devin Myers' office but stopped and returned to her own office to get the face mask that she knew her boss would want to see.

She walked through the labyrinth of "cell offices" created by head-high partitions, which provided just enough room for desks, chairs, laptops, and the ubiquitous framed photograph. It was eerie to see all the cubicles empty, as everyone was now working from home, trying to hang on. She had started out in one of those cells, but her value to the company had earned her a real office.

When she reached Devin's office, she stopped and clinched her fists, as if that action would steel her for what she was about to do. The door was open, and she saw Devin sitting there staring out the window.

She knocked lightly, and then entered without waiting for his response.

When he saw her, he raised his eyebrows but didn't speak.

"Carrie told me the latest," Javanna said.

"She doesn't know the half of it," Devin said. "Close the door and come have a seat."

"What has happened?" Javanna asked as she moved to a seat across from the big desk.

"I just got a call from Beverly. Edwin tested positive."

"Beverly's dad?"

"Yes, and the bad thing is, we moved him out of the nursing home. For the last week, he's been living with us, so..."

"That means you all have to go into quarantine," Javanna said.

Devin nodded his head. "And that means Carrie and anyone else who has been around me will be in quarantine."

Javanna began to inch her chair back without making a point of it. She was glad she had gone back for her mask, and she was glad she hadn't taken the chair that was closer to Devin.

"I don't think you are exposed, but if I were you, I wouldn't come back down here," Devin said as he ran his hand through his hair. "What else can go wrong in my life? First my business, now my family—where does this all end?"

"Will you shut down CDMI?" Javanna asked.

"I don't have a choice. I had planned to keep everyone on the payroll, but with the circumstances now, I just can't do it."

Javanna was sorry to hear what Devin had to say, but what she had planned to tell him when she walked in was now irrelevant. This revelation put her wishy-washy plan to either stay or quit, in the definite quit column.

"I know you are on your own, Javanna. Will you be able to make it without a paycheck? You'll be eligible for unemployment, but that won't come anywhere close to what you've been making."

"Thanks for caring, Devin. You know, you are the only boss I've ever had, and I've never thought of you as a boss—you and Beverly are two of my closest friends in Chicago."

"The feeling is mutual."

"When Dane died, and I was going through that horrible experience all alone, it was Beverly, and Carrie, too, who were there for me."

"If I remember right, his parents didn't even come," Devin said.

"That's right. In my mind, I rationalized it was because of the blizzard Montana was having, but down deep inside, I know it was because they blame me." She paused. "They could have come later, but they didn't. Only Martha Bryant came to be with me." Tears started to build in Javanna's eyes.

"All right, that's enough of that," Devin said. "We don't need to cry over water that's long past gone under the bridge. Now, tell me what you plan to do. Will you stay in your apartment?"

"Fortunately, my lease is up in September. If the rental agency will give me a month to clear out, I'll look for something a little less expensive," Javanna said, "and a little farther away from the riots."

"Do you want some advice from a friend?" Devin asked.

"Sure. I'm open to anything." She smiled. "Especially since you're not my boss anymore."

"I think you should go to White Sulphur Springs. You haven't been back since Dane died, and I think it would be good for you. Might give you a chance to settle some things." Devin said.

"Maybe you're right," Javanna said as she stood. "I'll clean out my office before I go."

"Hey, you don't have to do that. This place isn't dead yet—it's just taking a little hiatus."

Javanna cocked her head. "Look, buster, if I get back to Montana, I might just find me the most handsome cowboy you've ever seen, and I'll stay there forever and ever."

Devin laughed. "I wouldn't put it past you to pull something like that. You'd bail out on me, just when I'd need my best account executive to come back to work and bring in some money. You know Giorgio'll want you back."

"Who knows? Maybe I can work from Montana. This working from home is catching on."

When Javanna turned the corner onto Oak Street, she was surprised to see a boy standing in front of her building. He had a gas grill with a large pot on it. When she got closer, she saw that he was selling hot dogs.

"Now this is what I call being an entrepreneur," Javanna said. "How much?"

"Ten dollars."

"Ten dollars for a hot dog—what do you think this is? Wrigley Field?"

"If you don't want to pay my price, you can go to my competitor," he said.

Javanna laughed. "You have a point. I see a bright future for you. What's your name?"

"George Jenkins, the third."

"Ah ha! That's it, George Jenkins the second is standing right behind you." She looked up to see her doorman watching the exchange.

"All right, George Jenkins, the third, I'll take two hot dogs, and make sure you put mustard on them." She withdrew two twenty dollar bills and handed them over. "Keep the change."

The boy turned toward his father, his eyes wide. "Thank you, ma'am. That's the biggest tip I've ever gotten."

"How many hot dogs have you sold?"

"With your two, that makes five."

When she went into the building, George was shaking his head. "You didn't have to do that, Javanna."

"Oh, but I did. You are looking at the original 'old mother Hubbard'. My cupboard is definitely bare."

"You let me know if you need anything," George said. "We live in Skokie and for now, nothing's been touched in our neck of the woods. You just give me a list and I'll bring groceries to you tomorrow."

"Thanks, George, and I meant what I said. You've got a fine boy, there."

When she opened the door to her apartment her dog was waiting, her tail wagging.

"Hello, baby-dog," she said, as she took off her mask and leaned down to stroke her head. "It looks like you and I have some thinking to do? Do you want to move to Skokie? George says everything's fine up there. Or, how about this, do you want to go to Montana?"

Riley began barking incessantly.

"Is that a yes, or does it mean you want to go out?"

The dog started turning in circles.

"All right, we'll talk about this later."

Javanna got the leash and was going to take Riley outside, but she took her to the sundeck instead. She knew she would be safe outside, after all, she had just walked home from the Prudential Building, but she didn't want to make small talk with anyone, including George.

With her hot dogs eaten, and Riley fed, she moved over to the sofa. It was almost three o'clock in the afternoon, and now what was she going to do.

First things first. No matter where she went, she would be moving out of this building. She called the rental agency and gave notice that she would not be renewing her lease. They were quite accommodating and even gave her a month to get out of her apartment.

"We don't have many people clamoring to move in," the agent had said. "If we can get you to stay, you can pay on a month by month basis."

That was a relief. If she would have had to move in fifteen days, she would have gone crazy.

She looked around her apartment with a critical eye. Everything was Crate and Barrel chic—the sofa, the chairs, the rug, the tables, the sideboard—all her furnishings looked as if they had come out of a display window.

And there was a reason for that. They had.

Three years ago, when Dane died, she couldn't stand to stay in the condo they had bought in Lincoln Square. At the time, she was distraught and she didn't want anything that would remind her of that awful time. She had leased this apartment, and Beverly Myers and Carrie Cox had shopped for her. Within a month, she had moved into this building, never having seen a single stick of furniture until it was in place.

In hindsight, she probably should have stayed in

Lincoln Square a little longer. But so many emotions were haunting her. She just wanted out.

They had bought the condo, shortly after moving to Chicago in 2005. Dane was so excited to get a junior level position at the Chicago Mercantile Exchange specializing in cattle futures. He used to laugh and say his bosses thought anybody who came from Montana would automatically know all there was to know about cows. The closest he had ever come to being near a cow was when a bull got out of a pen at the Labor Day Rodeo and charged through the bleachers. His dad taught math at the White Sulphur Springs high school, and his mother worked at the library. Dane was as close to a "city" kid as one could get, when you considered that "city" had a population of close to a thousand people.

Thinking about Dane was good for her. She went into the bedroom and took a box off the shelf.

The first thing she took out was the urn that held his ashes. She had thought about what to do with them, but so far she hadn't made a decision. Dane's sister, Melissa, had told her that Barney and June were livid that they had not been consulted before she had had their son cremated. At the time, she had tried to get their input, but they were so hung up on blaming her for his death, that all communication between them had broken down. Last year, she had attempted to reestablish some relationship by sending a Christmas card, but she had not gotten a response.

Next, she took out their wedding album, and thumbed through the pictures. They had been married at Grace Gospel Church in White Sulph, as some people called the town. Her sister, Abigail, had been her matron-of-honor, and Melissa had been a bridesmaid. Dane had chosen his father and Gabe Bryant as his groomsmen. Again, to the consternation of June Caldwell. Because Gabe was already on the rodeo circuit, June was certain he was a bad influence on Dane.

Just as she was fitting the urn into the box, she hit a metal sign board. This time she smiled as she brought it out.

Giovanni's Pizzeria—the Star.

Luke Bryant had given this to her, and for a long time she kept it on her desk at work. Luke had written a play when he was a senior in high school. Javanna was a sophomore, and she had indeed been the star. Later, Luke had admitted the play was a take-off on Bus Stop, but Miss Kaiser, their English teacher, had been impressed enough that she had submitted it in a national competition. The result was that Luke had won a scholarship to the State University of New York in Binghamton where he majored in cinematography.

And now Luke Bryant's name joined two other notable residents from their little town who had gained some notoriety. Dirk Benedict, whose main claim to fame was being in Battlestar Galactica, and Ivan Doig, an author of several books, one of which, The House of Sky, was required reading in Miss Kaiser's class.

Under the sign board, was a note from Luke that he had written when he had sent it to her.

Dear Pete,

I thought I would send this to you, because if it had not been for you, I would never be doing what I am today. I'm not just saying that. If you hadn't been so good playing 'Giovanna,' Miss Kaiser would never have submitted my play.

Mom tells me you and Dane are in Chicago and that you both have established yourselves in successful careers. I should have known you would do well. It takes an effervescent personality to be a cheerleader, even if it was for the Hornets in White Sulphur Springs. Someday we'll have to talk about some of those long bus rides to away basketball games, but maybe not. Tia and Dane might not find them so funny.

All my best to you and Dane.

Luke

And one more thing. You know I produce movies now. If you ever decide you want to be a 'star' again, come to New Orleans. I did it once, and I know I could do it again. Javanna, even though you would never admit it, you did have talent.

Javanna folded the note and put it back in the envelope. No one but Luke Bryant ever called her Pete—it came from pizzeria.

She thought about his last line, even though you would never admit it, you did have talent. If anyone but Luke would have written that, she would have laughed. What if he had meant it when he said 'come to New Orleans?' Now would certainly be the time to try something like that, but then he was married to Tia Brown. Javanna had watched the movies Luke had produced, and Tia had starred in all of them. She was undoubtedly one of the most beautiful women she had ever seen.

"Javanna Caldwell, stop it!" she said aloud. "How stupid. When you traipsed around all over the ranch following him like a little puppy dog, he never knew you were alive. Except yes he did. 'Javanna, bring me a steel post, Javanna, back this truck up, Javanna, flake this hay, Javanna take the four-wheeler back to the shed. Javanna, chase that cow out of the trees.'"

Yes, she would have to say he knew she was there.

Chapter Four

New Orleans

Luke had been back in New Orleans for close to a month. The debacle in Natchitoches was his first failure, and yes he had to call it that. Maybe the mask controversy was what he was telling himself was the final blow, but if he really examined the whole project, it was awful from start to finish.

This was the first post-Tia production, and it was hard. In the beginning, he had thought they were in love, but hindsight told him there was never any true feelings between them. A perfect example was their wedding. While Virginia, her mother, had wanted a big splash, Tia had insisted that they should be married by a justice of the peace.

But Luke had balked at that. Even though none of his family was to be present, he had insisted that they be married in a church. And she had acquiesced.

Their marriage was marked by films—not by

anniversaries. They had been good together. He wrote scripts that built around Tia's personality; Tia did an amazing job of bringing his characters to life, and the bottom line was their bank account swelled over the nine years they had been together.

When the divorce was finalized, Tia had asked for nothing, but Luke had added a codicil to the divorce decree saying that she would get half the money they had accumulated. She did not turn it down, but she did not ask that their house in the Garden District be sold. And that was where Luke was now.

It was an old house, built in 1804, and he loved it. When they had first bought it, he had fantasized about what historical figures may have come through the doors—Aaron Burr, Andrew Jackson, Jefferson Davis—he had a whole list of people and for each of these people, he had written a story in his mind. Tia used to call it a writer's curse. One could live in the past but never in the future.

Tia was a native of New Orleans and she could never understand why Luke did not get into the whole Mardi Gras experience. She had served as the celebrity guest on several of the krewe floats and she had enjoyed the celebration. Because of her participation, Luke had gone with her to some of the balls that were around town. They were often photographed as one of the "beautiful people" couples, but Luke knew it was Tia who deserved the accolade.

Now at forty years old, Luke felt rudderless. Without Tia, LTN had become his family, that is his family in New Orleans.

He had a big family back in Montana, but he

hadn't been home since the divorce. In a way, he felt like the divorce was a failure, and that he couldn't face his parents. Dale and Martha Bryant were strong Christian people, and while neither of them had said anything, he knew they were disappointed in him.

As far as he knew, his commercial successes meant nothing to them. Occasionally his mother would comment that they had seen Tia on the Hallmark Channel. It was as if Tia somehow got projected on the screen without his having anything to do with it.

He knew his father had never accepted the fact that he had not come back to work at Crooked Creek. He had understood that when Luke won the scholarship to go to SUNY at Binghamton, he should go, but never did he even imagine that Luke would not come back to Montana.

Dale was an only child, born late in life to his parents. When his father died, Dale was only thirty years old. He had inherited a 125,000 acre ranch, and with a wife of twenty-eight and two small children and another one on the way, they had taken over the whole operation.

What Luke did to keep LTN in business was miniscule compared to what his father had managed to do for the last thirty-seven years. When anyone asked Luke about his background and he told them he had been raised on a cattle ranch in Montana, everyone immediately thought he had come from wealth. And on paper, he would have to say that he did, but in the real world, the profit margin was thin. Blizzards, droughts, floods, disease—all of these uncontrollable events could wipe out a whole year's income.

His father was not a windshield rancher, and while his boys were at home, neither were they.

Many was the time when Luke had been out in a snowstorm spreading hay from 800 pound bales, or chopping ice in the creek or one of the tanks, or cleaning out the jugs after a baby calf had been born, getting the pen ready for the next occupant.

The ranch was hard work, but just thinking about it made him homesick.

He had five brothers, and except for the two youngest, Josh and Matt, all of the others had left home.

Noah was two years younger than Luke and he was married and had a ten year old son. His mother never said anything, but reading between the lines, Noah's marriage was close to failure as well. He worked in Bozeman at an environmental think tank, while his wife, Patricia, was a lawyer, working as an environmental lobbyist in Washington D.C. Tyrone, or Ty as he was called, stayed with Noah, and he was the only grandchild.

If a family had to have a black sheep, it would be Gabe. For his whole life he had been fascinated with rodeos, and for the last fifteen years, he had been a member of the PRCA as a team roper. At first Dale had thought Gabe would be the one to come back to the ranch and take over, but over the years Gabe became more and more successful, and the chance of his settling down as a rancher was becoming less and less promising. Now, Gabe was traveling with a barrel racer named Dusty Valentine, at least that was the name she was using.

And then there was Sam. He had thought he had wanted to go to college at the University of

Texas, but upon entering a student body of close to 50,000, it was overwhelming to a country boy who had come from a high school with an enrollment of eighty kids. After the first semester, he dropped out of college and joined the Army, becoming a helicopter pilot. He had been deployed overseas to Iraq and Afghanistan, as well as a tour in Germany. While in Germany, he had met and married a woman who was a school teacher in the American Dependent Schools. Luke knew that his mother had adored Francine, and was more heartbroken than Sam was, when that marriage had ended in divorce.

Finally, there were Josh and Matt. There was a year's difference in their ages, but they were always thought of as a pair. And they were resentful of that. While they still worked on the ranch, they were in a constant state of competition.

Luke knew that his parents, but particularly his mother, said a lot of prayers for her sons. He knew that when he talked to her on the weekend, she would always ask him when he would be coming home. To stop the question, Luke had said he would try to get there for Christmas, but he knew he could always use the weather to get out of going.

All at once Luke was jolted out of his reverie. "You should go to White Sulphur Springs. Now."

It was as if God had spoken to him. And maybe He had.

Immediately, Luke called Sherman Morris, before he changed his mind. He asked if Sherman could come meet with him.

Luke was waiting in the courtyard, when Sherman came through the gate on the side of the house. He had two glasses of lemonade sitting on the table.

"Now this looks serious," Sherman said as he sat down. "I don't suppose I need to have my mask on?"

"Hardly," Luke said. "I don't care if I ever hear that word again." He pushed the lemonade closer to Sherman. "I want to know if you'd look out for this place for awhile."

"You know I will, but what's up?"

"Sherman, I would only say this to you, but I'm questioning my ability to write. In the last month, I have started a script at least a dozen times, and nothing is falling into place." Luke paused. "In the past, it was just as if the words were on automatic pilot, but now nothing works."

"Tell me," Sherman said, "is your main female character a beautiful blonde woman?"

"Hmph," Luke grunted. "That could be it. This is the first script I've tried to write since the breakup."

"You know, no matter what happens between you two, she can never work for LTN again."

"You mean our audience wouldn't accept seeing a star that they could have seen in the buff had they looked her up on Netflix or Amazon?"

"Yeah, I'd say you might be over the target."

"I've decided to take a little...vacation," Luke said.

"That's probably a good idea. You've been driving yourself for as long as I can remember, and a little relaxation will do you good," Sherman said.

Luke laughed. "It won't be much relaxing that I'll be doing."

"Now you've made me curious. What are you planning on doing?"

"Let's see, the first of October—the oats and barley are already harvested and in the grain bins, the hay's in the stackyard, but the fence needs fixin' and the cows need to be moved from the high ground. And I'll bet there's a truck or two that needs some kind of work. Maybe a transmission's out or an alternator needs to be replaced."

Sherman laughed. "You're going home."

Luke had a huge grin on his face as he nodded his head.

"I can't think of a better place for you to get your head screwed on straight. Have you told your mom?"

"Nope. I'm going to surprise her."

Chicago:

"Montana! You're going to Montana? Don't you know it gets cold there?" Jay questioned.

"Yes, I know. You seem to forget I lived there for the first twenty-two years of my life, and besides, you don't think it gets cold in Chicago?"

"It's not the same. Was it last year that we broke a record, and it was only minus twenty-three degrees," Jay said.

"There you go," Javanna said. "The average winter temperature in Bozeman is twelve degrees."

"I don't believe you."

"Look it up," Javanna said. "Now that we have that settled, I need your help."

"All right, what do you need?"

"This stuff." She swept her hand around her apartment. "I need to get rid of it."

"Everything?"

"Yes, everything."

"But if you do that, that means you aren't ever coming back," Jay said. He had a genuine look of disappointment on his face.

"Jay, you lived right next door when Carrie and Beverly brought all this furniture in here. Like I said, it's just stuff. I can always replace it when I come back."

Jay rolled his head as he looked around the room. "It is nice, and it is new."

"Yes...?"

"Are you going to sell it?"

"If I can. That's where you come in. If I list it on Craig's list and everything doesn't sell by the time I leave, will you let people in after I'm gone? I can keep paying rent as long as I need to," Javanna said.

"What if I bought your stuff?" Jay asked.

"I wouldn't sell it to you," Javanna said.

"Oh," Jay said, his voice deflated.

"But I'll give you everything if you want it."

"That's ridicules, Javanna. I won't take your furniture without paying for it."

"All right, make me an offer."

"Uh...I'm a little short on cash right now," Jay said.

"All right, we're right back where we started. What if I pay you a thousand dollars to haul everything to the Goodwill store for me?"

"That sounds better—what if you give me the thousand dollars and then I buy your furniture from you?"

"Sounds like we have a deal," Javanna said as Jay turned to leave her apartment.

Within five minutes, he was back at the door.

"Yes?" Javanna said when she opened the door.

"I just figured that out—you're actually giving me the furniture. Did you realize that?"

Javanna raised her eyebrows. "And just who is the accountant here? I need to get rid of the furniture. You want it. If it doesn't sell for two or three months, I pay rent. It's a better deal to give it to you, and let you deal with it."

"Do you think I can hug you, Javanna?"

Javanna looked around. "I don't see any mask patrol around, so why not?"

It took nearly a month before Javanna was able to get everything organized. She had helped Jay get her things into his apartment and it truly looked like a crowded junk store. He had suggested that he would pay her any money he would get from selling his own things, and Javanna had agreed that she would take the money. But if he got three hundred dollars for everything he had, he would be lucky.

The good thing, Jay had room to store her better working clothes. She would need those when she came back, and at this point, she was sure she would be back when CDMI was up and running. The stuff that she couldn't take with her, she gave to George. He had said that he would take it to the Goodwill store near where he lived.

The last morning she was in her apartment, with only her bed still there, Riley awakened her early. She knew something was up, and she had been restless the whole night, barking at every sound she heard.

After taking Riley to the roof, Javanna knocked lightly on Jay's door.

"Are you leaving already?" he said as he rubbed his eyes.

"I may as well get to the airport early. Who knows how Riley will act when she has to stay in this little bitty kennel," Javanna said. "We'll have to change planes in Denver, but I'll let you know when we get to Bozeman."

She noticed there were tears in Jay's eyes.

"I'm going to miss you," he said.

"I know. Me, too. But maybe I'll be back before Christmas."

"I hope so. Don't forget to send me a text."

"I can't believe you're really going, Javanna," George said when she got to the door. "I have a present for you." He handed her a mask with the Chicago Cubs emblem on it. "I don't want you to forget all about us."

Javanna laughed. "You know in Montana, I may never have to put this thing on. Big Sky Country is just that—wide open spaces. In Meagher County where I'm going, they've had fewer than twenty cases since this whole COVID thing began."

"Well, when you come back, I want you back in this building, you hear?"

"I do." She handed George an envelope. "I have something for you as well. You know my clients were all restaurants and one of the perks of the job were these gift certificates. I don't know how many there are, but if these restaurants ever open again, I want you and your wife, and George Jenkins the third, to use them."

George looked in the envelope. "There must be a hundred or more of these things? Are you sure you want to do this?"

Javanna chuckled. "I don't think they'll do me any good in Montana."

George shook his head. "Mrs. Caldwell, I have to tell you, you're one of a kind. I'm going to miss you."

"I'll miss you, too." She exchanged the mask she was wearing for the Cubs mask. "Go Cubs."

A slender, gray-haired man approached the door. He flashed a placard saying Uber.

"I believe that's your ride. Now don't forget us," George said as he picked up her luggage.

When her bags were loaded and Riley's kennel was safely beside her, the driver pulled away. He merged onto Interstate 90 as quickly as possible. She was glad the route didn't take her through the heart of the city, where so many memories were safely stored away. Both she and Dane had been excited twenty-two-year-old kids when they first arrived in Chicago. What a contrast from White Sulphur Springs, Montana. If the truth were told, they were both scared to death, but they had grown to love this place. Before Dane's accident, they had often dreamed of going back to Montana. Dane had said they would buy a ranch some place—not a working ranch, just a looking ranch. It would have mountains and a trout stream and they would fish all day if they wanted to, and they would have big strong horses that would pull a sleigh in the winter. So many dreams. All shattered.

Well, Dane, we're going home, Javanna thought. I just didn't know I'd be taking you in an urn.

She felt the tears sliding down her cheeks.

Chapter Five

New Orleans:

On the day Luke was ready to leave, Sherman came by at six-thirty in the morning.

"Have you changed your mind?" Sherman asked when Luke came to the door.

"Nope, I'm out of here," Luke said. He was wearing a white denim long sleeved shirt, jeans, a brown leather belt with the Crooked Creek brand, and boots.

"Where have you been hiding that get-up," Sherman asked.

Luke laughed. "Once a cowboy, always a cowboy." He grabbed a stockade jacket and put a navy blue Resistol hat on his head.

"Maybe I shouldn't say this, but boy oh boy, do you look good. If I were a betting man, I'd say you'll catch you a little lady while you're out West, and maybe you won't ever come back."

"Then here, this is yours." Luke tossed the keys

to his SUV to Sherman. "You do still have the key to the house don't you? Make certain the yard service keeps the courtyard up, and oh yes, the hurricane shutters are in the storeroom behind the garage. Hope that's where they stay."

"Don't worry, I'll take care of everything," Sherman said. "When do you plan on coming back here?"

"Right now, I'm thinking I'll probably stay through the calving season next spring. That's a busy time on a ranch, and if Matt and Josh will let me, maybe I can help."

"Well, come on, let me help you with your gear," Sherman said as he opened the back of his Highlander.

Sherman took Luke, not to Louie Armstrong Airport, but to the New Orleans Lakefront, the preferred airport for private planes. When he stopped the SUV, Sherman looked forward for a minute, while Luke was reluctant to get out of the vehicle.

"I meant it when I said this is what you need," Sherman said. "I've worked with you for a long time, and I know you've got it in you to come up with a blockbuster."

"Thanks, Sherman, I'm looking forward to this trip, but in the back of mind I keep thinking about Thomas Wolfe."

"You mean, You Can't Go Home Again."

"That's exactly what I mean," Luke said.

"Put that out of your mind. Just remember it's God's Big Sky Country you're going to, and if you let Him, He'll show you the way."

Luke nodded his head as he opened the door. "Keep in touch with the rest of the staff while I'm gone. Let me know if anybody needs help."

"I can do that," Sherman said. He extended his hand. "I know you'll come back a renewed person."

"I think so, too, but I'd better get the plane in the air."

As Sherman drove away, Luke headed toward the hangar.

He owned a Cessna 210, which was a single-engine, high-wing, retractable gear airplane. His flight to the ranch airstrip would be about eleven hours.

Technically, he didn't need a flight plan because he would be flying VFR, but he was a strong believer in having one. Getting a form from the operations office, he listed his destination as White Sulphur Springs, Montana, which was only twelve miles from the ranch. He listed the aircraft tail number, 543410, and type, Cessna 210, and the cruising speed of two hundred miles per hour. Reporting points would be Shreveport, Oklahoma City, Dodge City, Cheyenne, and Bozeman. His ETA would be 2300 hours Zulu time, or 5 PM Mountain Time.

With the flight plan filed, Luke went out to the aircraft which had just been fueled and pulled out onto the apron. He began his preflight inspection by first checking the oil and fuel, then manually checking the freedom of movement of the flight controls. Then he concluded with his pre-flight prayer.

"Lord, please watch over me during this flight.

Give me a good, trouble-free flight, and the awareness to know when the flight should be interrupted
whether for weather or mechanical reasons. Get
me there safely, amen."

As soon as he started the engine, he contacted
the tower.

"Lakefront Tower, Cessna four one oh, taxi and
takeoff."

"Four one oh, wind one five at one zero. Visibil-
ity one zero. Ceiling four thousand five hundred
broken. Temperature eight seven. Dew point seven
seven, Altimeter two niner six seven ILS-DME
Runway Departing Runway three six Right.

"Four one oh," Luke replied.

Luke taxied to the end of three six right, did his
magneto check, then called the tower for departure.

"Cessna four ten, clear for immediate take off."

Luke put the flaps to fifteen degrees, moved the
fuel lever to full rich, then pushed the throttle to
full power. The airplane raced down the runway
until it rotated then, even as he was climbing out
of Lakefront Airport, he retracted the gear, feeling
a sense of satisfaction and confidence when he felt
the tricycle gear tuck up into the fuselage.

Climbing to eighty-five hundred feet, he took up
a GPS heading of 335, soon leaving New Orleans
far below, and behind him.

He hadn't told anyone back in White Sulphur
Springs that he was coming home. He wondered
how they would receive him.

Abigail Baker pulled into the short term parking
area at the Bozeman airport. Checking her watch,

she found that she barely had time to get inside and check the arrival board. For her whole life, Abby had always had the habit of running late, and this time she intended to be on time. She was the mother of three children, and was now seven months pregnant. Her life seemed to be one continuous circus.

Except for the one stabilizing influence in her life—her husband.

Abby had married Paul when she was nineteen, and they had been married twenty years. As she was hurrying across the parking area, she pushed the button to call the Feed and Seed.

"You made it," Paul said as he answered the phone.

"Just barely. If her flight is the least little bit early her plane is on the ground already. What airline did you tell me she was coming in on? And what gate am I looking for?"

"Abby, take a deep breath. If you're late, Javanna won't care," Paul said speaking as calmly as he could. "Anyway you don't have to go to a gate. We told your sister you'd meet her by the bear. That's in the baggage carousel area on the lower level."

"Of course that's what we told her. Why am I so ditsy?"

"You're just nervous."

"I know. Since she became such a big shot at that advertising agency, she thinks she doesn't have time for me, or Mom, either as far as that goes."

"Honey, be fair. Javanna's been through a lot. Just let her take her time. You know she can't help but fall in love with the kids," Paul said.

"It'll be a new experience for her. In Lila's eight years, Javanna's probably seen her less than six months, and it's probably half that for Caroline," Abby said. "And poor Gavin—I doubt she even remembers we have a two year old. Oh, I forgot, I told your mother, I'd call her and see how she's getting along. Will you call her and check?"

"She's fine. Dad brought Gavy down to the feed store after his nap and he's been running the whole time he's been here. So you don't have to worry, he'll be on his best behavior tonight if he can stay awake. Now you'd better get to your spot, because you may not recognize your sister."

"Oh, there won't be any problem there," Abby said. "I'll just look for the one who is dressed like a Vogue fashion model. I'll find her."

"Well, honey, I've got a customer. Be careful."

"I love you," Abby said as she finished her call.

When Abby reached the baggage claim area, she checked the arrival board and found that Javanna would be delayed about twenty minutes. She was glad because it would give her time to pull herself together before she had to face her sister. Finding a comfortable chair she sat down and took a deep breath, and then sent Paul a text saying the plane would be a little late.

Abby didn't know why she was so intimidated by Javanna. She was two years older than she was, but even as children, Javanna could always do everything better than she could.

And their father hadn't helped matters. He had wanted a son, and when he didn't get one, he was determined to make Javanna as much of a tomboy as was humanly possible. From the time she and

Gabe Bryant were both eight years old, she could ride a horse as well as he could, and that was saying something, because Gabe was now a professional rodeo rider.

The older Bryant boys, Luke, Noah, Gabe, and Sam thought nothing of taking Javanna with them everywhere. Luke was a year older than Abby, and Noah was a year younger, Gabe and Javanna were the same age, and Sam was a year younger yet. But they never invited her to do any of the things the five of them did together. Consequently, Abby had let it be known that she wasn't interested in anything that had to do with ranching. Now, after her father had died, she was sorry she hadn't made more of an effort to get to spend time with Dallas Reed.

But as distant as the relationship between Abby and her father had been, the relationship between Abby and her mother had blossomed. Her mother and Martha Bryant had worked together to cook for the Bryant family, the Reed family, and all the cowboys. And Abby had learned to cook right along beside them. That training had served her well, when her mother had opened a restaurant, calling it Abby's Place.

But all of that was before her children were born.

Abby had not seen Javanna for three or four years, definitely not since Dane had died. And as she had told Paul, she was expecting to see her in the latest fashionable dress, but as passengers began congregating around the carousel, Abby picked her out immediately. She was wearing jeans, a plaid shirt, boots, and she was carrying a denim jacket. But what struck Abby the most was how fragile she looked, how thin she was. Her brown hair was shoulder length, and it looked as if it had noticeable gray streaks—not tinted, but natural gray. When she turned around as if looking for someone, Abby saw that her heavy brown eyebrows still looked the same. Even though she was wearing a Chicago Cubs mask, Abby would recognize those dark eyes anywhere.

Javanna had set something down, and was now retrieving her luggage as it came down the chute. She took a large case off and extended the handle, then retrieved the second bag and hooked it to the first with a luggage strap, all very efficiently. Then Abby watched as she moved toward the bronze bear statue.

"Oh my gosh, I should have helped her," Abby said as she hurried toward the statue. When she was close enough, she stopped. "Have you been gone so long that you don't recognize your own sister?"

Startled, Javanna looked toward her, and though Abby couldn't see it because of the mask, Javanna smiled.

"Abby, there you are," Javanna said and the two sisters embraced. Her eyebrows rose. "I didn't know about this."

"Yes, I'm pregnant again. You'd have known that if you'd keep in touch."

"Mom didn't mention it the last time I spoke to her, but then I always feel like I'm keeping her from something when we talk. Does she ever slow down?"

"Not really. She's running Abby's Place now, and

she keeps the bake shop going, and now she's added a catering business."

"What about the boot shop? Is she still a cobbler?"

"No, she gave that up. Now, Vincent sells his produce out of that side of the building," Abby said.

"I can't wait to see everyone, and I'm really looking forward to getting to White Sulphur Springs," Javanna said.

"After Chicago, I can't imagine why that would be," Abby said.

"Believe me, I'm ready for some quiet time."

Just then, a single bark came from the case that was sitting on the floor.

"Is that a dog?"

"It's my baby," Javanna said as she leaned down to talk to the animal. "Riley, baby, you'll get out of here in just a minute."

"Does Mom know you have a dog?"

"I don't know. I'm sure she's heard her bark when she's been on the phone."

Javanna picked up Riley's kennel, and then rolling the two suitcases, she started for the door. "Where are you parked?" she asked.

"Over there," Abby said pointing to an extended cab pickup.

Javanna left her bags by the truck, and then putting the leash on Riley, she led her toward a grassy patch on the other side of the parking lot. She was a bit concerned that Abby had questioned whether her mother knew that she was bringing a dog. Growing up on the ranch, there had been half a dozen dogs around, and everybody loved them, or at least, Javanna had thought that. But then those dogs belonged to the Bryants, and if they had gone in the house, it was up at the Big House. Did her mother not like dogs?

If that was the case, Javanna might not be able to stay until Christmas.

When Javanna got back to the truck, she hoisted the two bags into the bed of the truck, and put Riley's kennel on the back seat.

"Do you want to drive?" Abby asked as she offered the keys to Javanna.

"You don't want me to drive," Javanna said. "At least not this outfit. It's too big."

"I would think it would be easier than driving in Chicago. Once we get on 89, I'll bet we don't see a total of thirty vehicles the whole seventy miles up to White Sulph," Abby said.

"But you forget, I haven't driven in three years."

"What do you mean you haven't driven? You do have a car don't you?"

"No, I don't have a car. When Dane was alive, I had to have a van that was wheelchair accessible, but after he died, I sold it, and I haven't had a car since."

"Well how do you get places?"

Javanna laughed. "Mainly, I walk. Everything that I need is within three or four miles of my apartment, and if I want to go somewhere else, the bus stop is a half block away from me."

"You say 'my apartment'. Do you still have it?"

"Not the one I was in, but when I go back, I want to be in the same building."

Abby didn't comment. She got in the truck and backed out of her parking place.

Javanna pulled off her mask. "I'm glad to get out of that thing. Did you have many COVID cases in White Sulphur Springs?"

"The last I knew, Meagher County had nine since this all started." Abby said as she removed her mask as well.

They drove along in silence for quite awhile, neither really having anything to say. When they turned on Highway 89, it was a two lane road, and the speed limit was seventy miles an hour. Javanna was sure Abby was surpassing that, but she didn't say anything because she felt like Abby was in just as big a hurry to get out of this situation as she was. At least Riley was settled on her lap, and every so often she would reach up and give Javanna a kiss.

"That dog's important to you isn't he?" Abby asked.

"It's a she, and yes she is. When you live alone in a city, a dog is one of the best ways to meet people except for the people you work with."

"Well, I can tell you right now, Brooke is not going to like that dog."

"I thought she was enrolled at Montana State."

"She was," Abby said, "but when they said there would only be online classes, she withdrew."

"So she's at home? What's she doing?"

"Not much. You know how Mom protects her— or maybe you don't know."

"She was only four years old when I left," Javanna said. "Does she help out in the restaurant?"

"Only when Mom can't find anybody else. Brooke thinks she wants to be a country music singer."

"That's nice."

The two sisters rode in silence eating up the distance, going through the little town of Clyde Park, then coming into Wilsall.

Javanna saw the approach for Route 86. Then a small green sign: Flathead Creek Road, Bridger Bowl. Her eyes brimmed with tears.

Abby reached over and put her hand on Javanna's shoulder. "Are you all right?"

Javanna nodded her head and smiled.

After a few more miles, Abby spoke again. "Do you ever hear from the Caldwells?"

"Melissa calls every once in awhile, but I've not heard from either Barney or June since I told them I had cremated their son."

"You know you're going to have to face them."

Luke had been flying for a little over ten hours now, with fuel stops at Oklahoma City and Cheyenne. He had bought a ham sandwich and a Sprite in Cheyenne, and now opened the cellophane wrapping around the sandwich, and opened the Sprite. Looking just under the wing to the left, he could see the Rocky Mountains, but except for an occasional peak here and there, he was flying over relatively level land. It was isolated though, unlike Louisiana where, from ten thousand feet there was always some town in view, while here, the only connection with human activity below were the roads and interstate highways.

This would be the first time he had been home since he and Tia had flown up here shortly before she divorced him.

'Home'. It's funny that he still thought of Montana as home, even though it was half a lifetime ago when he lived here. Matt and Josh were here all the time, and though Gabe was on the rodeo circuit, he was here frequently, as was Noah, who lived in Bozeman. Only Luke, and his brother, Sam, made infrequent visits to the ranch. Sam's army deployments kept him away, and Luke told himself that he was too busy because of production schedules to spend much time at home.

Well, he had no production schedules now. And he had scrapped the script he was working on. If this time away did what he prayed it would do, he would return to New Orleans with a clear head.

He chuckled. Maybe he could come up with a screenplay about a ranch. He would make the ranch Crooked Creek and then he could claim this whole trip as a tax deduction.

His GPS told him that he was in Montana, and by the time he had finished his sandwich and Sprite, he could see Bozeman ahead of him, and he tuned his radio to Big Sky Approach control 118.975, then keyed his microphone which was a boom from his headset.

"Bozeman Approach, this is Cessna four one oh report Bozeman on a flight-plan out of New Orleans."

"four one oh, do you have a transponder?"

"Negative. My position is five miles south at 10,000 feet. I will not interfere with Bozeman flight operations."

"We have you reported four one oh. Destination White Sulphur Springs?"

"Uncontrolled private strip, Crooked Creek

Ranch, twelve miles west of White Sulphur. Bozeman, say now Density Altitude, please."

"Density altitude, six thousand ninety-two."

"I read six thousand ninety-two density altitude."

"Affirmative, four one oh."

"Thank you very much, four one oh out."

Luke throttled down and began to sightsee for
this last leg of the flight. Now he was in familiar
territory. He looked down and spotted the River-
side Country Club, the club where one and only
one time, he had shot a seventy-four. Then he
flew toward the Bridger Mountains, recognizing
various peaks: Saddle, Hardscrabble, Sacagawea,
Mount Baldy, and Bridger Peak.

Bridger Bowl was what was referred to as the
local ski resort, and how many times had he skied
those slopes. And then he thought of Dane Caldwell and the horrible accident that had befallen
him, just as his career was taking off. He wondered
about Javanna, what she was doing. He had meant
to write her when Dane died, but like so many other things, he had let it slide. He assumed she was
still in Chicago, and whatever it was she was doing,
she would be doing it better than anyone else.

As he got closer to White Sulphur Springs, he re-
duced his altitude. The little towns he passed over
seemed to be getting smaller. The stubble from the
barley and oats was golden yellow, while the alfalfa
fields after the last cutting were greening again.

Along 89, he saw the large round bales of hay
now lined up in rows, waiting for the winter feeding, and now he saw black angus cows in little
groups all over the pastures. There would be ten in

one place and close to fifty in another, but no herds the size of those at Crooked Creek.

He wondered how many head his father was running nowadays. When Luke left home, his father had wanted to get the herd up to 50,000 on his 125,000 acre ranch. He didn't know if he ever reached that number.

Looking down, he saw the Springdale Colony. If the other towns were getting smaller, it seemed the Hutterite colony was getting bigger. He counted about a dozen wind turbines and several extra-large buildings, that must house either a chicken or hog raising operation.

He smiled. Leave it to the Hoots to be the most progressive people in the area. They may not watch television or use the internet, but from what Luke knew, they devoured newspapers and books.

A unique culture, the Hutterites. What Luke remembered most about them was their work ethic. Many a time did Dale Bryant threaten to send his boys to Springdale to learn how to do a job and do it right.

And now he was right over White Sulphur Springs, the cemetery, the golf course, the high school, the spa, the Castle—all the things he remembered.

He dropped down a little lower to fly over the Peterson place. It was strange to think of Helen Reed as Helen Peterson. The Reeds and the Bryants had been like one big family when Dallas Reed had been the ranch foreman and Helen, and Abby, and his mother had been the cooks. They called themselves the "Hoodlum Girls", named for the wagons that followed the herd on long cattle drives.

Helen's husband, Vincent, had built himself a good business selling fresh produce. Looking down, Luke saw the pit his father had dug for him. It was covered with Plexiglas, an idea that Javanna had given Vincent, that allowed him to harvest vegetables even in the dead of winter. Javanna had called it some strange name that no one seemed to understand, but everyone was eager to buy his fresh produce.

When he saw the sharp right turn that Highway 89 made, Luke turned the plane to the left. He was within twelve miles of the ranch. When he passed over the Smith River, he began flying over the rolling foot hills of the Big Belts where he saw fields of snow on the mountain tops.

Within a few minutes, he was directly over the life-sustaining waters of Crooked Creek, and the sheltered valley that housed the sprawling compound that was home.

The gravel road that led up to the Big House, the huge shed that was the shop, the grain bins with the augurs run up to the tops, the stackyards, the tire shed, the scale shed, the calving shed, the horse barn, the cowhand's dormitory, the foreman's cabin, the runway, and the hangar. Then there were the pastures: the heifer pasture, the bull pasture, the yearling pasture, the cow pasture and the horse pasture. Crooked Creek really was like a self-contained little village.

A sense of excitement began to build in Luke. Why had he ever left this place, a place that was as vital to him as was the air he breathed?

He circled the airstrip one time to get the wind direction from the wind sock—then he set up his downwind leg, turned base, and then final for the ranch landing strip. He set the plane down making a smooth landing, then taxied back to the hangar where he saw his father's Cessna TTx was parked.

Killing the engine, Luke sat for a minute, taking in the majesty of this place. The sky was still as blue as only a Montana sky can be, with the puffy white clouds hugging the mountains. A hint of orange was beginning to brush the peaks.

"Hey there, are you going to just sit here, or are you going to get out," his brother, Josh, said as he yanked open the door.

"If I can get my old bones to move, I think I'll get out," Luke said as he grabbed his jacket and hat.

When he was on the ground, Josh embraced him. "Have I been workin' so hard that it's Christmas already, or else what are you doing here?"

"Would you believe me if I said I was homesick?" Luke asked.

Josh shook his head. "Not on a bet. You haven't been homesick in twenty years."

"What if I told you the state of Louisiana and the COVID virus shut down production on my movie project?"

"Now that I can believe. You want me to help you roll this baby into the hangar? Dad's got the Skycatcher out, but he should be coming in any minute now, and if your plane is in his way, you'll hear about it."

"I wondered where he was," Luke said.

"He's flying over the Wardlow property that he just bought," Josh said. "Said the fence is so bad, we can't put a cow on it until every mile of that fence has been walked."

"Is that where everybody is?" Luke asked.

"Yeah, except for Matt. He took the flatbed in to town to get some more steel posts," Josh said. "Everybody's fixing fence this time of year, and the supply is running low, but Paul Baker got in a tractor-trailer load this morning. He called and said he'd hold six bundles for us if we could get into town before somebody else bought 'em out from under us."

"Man, it sounds like nothing has changed since I left," Luke said.

Josh looked at him with shuttered eyes. "I wouldn't say that. Come on, we'd better get up to the Big House. Mom'll be wondering who landed on our strip. You want a ride?" He turned toward the four-wheeler that sat just off the runway.

"No, I think I'll walk," Luke said. "I need to get the kinks out."

The Big House which rose three stories, sat near the end of the runway. The north wall of the ground floor was built into the side of a hill. The other three sides were built of native stone, the front jutting out on one end in order to accommodate a three vehicle garage. The upper two floors were log timbers with a covered porch across the front and open decks on the back.

When Luke approached the house he was swept with a wave of memories. The banister around the porch that he had tried to walk on, like a tight-rope walker, where he lost his balance, fell, and broke his arm when he was six. The window on the ground floor he had broken by hitting a baseball through it when he was twelve. The porch swing that was still suspended under the porch, where he had been sitting when he had had his first kiss. He had been a freshman in high school and the girl was Amber Steedman.

He wondered where Amber was now.

When he got to the house, Josh was leaning over the banister. "Come on up, and I'll introduce you to the lady of the house."

"All right, it hasn't been that long since I've been here."

"I guess not. Three years isn't that long." Josh turned and opened the door as he yelled to his mother. "Kill the fatted calf! Your prodigal son has returned!"

"What in the world?" Martha started to say, as she looked up from the island in the kitchen. Then she saw Luke, standing just inside the front door.

"Luke!" she shouted in excitement as she dropped the pan she had just taken down from the pot rack, making a loud clatter. Shep, the old collie who had been sleeping near her, yelped and ran to the bedroom that was off the great room. When she got around the counter, she wrapped Luke in her embrace.

After, she clung to him for what seemed like a minute, she pulled back, not dropping her arms. "Sweetheart, why didn't you tell us you were coming? I could have cooked for you."

"You're not cooking tonight?" Luke asked looking down into her face.

"Silly, you know what I mean," Martha said as she playfully hit his chest. "I could have had a roast beef cooking all day—as it is you're stuck with venison chops."

"And that will taste wonderful. Do you know how often I get to eat venison in New Orleans?" Luke asked. "Anyway, I expect there'll be plenty of time to make a pot roast."

Martha got a concerned look on her face. "Oh, Luke, honey, what is it? Is something wrong?"

"Yes, there is something wrong. It's COVID 19."

"Oh, you don't have...you don't have the...?"

Luke laughed, and shook his head. "No, Mother, I don't have the virus. But I may as well have it. It seems that along with all the restaurants and hair salons that are shut down, the powers-that-be don't consider movie making an essential business. I think I told you I was shooting a movie in a town in northern Louisiana. Well, about a month ago, I had to kill the production."

"Oh dear, what about LTN? Do you still have your company?"

"I have it, but I had to shut it down."

"What did you do with all the people who work for you?" Josh asked. "You don't have to pay them if they don't work do you?"

"Technically, no," Luke said, "but I've said, if anybody gets in trouble, I'll bail them out."

"Humph, you didn't learn that on a ranch," Josh said. "If you don't work, you don't get paid around here."

"Now, Josh, that's enough," Martha said. "How long do you get to stay? Please say you'll be here for the holidays."

"I can guarantee you I'll be here that long," Luke said, "that is if I can earn my keep?" He looked toward Josh.

"You better believe you'll earn your keep," Josh

said. "I hope you brought some other clothes besides those fancy duds you got on now? How much did those boots cost? I can't wait to see you walking fence rows in those."

Martha let out a big sigh. "Boys, boys, let's have at least one night before all this gets back to normal. As for your boots, your room is just the way you left it. I'll bet there are even some well broken in boots down there."

"I got your bags out of the plane. I'll put 'em down below," Josh said.

When Josh was gone, Martha shook her head. "We go through this all the time. Matt and Josh are always at one another's throats."

"They always have been competitive," Luke said.

"But this isn't competition that drives them—I can't put my finger on what it is, but it's bad enough that your father and I have talked about breaking up the ranch."

"I'd hate to see that happen," Luke said. "Old Zeke put this ranch together and Dad has added to it hasn't he?"

"Yes, we've had the old Sawyer place for several years, and he bought the Wardlow pasture last spring. I think that brings the acreage up another 18,000 acres or so."

"After all that work, it'd be a shame if the third generation can't keep the place together."

"What we need is someone who could take over—someone who has some experience dealing with all kinds of people," Martha said, "even if those people were his own brothers."

"Mom, what are you trying to say?"

"Well, we know that person isn't going to be Noah. He's so involved with this environmental stuff he'd probably turn this whole place into a wildlife sanctuary. And Gabe—he'll never quit the rodeo, until...I don't like to think about that. Gabe is in the Lord's hands, and I pray for him every night. And Sam, too. Do you think he'll give up the army? I don't think so."

She looked out the window where some of the horses were up close to the fence that separated the horse pasture from the yard.

For the first time, Luke saw his mother when she appeared to not be in control.

"You have one more son, Mom. What do you think about him?"

"Honey, I don't know what to say about you. Neither your father nor I would ever ask you to give up your company, but maybe the Lord has sent this pandemic to make all of us get down on our knees and decide, not what we want, but what He wants us to do." Martha smiled as she patted Luke on the cheek. "I'm glad you're home."

When Luke went down the stairs to the lower level of the house, very little had changed since he had left home, except for a large screen TV that was hung over the mantle of the stone fireplace. The three brown leather couches were in the same places, the leather having become a little softer over the years, and the buffalo hide rug was still on the floor in front of the fireplace. To the right a bar and four stools faced a wall of cabinets, a sink, refrigerator, microwave, and a narrow stove. Beyond the kitchen area, was the door that closed off the ranch office.

On the other side of the open area was his room, one of seven bedrooms in the house. The front, of what was technically the basement, had windows and a walk-out door, which were often covered with snowdrifts in the winter. He smiled when he thought of the snow caves that would form when the escaping heat would seep out around the door.

Opening the door to his room, it was like stepping back in time. When he and Tia had visited, they had always stayed in the guest room on the main floor.

Luke's double bed looked so small compared to the king sized bed he was used to. Above the headboard were a couple of shelves filled with trophies—basketball, track, cross-country, rodeo competitions, even a debating trophy. He saw one framed certificate where his play, Giovanna's Pizzeria, had won the state competition for dramatic presentations.

He picked it up. How that single event had changed the course of his life. If it hadn't been for his scholarship, he would be living here on the ranch, probably married to some local girl. He would have built a house, maybe up by the pishkum, where long ago Indian hunters would stampede buffalo over the cliff. He and Javanna Reed used to ride out there together. She thought that spot was the most beautiful scene on the whole ranch.

It was strange when he thought about what an influence Javanna had had on his life. He wondered if she would be home for Christmas. It would be great to see her again.

Abby continued to drive north on Route 89, not meeting or passing more than ten vehicles. The two sisters found little to talk about, each waiting for the other to start a conversation. Javanna wanted to ask about her mother and Brooke, but she avoided that conversation, and Abby wanted to know exactly what had happened in Chicago and why Barney and June Caldwell were so upset with Javanna.

The Bakers, the Petersons, and the Caldwells all attended the Grace Gospel Church. For its most well-attended service, the church would number about seventy-five people. The minister, Owen Walker, and his wife, Deevy, had a full-time job keeping the church in harmony.

When they approached Ringling, Javanna noticed the town sign on the road. It said population, sixty.

"Didn't the sign use to say sixty-two?" Javanna asked as they sped on through.

"I think Bunkie Pippin died, and then Delores moved into Bozeman to live with her daughter."

It was all Javanna could do to keep from laughing out loud. Ringling was twenty miles away from White Sulphur Springs and yet Abby could say who and why the town had lost two residents. She took a deep breath. If she would have been a praying woman, she would have said, "Lord help me, what have I done?" but as she now considered herself agnostic, she kept her thoughts to herself.

The foothills of the Castle Mountains were all around now, and White Sulphur Springs was in sight. They passed the cemetery, and the golf course, and then Abby slowed down.

"Here it is," she said turning in to the first of three buildings. "The boot shop is shut down, but if anybody needs to have a shoe repaired, Mom still has the sewing machine. Now since Vincent has the deep greenhouse, he uses the space to sell fresh eggs and produce in the winter and Mom sells baked goods there, too."

"Oh, look," Javanna said pointing to the long open air building next to the shop. "I didn't know he was calling his business Vincent's Walipini."

"Yes, he does, thanks to you," Abby said. "Just how many times a month do you think we have to explain to people what that means?"

"When they find out the fresh tomatoes they're buying in January were raised not two hundred yards from where they're standing, are they impressed?"

"I guess, but the local people just take it in stride. They just say, 'what else is old Vincent going to come up with?' "

"And I'll bet he loves it," Javanna said. "Do you think Mom's at home?" Javanna put the leash back on Riley before she opened the door.

"Of course not," Abby said, "but she said to put your bags in the house before you come over to the restaurant."

The "house", was actually an extension of the storefront that had at one time been the boot shop. When Dallas Reed had died, Dale Bryant had taken the insurance money Helen had received, and then added a sizable chunk of his own money, in order to set her up with a business and a place to live in town.

The annex as they called it was quite livable for a widow and her two daughters. It had a state-of-the-art kitchen, that actually took up a third of the available living space, a large great room and two bedrooms. Dale had tried to talk Helen out of opening a boot shop, but she had insisted that repairing shoes was something she could learn to do. Because Helen had cooked at the ranch, Dale had tried to convince her to start a bake shop or a restaurant, but Helen wouldn't hear of it.

The shop and annex were built on land purchased from Vincent Peterson. Vincent, who was a bachelor, had a modest house with a greenhouse behind it that he ran as a seasonal business, raising and selling bedding plants and vegetables. Then on the remaining acreage, he had a truck farm where he raised fresh produce to sell in his open air shed. He also had a small horse barn surround by about five acres where he kept two aging horses.

After Helen and the girls had lived there a year, Helen and Vincent decided to marry. It was more a marriage of convenience than anything else, but within a year, they had a daughter, Brooke. When Vincent and Helen came to the realization that their combined businesses weren't enough to make a good living, they decided to take Vincent's house and remodel it making it into a restaurant.

The restaurant was called Abby's Place, and it was the intention that Helen and Abby would run it together, but as Abby had her children, the restaurant became Helen's alone.

"I'll take your luggage in," Abby said.

"I don't think so," Javanna said. "Didn't you tell me you're seven months pregnant?"

"Being pregnant doesn't make me an invalid," Abby said, and then when she saw the look on Javanna's face, she apologized. "I'm sorry. I guess that was a poor choice of words."

"It's all right. I learned to adapt to a lot of things when I lived with a man who was wheelchair bound."

"I know that was hard."

"It was...shall we say, challenging, but if I could snap my fingers and have Dane back, I would do it in a minute."

Riley was now on the ground, pulling Javanna to take her for a walk. "I'm going to take Riley over there for a minute."

When Javanna got to a patch of grass that ran along the highway she heard a familiar voice.

"There's my girl," Vincent said hurrying out of the produce building. "If you aren't a sight for sore eyes?"

He had his arms opened wide, and Javanna ran to meet him. It felt so good, so comfortable, to be in her step-father's arms. A knot began to build in her throat. "You don't know how much I've missed you," Javanna said.

"I've missed you, too, girl. I see you've brought a friend," he said as he bent down to rub Riley behind the ears.

"This is Riley, and she's the only thing that has kept me sane for the last little while."

"I know what you mean," Vincent said. "I still have Rosie and Prince, but it's been so long since I've been able to ride them, they've probably forgotten what it's like to have a saddle on their backs."

"Well, we'll just have to show them," Javanna said as she grabbed Vincent's hand. "I can't wait to go for a run so fast I lose my hat."

"Now wait a minute, you know you're talking to an old man, here. I'm going on seventy years old now," Vincent said.

"But you're not seventy yet. You won't be sixty-nine for two more months."

"All right, there you go. Then I'll be almost seventy." He squeezed her hand. "I'm so glad you're here. You'll keep me young." Then he added, "Have you seen your mother yet?"

"No."

"She'll be at the restaurant." Vincent said, letting out a deep sigh. "She may as well move in over there, she's there so much. You'd better leave your friend with me before you go see her." He took Riley's leash just as Abby came out of the annex.

"Are you ready?"

Javanna raised her eyebrows, but didn't say anything as Abby started across the parking lot.

Javanna turned back to look at Vincent. He gave her a thumbs up, as she followed her sister.

When she entered the restaurant, Javanna was surprised with how bright and fresh it looked. The tables were covered with red and white buffalo plaid cloth tablecloths with glass covers, and the chairs were black metal with padded seats. Black barn light pendants were strategically placed giving more than adequate lighting. The whitewashed shiplap and what Javanna had at first thought was hardwood, but was really a barn-wood tile, looked exceptionally pleasing.

"Abby, this is fantastic," Javanna said, "and I'm looking at this with the eye of one who has spent at least fifteen years doing nothing but promote restaurants."

In Javanna's mind, the only thing wrong was there weren't but two tables filled and it was close to five o'clock. She was going to ask if this was normal for this time of day, but she decided to hold her tongue. There would be time for her input later, especially after she had had a chance to look over the menu. She hoped her mother would be open for suggestions.

"You'd better wait over there, while I go tell Mom you're here," Abby said.

Just then a very attractive young woman came out of the kitchen. She was carrying a tray with two salads to one table where two elderly ladies were sitting. When she had served them, she came toward Javanna.

"I see you got, here."

Javanna did all she could to keep her mouth from falling open. "Brooke? I would not have known you if I would have met you on the street. You have changed so much."

"No kidding, you don't think four years will do that to you? You look the same except for your gray hair. I'd think you'd want to color that," Brooke said. "It makes you look old."

"I guess it does," Javanna said.

Just then Helen Peterson came out of the kitchen. Javanna noticed immediately that her mother had gained weight—not to the point of obesity, but definitely heavier than she had ever seen her.

"Welcome to Abby's Place," Helen said, when she

reached Javanna, who was now standing. "What do you think of the place?"

"I was telling Abby, how it looks exactly the way I would picture a restaurant in a western setting? Did you do this yourself?"

"Of course I did," Helen said. "Who else would do anything for me? You sure haven't been around."

"No, I haven't," Javanna said, "but I'm here now. I hope you'll let me help out around here."

"I know what you can do," Brooke said. "You can wash the windows every day. That's what she makes me do."

"I haven't done that for a long time, but I'll certainly be glad to do it," Javanna said.

"Well, if we're going to have any more customers, they'll be coming in, so I'd better get back to the kitchen. Old Bessie's the only help I've got tonight, except for Brooke here. Abby, do you and Paul want to come by and bring the kids? We could all eat here later, or do you want to wait till some other time?"

"Let me get home and see whether Jolene has fed them their supper before I make up my mind," Abby said.

"Well, don't wait too late. I don't want to cook anything other than what I already have for the special."

"Okay, I'll call you later."

"And you, Javanna, go on over to the house. Vincent will probably be coming in before long. You can talk to him until we decide what we're going to do here."

Javanna left the restaurant, walking dejectedly, back to the annex. "Welcome home, Javanna, I love you," she said. Her mother hadn't even hugged her. And Brooke, what was that all about. She had planned to go to Vincent's store, but the wooden drops had been let down and she could see that they were latched.

When she walked into the great room, Vincent was sitting in a big recliner, and Riley was snuggled up beside him. Both were sound asleep, but when Riley heard her, she jumped down and that disturbed Vincent.

"How was it, honey?" Vincent asked.

"The place is fantastic over there," Javanna said.

"I didn't mean how did you like the furniture. How was Helen, and how did Brooke treat you?"

"It's been a long time since I've been here. I can't expect them to fall all over themselves to welcome me," she said.

"Did they feed you?"

"No, and I have to say, I'm starved to death."

"I thought as much," Vincent said. "You know your mom has started a bake shop, too. She runs it out of her half of the old cobbler's shop."

"Does she run that, too?"

"No, do you remember Marie Bentley from church? She runs it most of the time, and when she can't, Amber White helps out. At least she does when it's her ex-husband's time to have the kids."

"I don't think I remember Amber White."

"Sure you do—she was Amber Steedman."

"Oh yes, I remember Amber Steedman. She was Luke Bryant's girlfriend in high school. When he would be sitting on the porch swing with her, Gabe and I used to sneak up and listen to them talking—that is if there was any talking going on."

"Oh, Javanna...that was bad. Did they ever know you two were there?"

"I don't think so. Unless Gabe told, because I certainly never said a word."

"Well, anyway, come over here and sit beside me." He walked to the

refrigerator and pulled out a bowl of chicken salad. Then he got a loaf of homemade bread and began slicing off four pieces of bread. "I fixed up a salad—some tomatoes and cucumbers with balsamic vinegar and olive oil. Do you want chives or basil?"

"I don't know if we should eat. Mom and Abby are trying to decide if we're going to get together over at the restaurant," Javanna said.

"Honey, you'd better eat now. If we do eat together, it'll be after the restaurant closes, and you can bet Abby won't bring those kids out that late. Now why don't you take your little dog out while I put this together for us?"

Luke had fallen across his bed, and before he knew it, he was sound asleep. After about thirty minutes, he was awakened by a clomping on the stairs. At first he was startled, because he thought someone had broken into his house. Then the light came on.

"Hey, boy, what you doing sleepin' in the middle of the day?" Dale Bryant yelled as he stepped into the room.

Luke jumped up immediately.

"Dad," he said, "I must have fallen asleep."

"I'll let it slide this time, but don't let it happen again," Dale said as he grabbed Luke in a bear hug. "You didn't tell anybody you were coming. Did you have any weather coming up?"

"Not a cloud in the sky," Luke said, "except for Montana's sky, and that's not weather, that's just beauty."

"I'm glad to hear you say that, Son. I was beginning to think you'd forgotten all about God's country up here."

"How can you say that? I think when we were little, you injected some Crooked Creek water in our blood."

"If I did, I don't think it took with a few of my boys," Dale said. "Come on up. I think your mom's about got eats on the table."

When Luke and his father got upstairs, Matt was just coming in off the back deck, bringing a plate of grilled venison chops.

"Look at those things," Luke said. "Those look as good as any chop I've had in New Orleans. Looks like Mama's bringing you up right."

"You'd better believe it. She's going to make it so women will be begging to marry me, just so they can eat my cookin'. And no woman will be runnin' out on me."

"Matthew!" Martha said. "There'll be none of that at my table."

"Mom, it's fine," Luke said. "Tia did leave me, and there's nothing I can do about it."

"I'm not sure I'd want her back," Josh said as he came down from his upstairs bedroom. "Have you seen her new movie?"

"I saw a little bit of it," Luke said.

"Ha! I know just exactly the minute you got up and walked out," Josh said.

Luke smiled. "I did do that."

"I'm hungry," Dale said. "Will you boys stop tormenting your big brother, and get this food on the table?"

"Bring those chops over here," Martha said. "I've got a sauce to put over them. Josh, you get the Brussels sprouts and sprinkle walnuts on them. And Matt, get the whipped cream out of the refrigerator. I've got hot gingerbread."

Luke laughed. "Man, it's good to be home. I've really missed all this."

"What I'm missing is eating," Josh said.

When they were seated, they all held hands, and Dale offered the blessing.

"Lord, bless this food that we are about to partake, and bless the hands who prepared it. We give thanks for the safe travels of our son and brother, Luke. May he be blessed with the peace in his heart that he so sorely needs. Watch over Gabe and Sam wherever they may be this night, and keep them safe. Bless Noah and Ty that they may continue in Your grace. In Jesus name, Amen."

When the prayer was concluded, Luke was taken aback by the petition his father had prayed on his behalf. Be blessed with the peace in his heart that he so sorely needs. Perhaps his father's words were prophetic. Maybe it was peace in his heart that Luke was seeking.

When the meal was over, Luke and his parents moved to the great room, while Josh and Matt took care of the kitchen and then went upstairs. It was cool enough for Luke to start a fire in the fireplace and he enjoyed the smell of wood smoke and the sound of crackling embers.

The conversation centered around the ranch and what had been done this past summer and what had to be done before winter. Dale talked about the Wardlow place, and how he thought he had paid too much for it, but it was a piece of property that had good water—Birch Creek ran through it. And the never-ending job of repairing the fence.

"We'll give you Saturday and Sunday off, but then you'll have to get right to it," Dale said. "I'll put you up at Wardlow running the fence line, or else you can pull up irrigation dams. Check with Russell and he'll tell you where to go."

"Russell Turns Plenty?" Luke asked.

"One and the same," Dale said. "A good man. He's been with me since before Josh and Matt were born."

"Is he your foreman, then?"

"For all practical purposes, he is. Jamal Harris is still the man whose name is on the line, but he had to go back to Nebraska about a month ago. He says he's comin' back, but he took all his personal belongings out of the foreman's cabin. I'd put Russell in charge in a minute, but your two brothers think they have to have a say in what I do."

"I'd say you're still the boss. You can do whatever you want to do," Luke said.

"Maybe you haven't noticed, but I'm getting old," Dale said. He stared at the flames for several moments before he continued. "It won't be too many more years before I have to take my boots off. When that happens, it looks like those two yahoos will be the ones to take over." He took a deep breath. "I have to let 'em take the reins sometime, but when I do..."

"Now Dale," Martha said, "they're just kids. Don't be too hard on the boys."

"You can't say that. Josh is twenty-eight and Matt is twenty-seven. My dad died when I was thirty years old and you were twenty-eight with a family. We took over this ranch and ran it, and nobody was around that we could ask for help—or to pay the bills for us," Dale said.

"But that was a long time ago," Martha said. "Things are different now, don't you think, Luke?"

"I suppose so," Luke said not wanting to bring up that he had been twenty-eight when he started LTN. Of course to his father's point, had the first picture failed, Elgin Brown would have paid the bills.

But the first picture had not failed, and every picture that Elgin had invested in had made money—that is all except But for the Grace of God. Luke had not taken the time to put a pencil to his own personal worth. With the money he had insisted Tia take when the divorce was final and the money he had personally put into Grace, he didn't want to know what the real bottom line was. He knew Sherman Morris would handle everything while he was gone, and when he returned, he could get back on the treadmill, forever chasing investors.

But for now he was going to enjoy his down time, and like his father had prayed, he was going to try to find peace in his heart.

"I've had about enough of this talking," Dale said. "I've got to be up at the crack of dawn, so I'm going to go to bed. If you and your mother want to palaver some more, that's up to her."

"Did you take your medicine?"

"No, I forgot," Dale said.

"Then you can't go to bed yet," Martha said as she headed for the kitchen.

Luke stirred the fire, separating the last of the embers. Then he moved to the French doors that led out to the deck on the back of the house. When he got to the railing, he saw that his mother had installed solar lights in and around the boulders and shrubs that many years ago, he had helped her put in place. Now they looked as if they had always been there.

He took a walk toward the barn, then heard a snort, and the lumbering sound of a horse coming up to the fence.

"Doc, is that you?" He couldn't believe his eyes in the shadowy effect of the solar lights when he saw a big Clydesdale horse coming up to the fence.

"It's him," Martha said as she brought Luke a jacket. "He's close to twenty-five years old, now."

"What about Tinker?" Luke asked. "Do we still have him?"

"We do. You'll see him come wandering up here in a minute. You never see one of those two without the other."

"Sort of like Josh and Matt," Luke said.

"You mean how they used to be. I worry about them," Martha said. "Your dad expects so much from them, and they're stuck out here on the ranch all the time. The only way they meet anybody, and by that I mean girls, is by going to church."

"Is the church as small as it used to be?"

Martha laughed as she moved over to sit in one of the chairs that had not yet been put away for the winter. "It's probably smaller—the only thing there are a few more children than there used to be. You'll see when you go with us Sunday morning."

Luke hadn't planned to go to church Sunday. He wasn't prepared to answer any question about why he had come home. But he would have to go sometime, so it may as well be now.

"Let's walk back so we can sit down and have a talk," Martha said.

Luke took the seat across from his mother. When she said let's talk, she meant you answer my questions. And even at forty years old, he would do that.

"What happened between you and Tia?"

Luke took a deep breath, knowing he would have to address this, but he didn't think the conversation would have come so soon.

"From the very beginning, I think we used one another, and I don't mean that in a bad way. I used her talent and she used LTN. We both wanted something from the marriage, but it wasn't a loving relationship. Never once did we talk about the possibility of having kids—that wasn't a part of the career path either of us was on."

"Did you love her?"

"I suppose so. I respected her."

"That's not what I asked. Did you love her?"

"I don't know. I do know, when I saw her naked on the screen, I was livid, but my thoughts weren't about me—it was how she would dilute the message that I've worked so hard to build. LTN is a faith-based business. When the 'franchise' as I called Tia, went off to Hollywood, and her first starring role is in an x-rated film—for that I don't think I can ever forgive her."

"Do you have any contact with her?"

"We were talking occasionally, and I have to say, in the beginning, I was happy for her, but then I went to see the film. You didn't see it did you?"

"No, but the boys drove into Bozeman to see it," Martha said, "and they told me. What are you going to do now? Are you going back to New Orleans?"

"Right now, I plan to stay here until at least next spring. Mom, I have another problem. I don't know if I can still write," Luke said.

"Have faith, son, have faith. You'll get through this and the whole family, the whole community will stand behind you." Martha stood up. "I love you, Luke. No matter what you do. But let's call it a night. I know you're tired."

Chapter Six

Just as Vincent had predicted, there was no meal with the Bakers at Abby's Place. Javanna had thought she may go back over to the restaurant, but Vincent and she were enjoying being together. He told her how well her idea for the deep winter greenhouse had gone and that he had even bigger plans for this year.

"Do you know that I have tomato plants that are going on three years old this winter? Nobody believes me when I tell them that."

"That's because you have such a green thumb," Javanna said. "I've been thinking about something else you might want to get into."

"Oh dear," Vincent said, "what do you have in mind?"

"Back in Chicago, you know my job was working with restaurants, and I was constantly going over their menus. One of the things that I noticed is that more and more people want healthier foods."

Vincent shook his head. "You'll never get people around here to give up their meat. Not when you're in cow country."

"Maybe not in White Sulphur Springs, but what about Bozeman?"

"I don't think I can grow enough tomatoes to pay somebody to drive them seventy miles," Vincent said. "What I've got going is enough to keep me busy."

"Vincent, you're forgetting—I'm here."

"I know you are, darlin', and I couldn't be happier to have you with us."

Just then Brooke and Helen came in the door, and Brooke went immediately to the sofa and flopped down.

"Mom, you've got to get some more help," Brooke said. "I don't want to work over there every weekend."

"I'll be glad to help," Javanna said.

"Maybe," Helen said. "We'll see. Did you eat?"

"Vincent took care of me."

"Good. I hope you don't mind, but I've got to get some things done before I go to bed. We'll talk tomorrow."

"That'll be good," Javanna said as she stood up. "I need to take Riley out before we go to bed."

When she came back in, Vincent and Brooke were gone and Helen was in the kitchen.

"Do you need any help?"

"No, I'm in a hurry and I don't want you in the way."

"Then I think I'll go on to bed."

There were only two bedrooms and one bathroom in the annex. She heard the water running and she assumed Brooke was taking a shower, so she went into the bedroom. When she and Abby had shared this room, there had been twin beds, but now those beds were replaced with a queen-sized bed.

Opening her bag, she took out her pajamas and put them on.

"Come on, baby dog," Javanna said as she lifted the dog onto the bed and then climbed in beside her. Riley liked to sleep in the curl of Javanna's legs, so she positioned herself to get comfortable.

Brooke entered the room with a towel around her head.

"I hope you don't kick, and I sure hope you don't snore," she said.

"I don't think I do," Javanna said, "but Riley may jump down and get a drink of water during the night."

"What do you mean?" Brooke said as she whirled around to face the bed. "Oh, no—there's not going to be a dog in my bed."

"But Riley always sleeps with me."

"Not here, he's not."

"She."

"Well whatever. There are some blankets in the closet. If you want to sleep with that dog, it will be on the floor or else go sleep on the couch."

Brook left the room, and Javanna heard the sound of the hair dryer.

Javanna found the blankets but no sheets or extra pillows. She grabbed one of the pillows off the bed, and went into the great room. By now, whatever her mother had been doing was finished and the room was dark, so from the light of the outside security light, she found her way to the sofa, spreading the blanket as best she could. She put Riley on the sofa first, and then she lay down, trying to move her body to conform to the dog's position.

As she lay there, her eyes wide open, she took a deep breath.

Why had she come here? What made her think things would be better for her here, than in Chicago? She had friends in Chicago, and it had been her home for half her life. What few accounts she still had, she had been servicing by using Zoom and Skype. She was certain that if she had stayed in her apartment, she could have made enough money to keep it. She knew Giorgio Moretti alone, would have advertised enough for that.

It had been the riots that had driven her out of Chicago, but for the last month, the Gold Coast seemed to have been spared. Psychologically, she knew the sheltering in place that the COVID pandemic had demanded, coupled with her already fragile psyche that she recognized was a residual of Dane's death, caused her to experience stress and anxiety. How many days had it been since she had had a good night's sleep? But had her life in Chicago been so bad that she should have come here?

She thought of Jay. She would call him Monday and tell him not to sell his furniture. Also, she would check to see if she could get her old apartment back. Anything but this.

Javanna was awakened the next morning by the banging of pots and pans in the kitchen. She sat up and when she did, Riley jumped down.

"What in the world are you doing on the couch?" Helen said when she saw Javanna. "Didn't you want to sleep with Brooke?"

It had been Brooke who wouldn't share the bed with her and Riley, but she didn't say so.

"It didn't seem comfortable," Javanna said coming around to the kitchen. She pulled out a stool and sat down. "What are you doing so early?"

"Saturday's the busiest day for the bakery," Helen said. "I've got to get the bread dough in the pans, so it will be ready to sell by eleven. Then I need to make some cinnamon rolls, and I've got to ice a couple of cakes."

"Do you ever slow down, Mom?"

Helen stopped for just a moment, and Javanna thought she was going to say something, but she didn't.

"Can I do anything?" Javanna asked.

"Yes, there's a storage room in the garage. Go out there and get me a half-dozen cardboard cake rounds. Oh, you're not dressed yet. I'll do it."

"No," Javanna said. "I need to take Riley out anyway."

"That dog's going to cause problems—you know that. What are you going to do with him when you come over to the restaurant? He for sure can't come in there, and you can't let him run loose in here. Technically, this is a commercial kitchen, and if the health department came and found a dog running around, they'd shut me down. You're going to have to get rid of him."

"It's a she."

Javanna's suitcase was in Brooke's bedroom, and she had to go in there now to get her clothes. Brooke was snoring, and she was lying in the middle, taking up more than half the bed. Javanna changed clothes as quietly as possible, and then left without awakening her sister.

As soon as she got outside, Javanna took Riley around back where the greenhouse was. The dog began barking and pulling on the leash. Then Javanna saw what the issue was. Vincent had added a chicken-raising operation that enabled him to sell free-range eggs. Javanna let Riley lead her back to the pen but Riley's barking wouldn't stop.

Near the back of the pit that was the walipini, Javanna saw a log that had been sawed so that it made a perfect bench. She picked Riley up to get her away from the chickens and headed for the log. When she sat down, she let Riley down, and she immediately ran out to the end of her leash, sniffing so many new smells.

Javanna put her head down, and the tears she had been holding back, began to flow.

Why? Why? Why? What had she done to deserve all this? Everybody was against her. Her mother, both her sisters, her in-laws that in a town of a thousand people, she couldn't avoid. Only Vincent had made her feel welcome.

She was glad she had made the decision to go back to Chicago, but she would have to get someone to take her back to Bozeman. She wouldn't ask Abby, because Abby had already made her feel it had been an imposition for her to meet her yesterday.

There was one person she could ask. Martha Bryant. Just after Javanna had moved into her apartment on Oak Street, Martha had come to Chicago to see her. Javanna had not shared all the details about Dane's death, and Martha had respected her privacy. She had taken Martha to CDMI, and afterward, everyone had assumed Martha was her mother. Javanna had not corrected them, because she was embarrassed and hurt that not one family member, either from Dane's or her own family had come when he died.

"Brighten the corner where you are! Brighten the corner where you are! Someone far from harbor you may guide across the bar; Brighten the corner where you are!"

Surprised to hear someone singing, Javanna looked toward the sound of the music and saw Vincent coming from his vegetable patch. He was pulling a wagon filled with pumpkins. Vincent was as surprised to see Javanna, as she was to see him.

"Well what have we here?" he asked, as Riley made her way over to him. He reached down to pet the dog, and was rewarded with several kisses.

"Good morning," Javanna replied, softly. "I'm glad you like my dog."

Vincent saw that Javanna had been crying and he dropped the handle of the wagon and walked over to her.

"Well now, it looks to me like somebody definitely needs her corner brightened."

Despite her gloom, Javanna smiled, and rubbed her eyes.

"You always did have a way of making me feel better, Vincent," she said.

"And what problem are we dealing with?"

"I can't point to one specific problem. It just a collection of events over the last..."

Vincent sat down on the bench beside her. He took Riley's leash and secured it to the pumpkin wagon.

"Do you want to talk about it?" He took her hand in his.

"I don't know where to begin. I feel so...alone. I thought if I came here, it would be different. I thought Mom would welcome me with open arms, but the feeling I get from her is that she'd rather I not be here. And Abby, she's so tied up with her kids and her husband. Brooke doesn't want me in her room. And this morning, Mom said I have to get rid of Riley."

"You don't worry about Riley. I'll not let anything happen to her," Vincent said.

"I don't think anybody but you understands what that dog is to me."

"I know, you got her after Dane died, didn't you?"

"Yes," Javanna said. "Not right away, but when nobody came, I didn't know if I could get through it, and then I got Riley. And there are the Caldwells. They hate me."

"Why do you think that?"

"Because they do. First of all they are mad because I had Dane cremated instead of bringing his body back to be buried here."

"Had they told you that was what they wanted?"

"No, but Dane and I had talked about it and that's what he wanted."

"Then you have nothing to feel bad about," Vincent said.

"There's more. They..." this time it was a sob that interrupted her narrative, "they think I killed him."

"No, Javanna, nobody thinks you killed your husband."

"Oh, but they do. Barney and June both think that. Neither one of them has spoken to me since I told them."

Vincent took a deep breath and squeezed her hand.

It seemed that action caused the dam to be broken and Javanna started to talk.

"It started with our skiing trip. It was my birthday, and he wanted to take me to the Alenia Restaurant. That's supposed to be the most expensive restaurant in Chicago, but no, I wanted to come back here and go skiing."

"Surely you don't blame yourself for Dane's accident. He tried to do a back flip, and he landed wrong. Skiing accidents happen all the time. You couldn't help that."

"He blamed me," Javanna said as she wiped away her tears. "He said I took his career away from him and I put him in a wheelchair for the rest of his life."

"But that didn't kill him. You're not at fault."

Javanna stopped and the tears continued to fall. Vincent wiped them away.

"Poor baby. You've been living with this for seven years. It's time you stop that."

"I called him just before lunch and he didn't answer. I should have realized something was wrong when he didn't answer, but I had meetings all afternoon, and I was too busy to try to call him again.

"On the way home, I picked up Chinese, and that took even longer. Then, when I walked in the condo, I smelled smoke, and I called out to him, but he didn't answer me. When I went into the kitchen, the burner on the stove was still on. I checked his office and the bathroom, and I couldn't find him. His wheelchair wasn't there, so I thought maybe one of his friends had come to take him out someplace, but then when I put my coat away, his coat was in the closet." Here, Javanna stopped as she gathered her composure enough to continue.

"There was only one other place he could be. There was a back deck on our condo—all the condos had the same kind and a stairway led down to the ground. I thought maybe he had fallen, but when I looked out, his wheelchair was there and he was still strapped in but all slumped over. It had been close to zero all day, and he had been outside since noon. Apparently, he had been cooking something, and when he took the pan out of the house, somehow he locked the door. He didn't have his cell phone or his coat. When I got out there, he was still breathing, but when they got him to the hospital, he never regained consciousness. I never got to tell him goodbye or that I loved him or anything.

"They told me he was suffering from hypothermia. Vincent, he froze to death, and it was my fault. I should have called and called until I knew something was wrong. I should have called an ambulance or the police or someone to go check on him...but I didn't."

Vincent lifted her up from the bench and put his arms around her, holding her as she sobbed into his shoulder. Finally she stopped, and pulled away from him and rubbed her eyes.

"Do the Caldwells know what happened?"

"I tried to tell June, but as soon as I started talking, she started screaming at me. To be honest, except for my boss and his wife, I have never told anybody this story."

"I'm glad you told me," Vincent said, "but there's someone else you need to talk to."

"Not Mom."

"You need to talk to God."

"Vincent, I know you are a Christian, and there was a time when I thought I was one, too, but now, I don't believe there is a God. Not after all this."

"You may not believe there is a God, but God believes there is a Javanna," Vincent said. "Will you go to church with me tomorrow? If nothing else, you can find a sense of peace there. And that's where you can start."

Chapter Seven

Luke was awakened the next morning to hear the sound of bawling cattle in the pasture down beyond the stackyard. Getting out of bed, he went out into the sitting area and headed for the door that led out onto the stone patio. When he stepped out, there was a smell in the air that was familiar. The animals, the dirt, all mixed in with the scent of cedar and pine. And beside him was a hanging basket filled with begonias, their yellow blossoms cascading downward.

Still wearing his boxers and barefooted, he shivered and he knew he was in Montana in the fall. A thermometer was hanging on the wall of the garage that formed the enclosure of the patio. The thirty-eight degrees forced him back inside.

Opening his duffle bag, Luke realized that Josh had been right about his clothes. Nothing that he had brought with him would be suitable for real work. His mother had said that everything in his room was just as he left it. Opening the closet, he saw that she was right. He pulled out a long-sleeved

flannel shirt and a pair of well-worn jeans. The shirt fit fine, but the jeans were too snug. He chuckled as he changed back to the pair he had worn when he arrived. What did he expect after twenty years?

In the back of his closet he found a pair of stockman boots that fit when he put them on, but the leather hadn't been oiled in years. He would need to go shopping.

Just then he heard sounds upstairs.

Climbing the stairs, he saw his father sitting in his easy chair, a cup of coffee in his hand. He was watching the news.

"I didn't expect to see you up this early," Dale said. "There's coffee if you want a cup."

"Thanks, Dad," Luke said as he walked over to the coffee pot.

"All these riots that are going on—how about where you are? Were they bad?"

"We had some in the early part of the summer, but for the most part, they were peaceful," Luke said.

Dale clicked off the TV. "Everything is so depressing: this virus, the riots, and then there are the fires. Could you see where the Bridgers burned when you were coming up?"

"Yes, I did see it," Luke said. "It looked like the fire wasn't that far from Bozeman."

"It makes you wonder if God isn't sending us a message. In 2 Timothy He tells us that in the last days there will come times of difficulty."

"I can't argue with that."

Dale took a swallow of his coffee. "Do you think you'll be able to save your production company?"

"I don't know, Dad. I hope so, but right now, it's just a game of wait and see."

Dale nodded his head. "I don't know if I've told you this, but your mother and I have been awfully proud of you, Son. Seeing your movies—it was just like being there with you. We could just imagine you standing over to the side directing everything that was going into the camera, and of course seeing Tia—she was so good. It's a shame..."

"She was good," Luke said in a subdued voice.

"Oh, I didn't mean to bring up a bad memory."

Luke smiled. "Because of Tia, The Angel of Bourbon Street won a major award and the movie brought in a lot of money for us."

"Luke, who wrote the script?"

"I did."

"Then it wasn't 'because of Tia'. If she hadn't had your story and your words, she wouldn't have been able to do what she did," Dale said. "Don't sell yourself short."

"Thanks, Dad."

"Now what do you plan to do today?"

"I think the first thing I need to do is go get outfitted. I thought I might drive down to Bozeman and get some clothes, that is if I can borrow a truck."

"Sure, take one of the F-150s but don't leave before you see your mother."

Sunday:

Sunday morning, the Bryant family drove the twelve miles into White Sulphur Springs to the church. Dale, Martha, and Luke were in a Ford F-150, and Josh and Matt were in front in another one, although it was several years older.

"This is just like old times," Luke said, "when the Bryants had to form a caravan to get their people to Grace Gospel. I guess I'm going to have to buy my own outfit if I'm going to be staying here any length of time."

"You don't have to," Dale said. "Crooked Creek has at least fifteen or sixteen vehicles either around the home place, or else up at Sawyer or Wardlow. We even have your old Manly Truck here someplace if you want to drive that."

Luke laughed. "Manly Truck is a 1978 Dodge with a gray paint job so faded out, that it looked like primer. It was a year older than I was when I inherited it."

"You loved that old truck," Martha said.

"Well, I guess I did. It was the first vehicle I ever owned. You say it's still around here?"

"It is," Dale said. "I think Jamal had Blake and Alejandro take the bed off and build a flatbed on the back. They use it when they take the irrigation liners out to the alfalfa fields."

"I'm surprised it's still running."

"You know your dad never gets rid of anything," Martha said. "If he can squeeze one more nickel out of something, he'll figure a way to do it."

By the time they reached the church, the parking lot was nearly full of extended cab pickup trucks with only a few SUVs and passenger vehicles scattered among them.

"I don't suppose Ken Pyron is still the pastor," Luke said.

"No, he's been gone about ten years and now we

have Owen Walker, and we just love him, but we really love his wife," Martha said. "Deevy is one of those women who can still the most troubled waters in a church."

"She probably learned to do that because of taking care of her twin boys. When they were little, they were a handful, but I think your friend, Kevin, has straightened them out," Dale said.

"Kevin Phillips—I haven't thought about him in a long time. Is he still teaching school?"

"He is. I think he's the athletic director now, and he coaches basketball. And Isaac and Ezra Walker are two of his stars."

"I'll have to catch a game or two while I'm home," Luke said as he got out of the truck.

Josh and Matt were waiting for them in the parking lot.

"What took you so long? Did you take a side trip?" Matt asked.

"You were driving so fast, I thought we'd hang back to get out of your dust," Dale said.

"Let's hurry," Martha said. "I don't want anybody to get our seat."

"Left side, third row from the back?" Luke questioned.

"Don't be smart, Luke Bryant," Martha said as she hit Luke on the arm.

"I'm just asking. What possible person would think of taking your seat?"

As they approached the front steps, they saw Vincent Peterson and an attractive woman just going into the church. Both of them were balancing two trays apiece.

"Looks like Helen has a lot of stale pastries to get rid of," Josh teased.

"You don't ever seem to complain," Dale said.

"Well, even her stale cinnamon rolls are good," Josh admitted.

"Is that..." Luke started, he stopped, stared more closely, at a woman wearing a black long-sleeved top with lace insets and loose draped camel pants. Every other woman was wearing typical western wear. Then he smiled. "That's Javanna Caldwell. How long has she been in town?"

"I don't know, this is the first time I've seen her," Martha said as she hurried up the steps to catch up with Javanna.

When they stepped inside, Vincent and Javanna had taken their trays into the fellowship hall where Martha found them placing them on the refreshment table.

"It is you," Martha said as she embraced Javanna. "I knew it had to be. You look fantastic!"

Just then, Luke stepped into the fellowship hall as well. "Pete!" he said with a happy smile, holding his arms open for a quick embrace. Javanna moved easily into his arms and kissed him on the cheek.

"You don't know how good it is to see you," he said. "Mom said she didn't even know you were in town."

"I just got here on Friday," Javanna said.

"Me too, I just got back on Friday. How 'bout that? Are you just here for a few days, or what?"

"To be honest, I'm not real sure." Javanna thought of the plan she had formulated in her mind, to call on Monday and see if her old apartment was still available.

Luke laughed. "I know what you mean. I'm sort of in the same boat myself."

Just then Barney Caldwell came in bringing a tray of cookies.

"Hello, Mr. Caldwell," Javanna said, hesitantly.

Caldwell glared at Javanna, set his cookies on the table and then turned abruptly to avoid being in the same room with her, but right behind him was Dane's sister, Melissa.

"Javanna," Melissa said, her greeting genuinely joyful. "When did you get here and how long are you staying?"

"I got here Friday."

"Oh, you must come over and...well, no, it would be better if we met somewhere. I know. We'll have lunch at Abby's Place."

Melissa's greeting was so effusive, and so genuine that the diss she had gotten from her former father-in-law was forgotten.

"I'd better get inside before papa gets upset," Melissa said as she rolled her eyes.

"Thank you, Melissa, I do want to get together," Javanna said.

"Me, too."

Luke had stood aside as first Barney and then Melissa Caldwell had reacted to seeing Javanna. He could see the animosity that Barney obviously felt for her, but he couldn't imagine what Javanna could have done to deserve that. He knew Dane had been dead for three years, and obviously, his parents would have been heartbroken, but why would there be hard feelings toward Javanna?

He had studied her while she was talking to Melissa. She had shoulder length brown hair, and he was surprised to see that there were a few streaks of gray which, strangely, made her hair more striking. She had thick eyebrows, and long dark eye lashes and dark eyes. The light spray of freckles that he remembered still played from cheekbones, across the bridge of her nose. They were so light that one would only see them if they were looking at Javanna as intensely as he was.

When Luke and Javanna moved out into the vestibule, he saw that his family had already gone into the church, and he didn't know if he should excuse himself and go inside or stay out here with Javanna for a moment longer. His dilemma was resolved when Vincent Peterson came out of the fellowship room, and offered his arm to his step-daughter.

Luke didn't know Vincent all that well, though he did know him. But as he followed them on into the sanctuary, he couldn't help but think of Dallas Reed. Luke had very much liked, and admired Dallas, and though he had nothing against Vincent Peterson, he wished it could be Dallas who offered his arm.

When they went inside to take a seat in the pew, Luke saw that the Bryant pew was full, so the logical choice for him was to take the empty seat beside Javanna. He took it happily.

Javanna was very aware of Luke's presence beside her as he sat there impeccably dressed in a crisp white shirt and khaki pants. He was as handsome as he ever was; his hair was a little longer than he had worn it in high school, and she noticed that unlike her own, he was showing a little gray. When he smiled she saw the fine lines around his eyes that betrayed his youthful good looks, but the dimples in his cheeks were as prominent as she remembered them to be. As casually as possible, she let her gaze take in his left hand where she saw no wedding ring. She felt like once again she was the school girl with the unrequited crush on Luke Bryant.

The service began and the choir processed in while the congregation joined in the singing of Praise to the Lord, the Almighty, the King of Creation. Among the choir members were Brooke Peterson, June Caldwell, and Amber Steedman, Luke's high school sweetheart. The Reverend Owen Walker followed the choir and when he got to the front of the church, he stepped up to the pulpit.

"I see some new faces with us today, and the people of Grace Gospel Church invite you to be a part of our family. And now, Brother Baker, would you lead us in prayer, please?"

As Howard Baker intoned the blessings of God on everyone and everything he could think of, his son, Paul and his family came into the sanctuary, arriving late as was their habit. Abby was quietly mouthing, "I'm sorry, I'm sorry," as her three children went their separate ways. Lila, the oldest, slipped in beside Vincent Peterson while Caroline squeezed in between Howard and Jolene, even while Howard was still praying, and the two-year-old Gavin ran down to the front of the aisle, to the suppressed giggles of several members of the congregation, before Paul retrieved him and sat him between him and Abby.

With Howard Baker's amen, Reverend Walker looked out over the congregation.

"And now that Gavin is here, our service may begin." The congregation twittered.

He picked up his Bible and began thumbing through it.

"Brothers and sisters, I'd like you to turn to the book of Matthew, chapter six. Look to verses eight through fifteen. This passage is one of the most familiar in the Bible—the verses you know so well. It is the Lord's prayer.

"Our Father, who art in Heaven, Hallowed be Thy Name, your Kingdom come, your will be done, on earth, as it is in heaven.

"Lord, we need that now. We need your healing hand to take away this virus that is plaguing so much of our country.

"I look at you who have come to our service today to worship God, and I am struck with sadness for our brothers and sisters in Christ who, in much of our country must wear masks, must avoid one another, and cannot even go to church.

"Thank you, Lord, that this affliction has not hit us in such a way. We are here, without masks, and in close fellowship.

"Many of our brothers and sisters are living in fear that their businesses may be burned or looted, that they themselves may be put in danger by the intemperate action of so many of the misguided who have turned their back on the teachings of Christ.

"We are thankful that no such evil has struck us here, but I ask you to think of, and pray for those people who were assailed by the terrible fires in

California, Oregon, and Washington, and even parts of our own state, and those who suffered through the hurricanes on the Gulf Coast.

"With all that is befalling this country, sometimes we think we are living in a horrible dream. Many of us are hoping we will wake up and say, whew, thank goodness I was dreaming. But we are not dreaming. It is only through God that we can come through these dark times. Dark times in our country and dark times in our hearts.

"Going back to the text in Matthew, many of us end with verse thirteen—that's the end of the Lord's Prayer, but read the next two verses: For if you forgive men for their transgressions, your heavenly Father will also forgive you. But if you do not forgive men, then your Father will not forgive your transgressions."

Reverend Owen paused for a long moment, looking at each member of the congregation.

"When you leave the service today, if you don't remember anything else, remember God forgives you, but He needs you to do your part. Forgive those who trespass against you."

The minister sat down and two men went forward to take the offering plates. Trenton York and Barney Caldwell. Javanna wondered if Barney had heard the last words the minister had spoken. Then she chided herself. Had she been listening?

When Javanna looked up, she saw Brooke moving out of the choir. She picked up a stool and a guitar and moved just behind the altar rail. She played the opening bars of The Lord's Prayer and then began to sing the familiar words. Her voice, the melody and the words touched Javanna. She had no idea Brooke could sing so well.

After the service, many of the congregants gathered in the fellowship room to enjoy the refreshments. Luke and Javanna were standing together.

"I'll bet you haven't had your mom's rolls in a long time," Martha Bryant said when she brought each of them a cinnamon roll.

"I know it's been a long time since I've had them," Luke said. "Remember when Helen used to have them hot out of the oven before we started out in the mornings?"

"She didn't have them every morning," Javanna said as she took a bite.

"I remember those days well," Martha said. "I miss having your family out at Crooked Creek. Do you think you'll get a chance to come visit us sometime?"

"I'd like that, but I'll probably be going back to Chicago soon."

"Why are you doing that," Luke asked. "I thought you just got here on Friday."

"I did, but..."

"But it's too crowded staying with Vincent and Helen," Martha said. "I knew when Dale built that place, he should have put another bedroom in it."

"It is small," Javanna said.

"And she had to sleep on the sofa last night," Vincent said as he came up to stand beside Martha.

"Well, I can take care of that. How would you like to come out to the ranch and stay in your old cabin? Jamal Harris is back in Nebraska and nobody thinks he's coming back," Martha said.

"I'd hate to impose," Javanna said.

"Nonsense. The cabin is just sitting there un-occupied. It's fully furnished and I wouldn't doubt but what a lot of it is stuff that was there when you lived there."

Javanna looked at Vincent as if she was asking for permission.

"Do it," he said. "You can drive my delivery van out there and come back and forth whenever you want to."

Martha shook her head. "I believe at last count we have at least fifteen outfits around the ranch. I know you can use any one of those."

"Maybe she can drive Manly Truck," Luke said, "that is when I'm not driving it."

Javanna laughed. "You don't really mean you still have that old Dodge?"

"I haven't seen it, but Dad says it's there."

"Then it's settled," Martha said. "I'll have my girl back."

"When do you want to move out?" Luke asked.

"Why not this afternoon," Vincent said. "Your mom won't be home until the restaurant closes, and then she'll be getting ready for tomorrow, so there won't be any visiting there."

"But what about you?" Javanna asked.

"We'll have plenty of time. I have a feeling you're going to be here quite awhile," Vincent said as he smiled.

"I'll move your things out now, if you want me to," Luke offered. "I'll get the keys from Josh and then he and Matt can ride home with Mom and Dad."

Chapter Eight

"I'm glad you're doing this," Luke said as they pulled out of the church parking lot.

"I guess I'm glad, too," Javanna said. "I was feeling a little like a fish out of water last night. If your mother hadn't offered the cabin, I think I would have been on my way back to Chicago tomorrow."

"That soon, uh? If you don't mind my asking what brought you home if you only wanted to stay for the weekend?"

"I can answer that in two words," Javanna replied. "COVID and riots. I can't sell advertising to restaurants that can't open, and we had a riot right in from of my building. Why did you leave New Orleans?"

"I can answer that in one word. COVID. You can't make movies, if all your actors have to wear masks."

Javanna nodded. "I can see how that might make it a little difficult. What about your wife? Did she stay in New Orleans or will she be coming out here, too?"

"There is no wife. Tia and I were divorced a couple of years ago."

"I didn't know that," Javanna said.

Luke pulled the truck into the parking lot of the produce market. "Looks like we got here before Vincent did."

Javanna walked up to the door of the annex where she heard Riley barking. She tried the door, but it was locked.

"That's new," Javanna said. "I never knew the house to ever be locked. I can go next door to the café and get a key from Mom."

"If we're going over there for the key, why don't you let me buy you lunch. I'm hungry."

Javanna thought about Riley on the other side of the door. She should let her out, but she could wait a little while longer.

"Sure, why not?"

All but two of the tables were full when they went into the restaurant, and they took the one right next to the front window. There were two menus in the middle of the table, and Luke picked one of them up, took a quick glance, and put it back down.

"That didn't take long," Javanna said with a little laugh.

"First thing I saw was chicken and dumplings. It's been a long time, but when you lived out at the ranch, I remember your mom's chicken and dumplings."

"If she made them, they are good," Javanna said as she put her menu down as well.

After a short wait a young waitress came up to

their table and took their order. She was wearing a name tag that read Katie.

"Katie, I guess my mom is in the kitchen, isn't she?"

"Are you the daughter from Chicago?"

"I am."

"Miss Helen said you'd prob'ly be here for lunch, 'n I wasn't s'posed to give you a bill. But I don't know about him." Katie nodded toward Luke.

Luke laughed. "Give us both a bill, young lady, and I'll pay it. That way you'll get a tip."

"Yes, sir," Katie said, smiling.

"Wait here," Javanna said. "I'd better go tell Mom what I'm doing."

"All right."

Javanna walked around the tables, then through the swinging double doors that led into the kitchen. She saw her mother, and an older, white haired lady working in the kitchen. Helen was lifting sandwiches from the Panini press and putting them on plates. Javanna hurried over to take one of the plates out of her way.

"Put some chips on that," Helen said as she set the other plate near a big container of homemade chips. "I didn't expect you back so soon. I thought Vince had some sort of a meeting today."

"I didn't come back with Vincent; I came back with Luke Bryant."

"Luke Bryant? I haven't seen him in a coon's age. What's he doing back in town?"

"Same thing I am, I suppose. COVID shut down one of his productions, so he's back out at the ranch." Javanna paused for a moment. "Where I'm going to be," she added.

"Where you're going to be? What do you mean?"

"Mom, the Bryants were at church, and Martha invited me to come live in our old cabin."

"That's decent of her," Helen said as she pulled another order slip and began filling it. "When will you be going out there?"

"Right after we leave here. Luke's having lunch with me, and he'll help me move my things."

"By things, you mean that dog, too, I guess."

"Yes, Riley will go with me," Javanna said.

Helen nodded. "Then I think that's probably best."

While Luke was waiting for Javanna to come back, Vincent and Brooke came into the restaurant. Luke waved at them, and they came over to the table.

"Thought you'd be here," Vincent said. "Saw your brother's truck."

"Why don't you join us?" Luke asked.

Vincent looked around. "It does look like she's got a good crowd today," he said as he pulled out a chair.

"Where's Javanna?" Brooke asked as she came over to join them.

"She's in the kitchen, telling your Mom that she'll be moving out to the ranch."

"Dad said she was moving out," Brooke said. "I guess that means she won't be doing any work around here."

Luke smiled. "I wouldn't count on that. When Javanna was young, she used to do almost as much work out at the ranch as my younger brothers. I wouldn't be a bit surprised if my father doesn't put her to work. He's already got half a dozen jobs lined out for me to do." Luke turned his attention to Brooke. "Brooke, you have one beautiful voice. Have you thought about singing professionally?"

"I'm going to," Brook said. "Sarah had accepted me as one of the side acts at the Red Ants Pants Festival, but it was cancelled this summer, because of the pandemic. But she says I should apply again next year."

"Sarah Calhoun, yes, I met her several years ago. She's a very enterprising lady, and you'll be an asset to the festival."

"She's more than that," Vincent said. "She does a lot for this community, and you wouldn't believe the money her music festival pumps into this little town."

At that moment Javanna and Katie came out of the kitchen, with Katie carrying the tray with the dumplings, while Javanna carried two glasses of iced tea.

"I didn't know you were here," Javanna said when she joined the table. "Brooke, you sang beautifully today. I can see why you practice all the time."

"Thank you," Brooke replied, as if a little surprised to get a compliment. "But what I really like to sing is bluegrass-country."

"I keep telling her not to turn her back on gospel music. You should hear her sing The Lord Has a Will. She sounds just like Amy Grant," Vincent said.

"I'd like to hear that," Luke said. "If I ever get back to producing movies, I'd love to have you send a demo to my composer."

Brooke didn't say anything, but the expression

on her face said she was pleased with Luke's comment.

"That looks good to me, today," Vince said to Katie as he pointed to the chicken and dumplings. "If she has plenty, that's what I'll have."

"And I'll have a chicken-salad sandwich," Brooke said.

"Go ahead and eat, don't wait on us," Vincent said. "We won't either one of us be going back to the house for a while. Brooke will stay here to run the cash register, and I've got to go over my produce to see if anything needs to be composted."

As soon as Luke and Javanna stepped into the house, a little blond fluff of fur came running to greet Javanna. The little cocker spaniel started jumping up on her, and when she held her hand down, Riley covered it with kisses.

"Well, somebody's happy to see you," Luke said.

Javanna scooped Riley up. "Luke, this is Riley. She's my baby." She held Riley out toward him.

"Will she let me hold her?"

"Oh, yes, she's a sweetheart."

Luke took Riley and held her just in front of his face, smiling as Riley examined him with deep penetrating eyes.

"Looks to me like you've got yourself a good dog here," he said as he set Riley back down.

"My things are in here, if you don't mind, I need to change my clothes."

"Sure, take all the time you want," Luke said as he sat down. "Dad said I could have the day off today." He picked up the Meagher County News and began perusing the local news.

Javanna came into the room then, having changed into jeans and a cotton shirt. "I'm ready."

Luke looked at her with more appreciation than he had had for any woman since Tia.

"Yes, I would say you are," he said with a smile.

During the drive out to the ranch, Luke was very aware of the woman sitting beside him. There was the scent of soap, and the suggestion of lavender, and of course the beauty, not the refined and carefully cultivated beauty of Tia, but a wholesome, natural beauty that required only minimum makeup.

"Tell me about Chicago," Luke said. He asked the question because he wanted to fill the awkward silence that filled the cab of the truck.

"Oh, I love Chicago," Javanna replied. "There is such a vitality to it. I think it was the best decision Dane and I ever made."

"Dane was a good man," Luke said. "I remember him from school. We were on the same basketball team, but if I remember he played football."

Javanna laughed. "Yeah, eight-man football. Dane used to talk about how lucky boys like him were to go to our high school. There were so few people that the coaches literally begged you to go out for a sport."

Luke laughed. "Well, he was probably right about that."

Javanna's hand was resting on the seat beside her, and Luke reached over to put his hand on her's.

"Javanna I can't tell you how sorry I was to hear that Dane had died. I know that had to be very hard for you."

Luke increased the pressure on her hand, very lightly, to illustrate his sincerity, then he took his hand away.

"Yes, when he died, it left a huge hole in my heart."

"But you stayed in Chicago and thrived," Luke said. "I was proud of you for that."

"You followed my career?" Javanna asked.

"A top level executive in CDMI, one of the top promotional companies in Chicago, which means it's one of the top level promotional companies in the whole country."

"Was one of the top level advertising firms in the country," Javanna said, with emphasis on the word was. "COVID did quite a job on us."

"On many of us," Luke said.

"Yes, I can see how it would have an impact on making motion pictures. Which you did very well, by the way."

"Have you seen any of them?"

"Of course," she said. "Dane and I used to brag that we knew you."

Luke chuckled. "It didn't hurt to have some notice in Chicago."

"There's Crooked Creek Road," Javanna said. They had driven west on Highway 360, where they turned south onto the gravel road Javanna had pointed out. This road ended at Crooked Creek Ranch.

Luke stopped the truck in front of the three-story Big House.

"We'll let Mom know we're here, then I'll take you down to your cabin. It's been empty for awhile so I expect it'll have to be cleaned out pretty well before you can move in," Luke said.

"All right," Javanna said connecting Riley to her leash.

When they reached the house, Martha was exuberant in her welcome.

"Oh, it will be so great having you out here again," Martha said. "You and the boys were so close; it was almost like you were my daughter."

"I remember well, being out here," Javanna said.

"I figure we probably should get the house cleaned up and aired before we move her in," Luke said. "Maybe she should stay in the guest room tonight."

"Oh, there's no need for that," Martha said. "Russell and Sage have been working on it ever since we came home from church. I'm sure it's all ready."

"Russell? Do you mean Russell Turns Plenty?" Javanna asked.

"Yes, and Sage is his fifteen year old son," Dale said. "A good worker and an all-around good boy."

"Oh, Luke, I was so excited about coming out here that I forgot to bring any food or bedding or anything else. The only thing I brought was Riley's dog food."

"You don't have to worry about that, honey," Martha said. "There are sheets and blankets on the bed and towels and wash cloths in the bathroom, and I put in a few groceries but I'd like you to come back here for supper tonight if you'd like."

"Thanks, and of course I'll be here for supper," Javanna said.

"Then let's go," Luke said.

The foreman's cabin was at the far end of a line of buildings that were in front of the air strip: the horse barn and corral, the dormitory for the ranch hands, and Russell's cabin.

This cabin was about a mile from the Big House, and as they stopped in front, Javanna stepped out of the truck to look at it. She experienced a powerful wave of emotion that she couldn't put into words. She had spent the first fifteen years of her life here, in this log cabin. It was two stories, with two dormer windows protruding from the steeped roof.

Luke grabbed her things from the back seat.

"Well, are you ready?" he asked.

As they started toward the house Russell and Sage Turns Plenty stepped out onto the front porch.

Other than the Bryants, Russell was one of the last people to see Dallas Reed alive, and Javanna ran to him and embraced him.

"It's been a long time since I've seen you," Russell said. "You just couldn't stay away."

"You may be right," Javanna said. "Looking around, I think things look the same and then I see something that wasn't here when I left."

"Nothing stays the same," Russell said. "This is my son, Sage. He's the same age you were when... well when the accident happened."

"According to Mr. Bryant, you are a hard worker," Javanna said to Sage.

Russell laughed. "Anybody who stays around here for very long has to work hard. I remember all the things you used to do. Are you up for bringing the cattle down from the high country?"

"I suppose so," Javanna said. "I haven't been on a horse for quite awhile, but I don't think that's something I would ever forget."

"Well, there's lots for you to do around here. Doris does most of the cooking for the guys these days," Russell said, "and she'd probably welcome your help."

"She may not want it," Javanna said. "It was Abby who did all the cooking."

"And your mom. I don't get into town all that often—at least not when it's time to eat, but when I have time, I always stop by for a piece of her lemon meringue pie."

"I know she's always glad to see you, Russell."

"I expect you want to get settled, so Sage and I will go on home. If you need anything, just come on over."

"Thanks," Javanna said.

While Luke was getting her bags, Javanna stepped into the open door of the cabin. The layout of the house was exactly as she remembered it: the great room with the stone fireplace, the rather small u-shaped kitchen and the two bedrooms on the side, one for her and one for Abby. The upstairs that was open to the great room, had a much larger bedroom that had been her parents' room.

Some of the furniture was the same that had been there for over twenty years. Walking into the back bedroom, she saw her old dresser and bed frame, as well as the nightstand.

"I expect you'll want your things upstairs," Luke said as he started for the stairs.

"What makes you so sure that's where I'll be sleeping?"

"Because that's the only bed that's been made up."

"In that case, I'll be sleeping upstairs," Javanna said with a little chuckle.

Javanna was standing in front of the fireplace when Luke came back downstairs.

"Ah, good, I see Russell, or more than likely, Sage, laid a fire for you."

"I may light it tonight," Javanna said. "Luke, if Russell becomes the new foreman, will he move in here?"

Luke laughed. "I don't see why he would want to. His cabin is exactly the same as this one so he wouldn't gain anything except the hassle of moving."

"What if Jamal Harris comes back? Where would I go?" Javanna asked.

"You'd stay here and Jamal could move into the bunkhouse. A few years back it was all remodeled, and now every hand has his own room. There's a kitchen and a dining room in there, too, so it's a much better layout than it was when you were here."

Javanna nodded her head.

"I'm going to let you get settled so I'll go on back to the house for a while."

After Luke left, Javanna sat down and looked around. It was as if her father would be coming in at any time. With all of her emotional capital spent on Dane and his death, she had not thought about her father in a long time.

Dallas Reed was a relatively small man in stature being less than six feet tall, but in spirit and will he stood above most men. He commanded the respect of all the hands who worked for him—they called him a cowboy's cowboy. Any task he asked a man to do, he could do himself and he could do it better.

When Javanna thought about her own experience at CDMI, she recognized many of her father's traits in herself. She was successful because she drove herself to be the very best. But now, for the short time she had been in Montana, she was lost. While she was examining her feelings, she decided she would give herself until Christmas, and then she would tell everyone she was going back to Chicago. Surely, the pandemic would be over, or at least some accommodation would be reached so restaurants could open up again.

The one bright spot was Luke Bryant. When she was growing up, Gabe had been the one whom she had competed with most often. She felt for a scar on the underside of her chin. She and Gabe had been racing back to the house across an irrigated alfalfa field, both of their horses jumping the ditches with no problems. But Gabe's horse had reached over and bit her horse on the neck. The horse reared and Javanna fell hitting her chin on a valve. She remembered bleeding profusely, and Luke getting very upset at Gabe. He insisted that Gabe had caused the whole thing.

Noah didn't tend to interact with Javanna, he being the more studious one, and Sam was younger, so he tagged along often getting into just as much mischief as she and Gabe.

She smiled. At the time, she idolized Luke, and some of the daring things she did might have been in an attempt to get his attention. More often than not, he took her side when she and Gabe got into trouble.

Chapter Nine

Javanna had no more than gotten settled in before there was knock on the door.

"Javanna, it's me," Luke called.

"Me, who?" Javanna teased.

"Luke Emerson Bryant," he replied, going along with her joke.

"Come in, Luke, I'm almost finished unpacking," she said with a chuckle.

"You're staying in this room?" Luke asked, noticing she was going into the back bedroom. "I thought you were going to use the upstairs bedroom."

"I found some sheets for this bed," Javanna said. "This was my room when we lived here, and there's something comfortable about it. Also, it will be easier to take Riley out. I expect it will take some getting used to for her. She's not heard too many cows bawling in Chicago."

"I know what you mean about your old room being comfortable; I'm in my old room, too. If I stay very long, I may put away some of the high school stuff. Seems sort of juvenile for a forty-year old man to be sleeping with a Hornet's pennant above his bed."

"At one time all that stuff was sort of important, but I don't expect any of my things are left. Mom's pretty good about getting rid of stuff."

"If she was still in this house, maybe she would have kept things," Luke said. "Do you have anything you want to do this afternoon?"

"Not really."

"Then how would you like to take a ride around the place? One of the boys is saddling a couple of horses for us. That is, unless you've forgotten how to ride a horse, being in Chicago for so long."

"You mean as opposed to all the horses you ride in New Orleans?"

Luke winced, and smiled. "Touché," he said. "Who knows, we may both wind up walking back."

Javanna followed Luke out to the corral, where one of the ranch hands, stood holding the reins to a couple of quarter horses, one white and one black.

"All ready for you, Mr. Bryant," the young man said.

"Thanks," Luke said. "You're Carter, Carter Lynch, right?"

"Yes, sir," Carter said.

Luke laughed. "Save the sir for my dad, I'm just plain Luke, and this is Javanna Caldwell. Her dad was foreman here about twenty years ago, and she's going to be staying in Jamal's cabin for awhile."

"Yes, ma'am." In keeping with the history of Western cowboys, Carter was a young man who was no more than twenty or twenty-one years old.

"Did you pick out a couple of broncos?" Javanna asked.

"No, ma'am, these are two of the best on the ranch," he said handing the reins to Luke.

"Which one do you want?" Luke offered.

"This one will be all right," she said, taking the reins of the white horse. "What are their names?"

Luke chuckled. "Something really original. Salt and Pepper."

"Okay, Salt I guess you and I..."

"Huh, uh," Luke said. "That one is Pepper, this one is Salt."

"What?" Javanna asked, surprised by the revelation.

Luke chuckled. "No, wait. The white one is Salt. I got them mixed up."

"I'm sure you did," Javanna replied, laughing as she mounted her horse.

"Well, as least you haven't forgotten how to get on a horse," Luke said as he threw a pack onto the horse and then climbed into the saddle.

"I always could ride better than you. Even Gabe said that."

"Carter, you'd better open the gate, or she'll jump it, just to show me up," Luke said.

Carter laughed as he swung open the gate to let the two riders out.

Luke and Javanna rode side by side for a while, following the Sawyer Trail until it twisted out into a meadow. Looking down toward the creek, the red willow still held some of its leaves while the golden grass was in contrast to the darker brush. To the east were the rolling foothills and to the west there were mountains on the horizon.

"I've forgotten how beautiful this is," Javanna said.

"Makes you wonder why we ever left, doesn't it?"

"Jobs? Careers? Had either one of us stayed here, what would we be doing?"

"Look at Josh and Matt. They are at one another's throats all the time," Luke said. "When you think about it, Dad has worked fourteen to sixteen hours a day, six days a week for as long as I can remember. What young person wants to do that?"

"Someone who loves the land," Javanna said. "Would you ever think about coming back?"

Luke was quiet for a long while. "If I could figure out some way to make it work. My company is in New Orleans because of Louisiana tax incentives, but my people could run everything there without me. When a movie is in full production, if everything goes well, it takes between two and five months and that's the only time I would absolutely have to be gone. What about you?"

"I've never given it much thought. Working for Mom at Abby's Place isn't quite the same as you running Crooked Creek."

"You could do advertising campaigns from anywhere. Look at all the businesses that have found out they don't need physical offices. I'll bet your boss would love to be able to let his downtown Chicago office go and do everything remotely."

"That's probably true," Javanna said, "but right now, I'd have to have a reason to stay."

"Maybe we could find some reason," Luke said. "I'll race you up to the ridge." He kicked his horse and galloped ahead of her.

Luke was waiting for Javanna when she caught

up with him. He was untying the pack he had brought with him.

"Did you bring us a lunch," Javanna asked as she slid down as well.

"I should have," Luke said. He withdrew two fleece-lined hooded jackets and putting one on himself, he handed the other one to Javanna. "If we go any higher, you'll need this."

"Thanks," she said as she took the coat. "You always did take care of me."

"I've always tried to." He looked at his watch. "We've got time. Do you want to go on up to the pishkun?"

"We may as well," she said.

The pishkun was a cliff that archeologists had determined was probably used by Blackfeet Indians. These buffalo jumps were found in many spots in Eastern Montana, and as children, the boys and Javanna had often played that they were driving the buffalo over the cliff. The view from this site was one of the prettiest vistas on Crooked Creek Ranch.

When Luke and Javanna got there, they let the horses graze for awhile and went over to sit with their legs dangling off the cliff.

"I love this place," Luke said. "It would be a perfect place for a cabin."

"If you would build it, I would live in it," Javanna said.

Luke had a quizzical look on his face. "It's a little out of the way, don't you think?"

"That's what I want. You'd bring me food and water if I needed it."

Luke was pensive before he spoke. "You've not

said as much, but at church this morning, I thought there was some tension between you and the Caldwells."

"There is, and I don't know how to resolve it."

"If you'd like you can tell me about it and maybe I can help you."

Luke put his arm around Javanna's shoulders and pulled her close to him.

For the next hour or so, Javanna poured out all the details of Dane's accident, his death, her self-described involvement with his death, and the relationship she now had with Dane's parents. She told the story without emotion, as if she had told and retold this narrative to herself many times.

When she was finished, Luke took her hands in his. "Would you mind if we prayed? I don't know the answer, but I know God will help you."

While Luke prayed, it was only then that Javanna shed tears. He wiped them away with his thumb.

"We probably need to start back, now," Javanna said.

"All right, but on the way let's go down by the pines. We should start marking out the best Christmas trees. Do you remember when your Dad used to load us all into the sleigh and come out here and cut trees for all of us?" Luke asked.

"Do you remember how he always tried to cut the biggest one he could find for the church?"

"And how we would always have to cut the bottom off just so we could get it in the building."

"I wish we could do that again," Javanna said.

"We will. I think I saw the sleigh in the horse barn and I for sure saw the Clydesdales in the pasture the other night."

Javanna had been invited to take supper with the Bryants that night, and she agreed, provided Martha let her do the cooking.

"Well now, that's a proposition I'm happy to take," Martha said as she settled back onto the sofa. "Use anything you can find."

"Wait a minute, what if she isn't a very good cook?" Matt teased.

"You can always eat peanut butter and jelly sandwiches," Martha said.

With the others watching TV Javanna got busy in the kitchen. She took a quick survey of the ingredients she had to work with, and after checking a few things, she decided she wanted to cook something her father used to put together when for some reason her mother was gone. She smiled and got ready to work.

The first thing she did was cut potatoes into as small a dice as she could, then she did the same thing with an onion, and a bell pepper. Putting olive oil into a pan, she began to cook that concoction. Then she got ground beef out and began browning it, cooking it with cut up black and green olives, and some jalapenos she took from a jar.

When both the potato mixture and the ground beef were cooked, she stirred them together adding Worcestershire sauce and crushed red peppers.

While the hash was cooking, she was toasting

bread and frying eggs over easy. She put the hash, the eggs and the toast on plates, and when she was finished, she began carrying them into the dining room.

"Have you served up all the plates?" Martha asked.

"Yes, ma'am."

"Well then, let me help you bring them out."

"I'll do it," Luke offered. "You just sit, Mom."

When the table was set, all took their seats. Javanna started to pick up her fork, but realized that someone in the Bryant family would give the blessing. The task fell to Luke. Javanna was sitting between Luke and his mother, and when they reached out to join hands, she took them.

"Lord, bless the food that this wonderful young lady has set before us tonight, and know that we welcome her, not only to this ranch, but to this family, amen."

Matt was the first one to take a bite. "Hey, what do you know?" he said. "She can cook after all."

Javanna and the others laughed.

As Javanna lay in bed that night, she replayed the day. She had not wanted to go to church, but now she was glad she had gone. She wished she could get some comfort from a God that everyone around her seemed to accept without question, but she couldn't get over the feeling that God had either deserted her, or that there was no God at all.

Despite the religious vacuity of her time in church, her visit wasn't without benefit. She had reconnected with the Bryant family, and especially, with Luke. She had told herself that there was no room in her heart for anyone but Dane, and even though he was gone, his memory was still very much in her heart. And, although nothing had been said, she felt certain that Luke still had feelings for Tia.

Still, when all had held hands before the blessing, she felt a warmth from Luke's touch.

The next morning, Javanna and Riley walked down to the Big House. The air was crisp and cool and she was glad to have the jacket Luke had loaned her yesterday. She definitely needed to pick up some things in town.

"There you are," Martha said when Javanna came in the back door. "I've got some coffee if you'd like a cup, and I think there may be some scrambled eggs left."

"That sounds great," Javanna said as she opened the cabinet and took out a cup and a small plate. It didn't occur to her to ask. She knew Martha would approve.

"You looked like you slept well. Luke said you are in your old room."

"I am. It just felt right."

"I understand. Tell me how is your mother? I see Vincent a lot at church, but your mother seldom comes."

"I think she's busy most of the time," Javanna said. "I really haven't had an opportunity to talk with her since I've been back."

Martha furrowed her brow. "Oh, honey, that's not good. So many things can happen in this life—

as you more than anyone, can attest to."

Javanna looked away. "Maybe I'll get to talk to her this morning. Are the keys to one of the trucks down at the shop?"

"You take my Jeep," Martha said as she retrieved the key from a hook under the cabinet. "It's in the garage under the porch."

"I plan on staying in town most of the day," Javanna replied. "Won't you need it?"

"Don't worry, if I need to go somewhere I'm sure I can find an available truck, or else an available driver with a truck," Martha replied with a little chuckle. "Why don't you leave Riley with me? That way you won't have to bother with her while you do your visiting."

Javanna smiled. "That would be great. Not everybody loves her as much as I do."

"She and I will do fine," Martha said. "You have fun today—and say hello to your mother for me."

After no more than a twenty-minute drive, Javanna stopped in front of Abby's Place. There were a few cars out front, but Javanna went around to the back so she would enter through the kitchen.

"I thought you might come in today," Helen said. "How did it go out at Crooked Creek?"

"It's good. I slept in my old room and it really brought back the memories."

"We had some good times out there," Helen said. "It's too bad we had to move."

"I'd say there wasn't much choice. I'm so glad you've kept the friendship with the Bryants going."

"Yes, but over the years we've sort of drifted

apart. Not because of anything in particular, but just because our lives have all changed."

"Do you see them at church?"

"Not really. You saw how busy I was on Sunday."

"Why do you do it?"

"What do you mean?" Helen asked.

"Why do you work so hard? The bake shop, the produce market, and the restaurant—surely between the three, you have more than enough to get by," Javanna said.

"I could ask you the same thing. Why do you work so hard? We almost never get to talk to you. Until this trip, you've never even seen your nephew, and Abby said you had no idea she was pregnant. Now that Dane is gone, we are all you have for a family, and you don't seem to care about us at all."

"I do care, Mom. It's just that there are things you don't know about what happened when Dane died."

"Vincent told me some of what you told him, and I'm not asking you to tell me—not until you're ready, but from what he said, you have nothing to feel guilty about. You didn't kill Dane any more than I killed your father. Accidents happen. We don't understand why, but they do. And as for the Caldwells and the cremation. Isn't that what Dane wanted?"

"Yes, we talked about it right after the skiing accident."

"Then they need to get over it. Right now," Helen said. "Where did you spread his ashes?"

"I didn't. They're here with me."

"Well it's time you took care of them. Spread them on the football field, or inter them in the cemetery, or take them to Bridger Bowl, or give them to the Caldwells. You can't get on with your life until

you put your life with Dane Caldwell behind you. Do you think it was easy to go on without Dallas Reed? Let me tell you it was not. But there is no finer man than Vincent Peterson, and maybe it's not the same kind of love I had for your father, but I love him and I know he loves me. Javanna, give yourself a chance, do you hear me?"

When Helen was finished, Javanna just stood there. So much of what her mother had said was true, but it was hard to hear.

"I'm sorry," Helen said. "I probably said too much."

"No, Mom, you didn't." Javanna sighed. "Maybe I've been using Dane's death as a crutch. Anything that doesn't go exactly right, I can blame it on him. And that's not right. I think I'll go see Melissa today."

"That's a start."

Luke was helping Josh push the Cessna 150 out of the hangar.

"Now why are we going to Townsend and not into White Sulphur?" Luke asked.

"Because Dad said. You see that elevator that's run up to the top of the number three grain bin. And do you see that tractor trailer full of corn that's just sittin' there. The sprocket on the augur's broken and Dad wants it in a hurry. He called over to Nailing Truck and Tractor and they've got several sprockets on hand. We're supposed to pick up some extra chain, too, just in case," Josh said.

"It's good flying weather," Luke said.

"We wouldn't be going if it wasn't VFR.

Townsend's an uncontrolled field with one runway, one-six and three-four," Josh replied.

"I haven't flown a one-fifty since I was taking lessons," Luke said.

Josh chuckled. "You still haven't. I'm flying."

"All right," Luke said suppressing a smile. "The left seat is yours."

The two men climbed into the airplane, Josh started it, then with no more of a preliminary than a magneto check, took off.

"Mom said you and Javanna went out riding yesterday," Josh said after they reached cruising altitude. Both men were wearing headsets, and by using the intercom it was very easy for them to talk.

"We did," Luke replied.

"I was only four years old when her dad died, so I don't really remember them living out here. But Mom said she used to hang around you, and Noah and Gabe. She said Javanna was a tomboy."

Luke chuckled. "I guess you could say that."

"But the two of you never dated or anything?"

"No, we never did."

"Why not? As pretty as she is now, she had to be pretty when she was in high school."

"She was pretty back then. In fact, I'd say she and Amber Steedman were the two prettiest."

"It's Amber White now. She married Eddie, but they're divorced," Josh said.

"Oh, what happened?"

Josh shrugged his shoulders. "Who knows what causes people to get divorces." He looked squarely at Luke. "Maybe you should get back with Amber if you're going to stay around here—that is, unless you're wanting Javanna."

"What is this?" Luke asked as he chuckled. "My brother who is twenty-eight and hasn't had a date in how long? That's who's coaching me about my love life."

"That's just it. Matt and I both want you to find some woman to marry and stay here and help run the ranch. Dad wouldn't tell you what to do all the time like he does us."

"And what makes you say that? Am I not assigned a fence to work tomorrow?"

"That doesn't count," Josh said. "Every hand on the place has to do that." He laughed. "I sometimes wonder if when Carter and Blake and Jeff signed up to be cowboys, they understood that they'd be mechanics and truck drivers and fence builders first."

"They're definitely cowboys when it's calving season," Luke said.

"Getting back to you. Will you be around for that?"

"I plan to be."

"All right then—that gives you November, December, and January to find youself a wife."

"Josh, slow down. Who would I find in that length of time?"

"Javanna. I'd take her over Amber," Josh said. "Besides you really know all about her." Josh started nodding his head. "Yes, Javanna's the one. You know Mom likes her. You work on that."

They were approaching Townsend, and Josh turned his attention to the business of flying.

"Any aircraft in vicinity of Townsend, Cessna one-fifty, tail number two seven five, downwind for three-six."

They didn't speak again until they were on the ground and taxied up to the Fixed Base Operator's office.

"I'll get us a car from Petey; he keeps one here for the transient pilots," Josh said.

Luke was still thinking about Josh's comment.

A moment later, Josh pulled up in a Ford Fiesta. "Do you think you can fit in this car, or do you want to stay with the plane?"

"I think I'll stay here."

A wife. A wife before the calving season.

Wouldn't Sherman and the others back in New Orleans have a good laugh if they'd heard what Josh had just said? They'd give it the ax if he wrote that conversation as dialogue.

When Javanna left Abby's Place, she went to one of the outfitters in town and bought some warmer clothing: a shearling jacket, Cowboy Pac boots, a pair of quilted coveralls, some long underwear, a pair of heavy mittens, a wool sock hat and a balaclava to go under it. She even bought some leather chaps. If she was going to be riding up the mountain to bring the cows down to closer pastures, she'd need them if she had to ride through the trees.

As she was checking out, she thought about all the work clothes she'd left in Chicago. The first day she was all dressed up for work here, she'd have Luke take a picture so she could send it back to Devin and Jay. They'd get a kick out of seeing what she was doing while she was in their words, getting her head on straight.

The conversation with her mother was the first step in doing just that. When her mother was talking to her, Javanna had felt like she was back in high school, that she had just been "taken to the wood shed". But what was strange was that she did feel like a weight had been taken off her heart.

Telling both Vincent and Luke the events of Dane's last days had been cathartic. At one time, Devin had suggested she talk to a psychiatrist, to help her get over Dane, but she had insisted she could work through this without help.

Both Vincent and Luke had said she should turn to God to ask for help. She wasn't ready to do that yet, but who knows. Maybe people were praying for her, asking God to help her heal. Whatever had happened, she felt better today.

Javanna was passing the White Sulphur Springs Ranger District Station. She knew Melissa Caldwell worked there and she turned into the parking lot. When she got inside there were only three people there.

When Melissa looked up, she had a genuine smile on her face when she saw Javanna.

"What a surprise," she said coming around the counter to give Javanna a hug.

"I should have called," Javanna said. "Are you right in the middle of something?"

"I am, but it can wait."

"No, no, I'll come some other time," Javanna said.

"Nonsense. Do you know what I'm working on? I'm writing out a program for kids telling them about life after fire in the forest. Do you know bears like forest fires? Why? Because it brings the huckleberries. Huckleberries like sunlight, and when the fires are out the huckleberries resprout."

Javanna laughed. "All right, all right. I guess you can put that aside for a moment. Is there someplace we could go to talk?"

"How about let's go out and sit around the picnic table?" Melissa said as she grabbed her coat.

When the two were seated, Javanna started the conversation, immediately getting to the point.

"I know your parents are very upset with me."

"I won't argue with that," Melissa said.

"Why? They say it was because of the cremation, but that was Dane's choice. We talked about it a lot."

"I know that," Melissa said. "You probably don't know this but I called Dane almost every day."

"He didn't tell me that."

"There are a lot of things he didn't tell you. Do you know he was thinking about divorcing you?"

"I don't believe that," Javanna said. "He loved me and I loved him."

"It's true, believe me. He was bitter about the accident, and he was jealous that your career was going so well, while his was stagnating, if not going backwards."

Javanna put her head in her hands. "If that is how he felt, then when I didn't go check on him when he was locked out of the house—how horrible he must have felt. I really am at fault."

"Javanna, I have something to say, that I've not told anyone—anyone except God. If you blame yourself for not calling him, then I have to blame myself as well. You see, when he was frying the hamburger, it was me he was talking to. He said 'oh my God, I have to go. The place is filling up with smoke.' I didn't call him back either. Does that make me as guilty as you think you are?"

Javanna came around the table and the two held one another for several minutes, neither saying anything.

"But now, that brings us back to Mom and Dad. I think they are over the cremation, because I told them what Dane had said, but the problem is they don't think his life and death was memorialized in the church."

"They want a funeral? Now?"

"I think they would want a memorial service. Why don't you go talk to Reverend Owen?"

Javanna took a deep breath. "This has been an eventful morning."

"I'm serious, Javanna. There needs to be some closure—for them, but for you, too."

"Melissa, you do not know how much I appreciate what you have told me."

"You don't have to go see the pastor yet. Pray about it and you will make the right decision."

Chapter Ten

Over the next few weeks, Javanna's routine had been pretty much established. She went into town early in the day and helped Vincent water and harvest his vegetables from the walipini. She thought back to how hard it had been to convince him that digging a pit in the ground and covering it with Plexiglas would allow him to raise vegetables in the middle of a Montana winter. But now, everyone accepted that Vincent would have fresh organic vegetables anytime of the year.

Raising chickens had been his idea. He had had Dale Bryant dig a smaller pit for the chickens to use in the winter, but for the rest of the time, Vincent had a chicken house and a fenced yard. It was Javanna's job to gather eggs and clean out the coops, and even though it was mundane work, she tended to enjoy it.

When she was finished, she spent some time with her mother and Brooke and then got back to the ranch in time to help Doris Turns Plenty prepare lunch for the hands.

Javanna had fond memories of Russell and Doris. She could remember going to their wedding which was held at a church on the Crow Indian Reservation. Both of their children, Cedar and Sage, had been born after Javanna had moved into town, so while she had seen Cedar as a young child, she had not seen her since Javanna had moved to Chicago.

"Cedar is going to Little Big Horn College now, but when she's done there, she'll be going to Montana State," Doris said.

"You must be very proud of her," Javanna said as she helped to pack the hot boxes to take out to the men in the field. "What does she want to do when she's finished?"

"She wants to be a teacher. It's hard to believe, my grandmother could speak no English, my mother lived her whole life on the reservation and could only attend a BIA school, and now my daughter will be a teacher, not just in Indian schools, but in any school."

"Well, it's only fitting that she be a teacher. You taught my sister and me many things."

"I taught you how to stay out of trouble," Doris said, with a laugh. "Now take those hot rolls out of the oven."

Javanna did and Doris tasted the brisket stew before she helped fill the containers to go to the field.

All the hands who were near the dining hall came there for their lunch meal. The dining hall was part of what the ranch hands referred to as the bunk house, however, as there were individual rooms, it would more correctly be a dormitory.

Blake Coleman, Jeff Graves, and Luke were

working away from the ranch complex and it fell to Javanna to deliver their meals to them.

She put four meals into the hotbox, lashed it to the four-wheeler, then started out onto the open range with them.

Blake and Jeff were up at the Sawyer place, looking for some cows Dale had seen when he had flown over the rim pasture. They had apparently wandered through a section of downed fence. Luke was at the heifer pasture, walking the fence line replacing steel posts and stretching, splicing, and stapling the barbed wire into place.

Every ranch hand had a small, two-way radio, and as soon as she was within range, Javanna called out to them.

"Blake or Jeff, this is Javanna, come in."

"This is Jeff." The response was small and tinny sounding, but easily understandable.

"I'm bringing your lunch. Where will I find you, over?"

"Keep comin' up the Sawyer Trail until you see our four-wheeler parked by the green tanks. We'll meet you there, over."

"I'll be there soon, out."

She put the radio on the seat beside her, and a moment later saw, first the green tanks, then the Honda ATV. Blake and Jeff were standing beside it as Javanna drove up to them.

"Well, now, you're a welcome sight," Jeff said. At twenty-eight, Jeff was one of the older ranch hands. He was also married and lived in White Sulphur Springs.

"Why don't you join us?" Jeff invited.

"That wouldn't be fair to Luke, would it? He'd

have to wait on me."

"He wouldn't care. He's probably sittin' under a tree somewhere just takin' it easy," Blake said.

"I'll tell him you said that," Javanna said.

"No, no, you don't have to do that."

With a friendly wave, Javanna turned the four-wheeler around and started down toward the heifer pasture. She was continually amazed at just how big the Crooked Creek Ranch was. She knew she was several miles away from where she expected Luke to be.

She picked up the radio again. "Luke, do you hear me? Come in, over."

"Luke, here."

"Where are you?"

"Down by the creek bottom. Lots of washout here."

"Can I get to you on the buggy?"

"Don't try it. Lots of deadfall."

"What about your lunch?"

"Wait at the hollow below the ridgeline. I'll get to you."

"I'll be there."

Luke responded by breaking squelch twice.

When Javanna arrived at what she thought would be the hollow Luke had referenced, she turned off the machine and waited. After a ten minute wait, she saw Luke making his way up the hollow, carrying a machete as he chopped brush away in front of him.

When he got there he plopped down on the seat beside Javanna.

"Now tell me again just exactly why I'm here." He took off his glove and wiped sweat off his forehead.

"Uhm...is it because your gym membership was cancelled because of Covid?"

"That's it! You cannot guess how much my legs ache after a day out here."

"Well then you need some energy—some protein," Javanna said as she unzipped the hotbox and removed two covered plates.

"Two plates? Did Doris know how hungry I would be?"

"Not really," Javanna said as she unscrewed the insulated covering. "I thought I'd have lunch with you if you don't mind."

"Mind? I can't think of anything I'd rather do than eat with you," Luke said. He looked around. "Unless it would be eating with you at a table in a fine restaurant."

Javanna nodded her head. "I accept."

For just a second, Luke was taken aback, until he realized that he and Javanna were going to have a dinner date.

"All right, that works for me. How about the Rustic Rock in Bozeman tonight? Or would you rather eat at Abby's Place?"

"Luke, you know I was teasing."

"Maybe you were, but I'm not. Seriously, how about going to the Rustic Rock tonight?"

"Silly, that's a hundred fifty miles we would drive tonight. If you're as tired as you say you are, we'd never make it," Javanna said.

"Who said anything about driving? You forget there are three airplanes on this ranch and I've barely flown in three weeks. Dad flies almost every day and when I hint that I'd like to do it, he says, 'no son, you don't know where to look. Cows could be hiding anyplace and I don't think you could find 'em'. Then he says you've only got ten more miles of fence to cover, or you need to get that grain bin cleaned out, or we'll be needin' to weigh the yearlings in a few weeks and the shed needs cleaning."

Javanna laughed. "Mr. Bryant, it sounds to me like you need a mini vacation. I'll be happy to accompany you to Bozeman tonight, but only if you promise me the dinner can top this brisket stew, which by the way, is going to be cold if you don't stop talking."

Luke would normally have worked until the sun went down, but he stopped about four-thirty and made his way back to the house. Going through the downstairs door to his own room, he headed for the shower, because just as he had told Javanna, he hurt in places he hadn't felt in a long time. Even so, he began to sing.

When he went upstairs, he was dressed in better clothes, still Western wear, but not the usual jeans and shirt he would have had on for a family dinner.

"My, my, Luke, you sure seem happy," Martha said. "Did I hear you crooning in the shower?"

"You did."

"What's got in to you tonight?" Josh asked when he came in from feeding the horses. "Look at him, Mom, all gussied up just for us."

"I doubt that," Martha said. "What's going on?"

"I'm taking Javanna out to dinner," Luke said.

"That's nice. If it's not too late when you come home will you stop by Mathis' and bring me a couple of boxes of brownie mix? I meant to ask

Javanna to get it for me, but I keep forgetting it, and I promised I'd make brownies for the fellowship hour Sunday morning."

"Sorry, Mom, we're going to the Rustic Rock tonight."

"The Rustic Rock in Bozeman?" Josh asked.

"That's it," Luke said. "I guess the landing strip lights are working."

"I think so. Dad had Ray check the bulbs not too long ago."

"Well, I'm going to turn them on before I leave. Don't let anybody turn them off," Luke said.

"How late do you plan to be?" Martha asked.

Luke smiled. "It just depends on what we can find to talk about."

Javanna was excited about her "date" tonight if that's what it would be called. She thought about calling Abby and telling her about it, but now would be the time she was getting her kids corralled, either for dinner, or for baths, or even getting them ready for bed.

And she couldn't call her mother. She would still be at the restaurant, and Brooke would be off doing whatever it was Brooke did. She could tell Vincent, but he wouldn't appreciate the significance of the date.

There was one person who would be pleased about this spontaneous trip to Bozeman—in a plane—for no other reason than to go out to dinner.

She picked up her phone and called Jay.

"Javanna! It's good to hear from you, girl. What's happening? How are things going for you out there?" He answered without waiting for her to say hello.

"You don't know how good it is to hear your voice," Javanna said.

"Oh, the Big Sky getting to you. Are you ready to come home?"

"Now, Jay, don't start drawing conclusions. I've not had enough of it yet. In fact, things are going quite well. Mom and I have sort of come to an understanding. I stay out of her way, and she's fine with that."

"What about you and the Caldwells?"

"That's not resolved yet, but I have an idea. It's just I'm not ready to tackle that right now."

"Well how are you getting along bunking with your little sister?"

"You'll never believe it. I'm living in the cabin I lived in when I was a little girl. I'm out at Crooked Creek Ranch."

"So, are you a cowgirl yet?" Jay teased.

Javanna laughed. "I am. Horses, four-wheelers, cows, fence-lines, I'm all in for it. I'm even one of the cookies."

"Cookies? I don't understand," Jay said.

"I cook. I cook for the cowboys."

Jay laughed uproariously. "I don't believe it. The whole time I've known you, I never saw you cook anything. You mean they don't have take-out anywhere close?"

"They don't. In fact, I'm going out to dinner tonight, and we're flying in to Bozeman."

"Did you say flying? You mean in a plane?"

"Jay, yes, that's how it is out West. There are lots of miles between towns."

"Okay, tell me about this date of yours. I assume it's a man you're going with."

"Yes."

"Is it somebody you've just met?"

"No, I've known him all my life. It's Luke Bryant."

"The movie producer?"

"Yes."

There was a long pause on the other end of the phone.

"Jay? Are you still there?"

"I am, but I'm concerned for you. You sound excited and I don't want you to get hurt. This is just a friendly night out isn't it?"

"What are you getting at?" Javanna asked.

"When we watched The Angel of Bourbon Street together, you told me the beautiful blonde was his wife. Is she going with you?"

"He's divorced."

"Oooooh, then that's different," Jay said. "What are you going to wear? You left all your good clothes here."

"I'm going to wear a better pair of jeans and a silk shirt if you approve."

"Jeans! You can't wear jeans on a date with a movie producer."

"Don't worry, they're stylish jeans," Javanna said.

"What about perfume? Do you have perfume to wear?"

"I have some." Javanna bit her lip to keep from laughing. She thought about the "perfume" she wore when she came out of Vincent's chicken house.

"Well put it on, and make sure your hair is calmed down. You know how you wear it sometimes with the French roll in the back? Do that."

"All right, but if I'm going to get all fixed up, I'd better hang up and get busy," Javanna said.

"One more thing. You tell Mr. Luke Bryant if he doesn't treat you right, I'll come out there and knock the stuffing out of him."

"Jay, he's six feet three, with shoulders the size of an axe handle."

"You tell him if he doesn't treat you right, I will come out there and speak harshly to him."

Javanna laughed. "It was so good talking to you tonight, my friend. Take care, and don't get into any trouble."

When Javanna hung up, she thought about Jay. There was absolutely nothing feminine about him, but he was clearly as close a friend as any woman could be. In fact, except for business associates, he was her only friend in Chicago.

Chapter Eleven

Luke helped Javanna into the Cessna 210, then walked around and climbed in himself. He looked at the wind sack and within a couple of minutes they were in the air.

"I think this is a first for me," Javanna said as she put on her headset.

"It can't be the first time you've been in a small plane. Dad used to take us all up at one time or another when we were kids," Luke said.

"No, I mean flying in a small plane at night."

"Well then you're in for a treat," Luke said. "You don't have the heat convections coming up from the ground, so the air is stable and the ride is smooth."

"Then I won't need to hunt for a barf bag," Javanna said.

"I do remember that," Luke said. "You used to get sick just about every time you went up, but when Dad tried to make you stay back, you'd say 'no, no I won't get sick this time', and every time you did."

"I guess I was a pest back then," Javanna said. "No wonder you never paid any attention to me."

"What do you mean I never paid any attention to you? Didn't I always take up for you when Gabe got you in trouble? And who was it who saved your life when he made you climb into the hopper of a combine and then you couldn't get out?"

Javanna laughed. "Why did I listen to Gabe? No wonder he's still cheating the devil. Has he ever been hurt?"

"Oh yes, broken collarbone, twisted ankles, a strained back and I think he broke his leg once. At least he's not riding bulls anymore, and Mom's thankful for that. She must have calluses on her knees from praying for him. And for Sam, too, but now Sam's back at Fort Rucker so she doesn't have to worry about him as much. I think both of the wayward boys will be here for Christmas, so you'll see them."

"What about Noah?" Javanna asked.

"You never know about him. We thought he and Ty would be here for Thanksgiving, but now he's said Patricia isn't coming home, so they're going to Washington D.C. to be with her."

"That must be hard for your parents not to see their grandson all that often."

"It is, but sometimes on Sunday afternoons Dad and Mom fly down there and spend time with him. He's ten, I think, but I haven't seen Ty for several years. It's too bad."

Within twenty minutes the lights of Bozeman were in sight and Luke was calling for clearance to land at BZN, Bozeman airport.

Once he had the plane parked, they rented a car at the airport, then drove to the Rustic Rock on South Bozeman Avenue. True to its name, the restaurant was constructed of native rocks that were fitted together as neatly as if they were the pieces of a jigsaw puzzle.

"I haven't been here since the day I graduated from college," Javanna said. "Dane and I came for..."

Javanna stopped in mid-sentence, and Luke realized that she was having a difficult moment. He reached over to take her hand in his.

"Javanna, do you want to go someplace else?" Luke asked. "I'm sorry, I wasn't thinking about the memories coming here might cause."

Javanna smiled, a soft smile. "Don't be silly, Luke. Any memories I have of this place are pleasant," her smile brightened, "and now I'll be making a new memory."

They were taken to a table near the fireplace, where, because the weather was nippy, a fire was going.

The waiter who brought the menus, like the maître de who seated them, was wearing black trousers and a white shirt with the Rustic Rock emblem, interlocked Rs, on the left pocket of his shirt.

"Will you be wanting to see the wine list, sir?"

Luke looked at Javanna and she gave a subtle nod.

"We will, thank you," Luke said.

While Luke perused the wine list, Javanna settled on a caprese crostini as an appetizer.

"Do you see anything that looks good to you?" Luke asked.

"I want the blackened bison," Javanna said. "That's something none of my clients served in Chicago."

"All right, we'll make it easy. We'll both have the bison," Luke said to the waiter, "and we'll pair that with the St. Emilion Merlot-Cabernet Franc."

"A good choice, sir."

Javanna looked around the restaurant. There were diners sitting at tables enjoying themselves with no facemasks and no Plexiglas dividers. She wondered if the restaurants in Chicago were coming back, and for a moment, she regretted her decision to leave the city, but then she looked over at Luke.

"May I make a confession?" Javanna asked.

"Yes, my child, what is your confession?" Luke replied in a solemn tone.

Javanna laughed. "Well it won't be that kind of confession, but I have to say this is the first date I've been on since...well in three years. Unless you count Jay—we've gone out together several times, but I don't regard those outings as actual dates."

"Who's Jay?"

"Jay Butler, my neighbor. He's ten years younger than I am, and I think he looks at me like an older sister."

"You mean the way you look at me as an older brother?" Luke asked.

"That's not true—at least for sure, not now," Javanna said. "Maybe when I was young I guess it was a case of hero worship."

"Really? And here, all this time, I thought it was Gabe you were after."

Javanna laughed. "Gabe was a lot of fun and since we are the same age, we were always together in school. And when Gabe would do silly things, Dane would laugh at him and then Gabe would make everything worse. I wonder how many times your mother had to come to school to pick him up after he got in trouble?"

"He was a handful," Luke said, "but Dane wasn't like that was he?"

"Oh, no, Dane didn't do anything exciting...and when he did try to do a flip look what happened? If he had just skied like he always did, he'd probably be alive today."

"Were you happy?"

"I thought I was, but I saw Dane's sister the other day, and she told me something I would never have thought possible. She said Dane told her he wanted to divorce me."

"You had no indication?"

"No, what happened in your marriage?"

Just then the sommelier brought the wine and Luke turned his attention to him, not answering Javanna's question.

The waiter brought two small plates and the caprese crostini.

"Ah," she said, "the Rustic Rock is at the forefront of nouvelle cuisine."

"What do you mean? Caprese has been around for a long time."

"Not the caprese—the microgreens. This is basil," she said, indicating the little green leaves that were on top of the tomatoes and mozzarella.

"All right, so those little leaves are basil. What's so special about that?"

"Luke, you don't understand, it's a whole new way of eating. These plants are ready to eat within about fourteen days. You plant them, they come up, and you cut them before they are more than one or two inches tall, depending on what plant you are wanting. And the nutritional value is phenomenal."

"You sound like a walking commercial for this stuff."

Javanna laughed. "Maybe I am. I've certainly written enough advertising copy about microgreens."

Luke took a bite. "It tastes like it's supposed to. I wonder where they get these, especially in Montana in November."

"Yes," Javanna replied, getting an idea. "Where do they get them?"

The strip lights weren't bright enough to illuminate the airstrip itself, but Luke turned on the landing light when they were on short final, and the powerful beam made the turf landing strip clearly visible.

"It's only eleven o'clock and all the lights are off," Luke observed as he walked her to her house. "Everyone must be in bed."

"Well, that comes from working from sunup 'til sundown," Javanna said. "If we hadn't gone out tonight, I'd be in bed, too."

"I guess you're right," Luke replied. When they reached the door, Riley began barking immediately.

"I think your baby thinks you abandoned her. Do you want to take her for a walk?"

Javanna opened the door carefully. "Let me get her leash." She found it on a hook by the door and attaching it to Riley's collar, let the little dog outside.

"Do you want to walk along the air strip?" Luke asked. "I'll walk with you."

He took Javanna's hand as they walked about a hundred yards from the house. Riley stopped and did her business, but Luke wasn't ready to go back yet.

Javanna pulled her coat around her more tightly and Luke moved closer to her, wrapping his arm around her.

"Luke, I can't tell you how much I enjoyed this evening."

"I know. I did, too. You said this was the first time you've gone out in three years. Well, this is my first time out since Tia and I were divorced. I couldn't have chosen a better date," Luke said. "I don't exactly know how this date came about, but I want to do it again. Would you be up for that?"

"What do you think, Luke Bryant?"

"Before I answer, let me check on something," Luke said. He turned toward her, and he put his finger under her chin, lifted her head, and then came down to join his lips with hers. It wasn't a deep kiss, but there was enough pressure to make it more than a casual buss. "I think you just said you'd go out with me again."

They walked hand in hand back to the cabin. When they reached the door, she opened it and Riley ran in.

Luke took Javanna in his arms, and this time he kissed her, unlike any kiss she could ever remember. It was not the kiss of friends. It was the hungry kiss of lovers.

He separated from her and in the moonlight, Javanna knew he was looking into her eyes.

"Goodnight, Pete, I'll see you tomorrow."

He turned and she watched him for as long as

she could see the form of his body in the darkness. Then she went inside, and closing the door, she slid to the floor, her back resting against the wall. Riley came bounding up to her, her leash dragging across the floor. Javanna unhooked her, and the little dog began kissing her profusely.

"Riley, baby, I don't know what just happened, but I think I like it. I hope you learn to like the snow, because I think we might be here for awhile." She buried her face in the dog's coat as she hugged her close.

When Luke returned to his room he was shaken. What had he just done? These past weeks, he had been thoroughly enjoying Javanna's company, and now he had kissed her—not once, but twice. She had said he was her first date, and he had told her it was the first time he had gone out with anyone since his divorce. What did he know about rebound relationships? Was this one for both of them?

At the restaurant, Javanna had asked what had happened to his marriage, and he had ignored her question.

When he and Tia had married, it had been almost like a merger—she was his star performer, and he was her conduit to movies. It just seemed natural that they would marry. Her father had supplied the start-up money, and while it had never been openly discussed, it was assumed that Luke's movies would have Tia as the star, and that business model had been most successful. They both had gotten what they wanted.

But Javanna had asked what had happened to

their marriage, a totally different question.

The decision to accept the offer made to Tia by Magnum Pictures was hers alone. Luke had tried to make some accommodation to further her career. Had they ever really discussed it seriously, he would have opened a branch of LTN in California, and kept the parent company in New Orleans. He spent several months of the year writing scripts. All of those could have been written while he lived in California, but he remembered her words: "Luke, I need to be in Hollywood...and I need to be alone."

She needed to be alone. That was the hardest part for Luke to accept. It was a total rejection of him, and nothing that he could do or say would change her mind.

And now that brought him to Javanna. He had kissed her and he knew she had returned his kisses. But what if she was "acting", just as Tia had done?

Luke decided he would need to step back a little from his relationship with Javanna. He had known her his whole life and there was no doubt he enjoyed being with her, but he could not stand it, if he entered into a commitment, and then she decided she wanted to go back to her old job in Chicago, and "she needed to be alone".

From those thoughts that were tumbling through Luke's mind, came something that had, for some time now, lay dormant. He felt like writing. Opening his laptop, he began:

IN GOD'S HANDS
Film Script by
Luke Bryant

SCENE ONE:
INT
SOUND: Organ music
Church altar
ECU

An attractive young woman is kneeling at the altar. This is KATHY MORRIS and she is praying softly, but loudly enough that someone close can hear.

KATHY

While He was on the cross, your son cried out: Father, Father, why hast thou forsaken me? I now make this same cry. If you are not real, this will be but a cry in the wilderness. But if you are real, why have you taken from me the one that I loved. I don't believe a loving God would do that, so these words that I am speaking in hurt and anger, are but a cry in the wilderness, because there is no God.

CUT TO:

PHIL BARKSDALE, a young man who, because he was working on something behind the organ, was unseen by Kathy. He has heard Kathy's words of grief.

PHIL (quietly)

Lord, give this woman solace, and restore her faith. Amen

The next morning, Javanna was up earlier than usual, and she was happier than she had been at any time since Dane died. Taking Riley, she stepped out of the cabin, and she was greeted by huge flakes of snow, the first of the season. She knew that it wasn't cold enough for it to stick, but she was as excited as she had been as a child.

Her first instinct was to go find Luke, so she hurried to the machine shed where she expected him to be.

"My, my, what have we here?" Russell Turns Plenty said when he saw Javanna. "On a morning like this, I'd think you'd be snuggled up in bed, especially since I heard Luke's plane come in late last night."

"Eleven o'clock isn't late," Javanna said.

"Maybe not for you city folks, but it is for us old cowboys. What do you need?"

"Nothing really, I was just looking for Luke."

"You missed him. He took the F-150 over to the Colony to see if we can get some of the Hutterites to come help with the gather," Russell said. "Dale thinks there's nobody better than the Hoots to help out, but he doesn't pay them, so it's up to Luke to decide what we can trade."

"Oh, well maybe I'll see him later," Javanna said.

"If you don't, you'll for sure see him tomorrow. You are going to help bring the herds down from the high country, aren't you? That is, unless you've forgotten how to do it."

"I don't think that's something you forget," Javanna said. "There's no telling how many times I did that growing up, but you'd better not stick me as a gate guard."

"Wouldn't think of it," Russell said. "That's Sage's job."

"Poor Sage," Javanna said as she left the shed and started for the Big House.

After having a cup of coffee with Martha and leaving Riley for the day, Javanna drove into town. Since she was early, she went immediately to the chicken house without going to see Vincent first. She saw that one of the waterers had been over-turned, so she replaced the wet wood shavings and then refilled the waterer.

Then she gathered the eggs and took them into the candling room, which was a small dark clos-et on the back of the produce market. Not seeing Vincent anywhere, she turned on the light which was in a little box, and very carefully put each egg in front of the light, checking for any impurities or blood spots that would make the egg unsalable.

When she was finished, she went to the house looking for Vincent or her mother, but when she didn't find them, she walked over to the restaurant. Brooke was putting the chairs down after having mopped the floor.

"I didn't see Vincent or Mom this morning," Ja-vanna said. "Do you know where they are?"

"They went in to Bozeman," Brooke said. "Mom had a doctor's appointment."

"Is something wrong?"

"You know Mom. She didn't say," Brooke said. "Since you're here, roll up some of the silverware in napkins and make sure the salt and pepper shakers are filled. Then you can..."

"I know. Wash the windows," Javanna interrupt-ed. "What is it with that woman and windows?"

"She likes them clean. She says if you have dirty windows, you have a dirty restaurant."

When Brooke had finished her job, she came over and sat across from Javanna helping her wrap the silverware.

"Do you miss not being at Montana State this year?" Javanna asked.

"I wouldn't say I miss it, since I've never been there," Brooke said. "I know you don't believe me, but I want to be a musician."

Javanna smiled. "Would you be surprised if I told you your singing is the only reason I go to church? You really are good."

"Thanks. Nobody around here gives me much encouragement, they just say, oh that's just what Brooke plays around with. The only one who really thinks I can sing is Sarah."

"You mean Sarah Calhoun?"

"Yes, you ought to meet her. Her Red Ants Pants Foundation is something else. Last year I got to go to the chainsaw workshop, and it was one of the most fun times I've ever had. She made me think that maybe a woman can do things that she never thought she could."

"That's good," Javanna said.

"Everybody thinks that I have to go to college, but I don't know if I want to."

"Is it that you don't want to go to college, or is it that you don't want to go to Montana State?" Javanna asked.

"Maybe both," Brooke said.

"Look at Luke Bryant. Who would have thought that going to an unknown school to us—the State University of New York at Binghamton—would have led to all that he has accomplished. A screen writer, a movie producer, not exactly the career path you expect from a cowboy from White Sulphur Springs, Montana, population 944," Javanna said. "Let's see if he has a suggestion for what you could do."

"I'm glad you came in this morning," Brooke said, "and I'm sorry I was so mean to Riley. She really is a good dog."

"She is," Javanna said. "I think she likes living in the country."

"If you want, you can share my room with me. And Riley is welcome too."

Javanna thought of her date with Luke, and the kisses last night.

"I appreciate your offer, but I think I'll stay just where I am."

"Humm, something must be happening out at Crooked Creek."

"All the time," Javanna said. "In a few days I'm going to be riding up into the mountains to bring the cows down for winter pasture. Now that's something a girl who took a class in chainsaw ought to jump at the chance to do."

Brooke laughed. "I'm a 'city' girl, no cow chasing for me."

Javanna felt good about her visit with Brooke. She could understand how Brooke could be anxious about her future, especially if she did have the talent and the will to become a musician. The Red Ants Pants Festival was not enough to propel her into a career, unless she was extremely lucky.

Javanna supposed someone could be "discovered" from playing at that venue, but the likelihood of that happening was slim.

Javanna had been serious when she had said Luke may have a suggestion for a path Brooke could follow. She knew that he had a composer on his staff, and perhaps there would be avenues that neither she nor Brooke had thought of.

Because Vincent and her mother were gone, one of the women from the church was running both the produce store and the bake shop that were in the front of the annex. It had been Javanna's plan to have a talk with Vincent about the possibility of adding microgreens to his repertoire of produce he could raise in the walipini, but since he was gone, she would do it another day.

Javanna had been in White Sulphur Springs for a little over a month and she had not been to Abby and Paul's house yet. They lived in an older house in the section of town behind the high school. The two story house sat on a little rise, giving them an excellent view of the Castle and Big Belt Mountains. Pulling into the driveway that was behind the house, she went up to the back door.

"Mama, it's Aunt Vanna," Lila said as she threw open the door and hugged Javanna.

"Lila, I didn't expect you to be home today. Why aren't you in school?"

"I went, but I had a temperature, so the principal sent me home. Now I have an online learning day," the eight-year-old said.

"Then I'm glad I came to visit you. Where's your mama?"

"She's in the living room," Lila said leading Javanna through the kitchen.

Javanna couldn't help but look around. There were cereal bowls in various stages of being eaten on the table, crusts of toast were on the floor next to the booster seat, and several dirty dishes were in the sink.

When she got to the living room, Abby was sitting on the floor with an overflowing basket of laundered clothing. Several piles of clean clothes were spread out around Abby and on the sofa behind her.

"Hi," Javanna said as she sat down on a foot stool opposite her sister.

Abby looked up at her, her lip quivering as her eyes filled with tears. "I am so tired."

"Can I do something to help you?" Javanna asked.

"You don't know anything about kids. How can you help?"

"I agree, but I'll bet I could handle one of them. Why don't you and the girls go somewhere this afternoon? Maybe out to the carriage house behind the castle. Lila, have you seen the old schoolroom that's part of the museum?"

"Yes, ma'am. My class went out there last year," Lila said.

"But what about Caroline. Has she ever been there?"

Lila shook her head. "I don't think so."

"All right, then you are about to go on a field trip with your mama. Now, Abby, just go. Get out for a little while and I'll stay with Gavin. I need to get to know him anyway."

Abby was like a lumbering bear trying to get off the floor while being seven-plus months pregnant.

"You don't have to do this," she said.

"I know that. I didn't have to stop by here either, but I'm here and I may as well help."

After Abby and the girls left, Gavin and Javanna went outside in the cool crisp air. They walked down to the high school and around the football field. She let him run on the field and she chased him, pretending to tackle him and then she let him tackle her. Finally he asked to be carried, but she continued to let him walk the few blocks to Abby's house.

When they got home, she put him on the booster seat and made him a peanut butter and jelly sandwich. He could barely keep his eyes open while he ate, and finally she carried him into his room and put him into his bed. Before she was out of the room, he was asleep.

From there she went to the kitchen, and quickly had the table cleaned and the dishes done. Then on to the mountain of clothes. Javanna wasn't as sure of herself with the sorting, but she made piles of folded clothes, according to the sizes. Then she placed the piles back in the basket waiting for Abby to put them away. When she was finished she found the vacuum cleaner and ran it in the kitchen and living room.

She had just sat down to take a breath when she heard the back door open. Lila and Caroline came bounding into the living room.

"We had so much fun," Lila said. "Caroline tried to climb on one of the stagecoaches, and Mama had to have the woman get her down. She didn't know she couldn't do that."

"Well, Caroline, what else did you see?" Javanna asked.

Caroline put her head down, but she didn't answer.

"She saw lots of things, but she doesn't know what they are," Lila said.

"You're the big sister, so you took care of Caroline, just like your mama used to take care of me when I was little," Javanna said.

"It looks like you took care of me today," Abby said. "You don't know how much I enjoyed this afternoon." She came to Javanna and as much as possible with her condition, she hugged her. "Thank you."

"Maybe I'll have to do this more often," Javanna said. "Gavin and I had a lot of fun, but I'll say one thing—that child has a lot of energy."

Chapter Twelve

It had still been warm when Javanna left Chicago for White Sulphur Springs, but now it was the beginning of November, and the temperature had dropped into the thirties. She was lying in bed in the gray light of early morning, thinking that she needed to turn the heat up and then take Riley out. She pulled the down comforter up around her neck and closed her eyes in hopes of sleeping a few more minutes before Riley started demanding to be taken out.

But then she remembered what was going to happen today. It was the first day of the gather, and every hand on the ranch, plus half a dozen more, were going to start moving cattle down from the summer grazing fields. The cattle would be kept together in various groupings—the bulls in one pasture, the yearling steers in another, the nursing mothers, the feeder cattle, and the fats in still others. The yearling heifers would be the closest to the calving shed so that they could be watched more carefully.

Jumping out of bed, she pulled on her long underwear, then a flannel shirt and jeans. In addition she got out her chaps, her wool sock hat and her balaclava. She wasn't sure she would need the face covering today, but she was going to take it in case the wind was blowing. Finally, she pulled on her new Cowboy Pac boots and laced them up over her jeans.

Last night, Dale had gathered everyone together and assigned various jobs. Some of the hands would be riding four-wheelers while others would be on horseback. Luke and Matt had gone over to Springdale Colony to pick up six additional men. Even though they would be riding Crooked Creek horses, Luke pulled a horse trailer behind his truck. In exchange for their work, Dale would send several steers back with them.

Javanna had agreed to help Doris fix breakfast, and she hurried to the dormitory dining room. Several of the men including Luke and Matt were already there drinking coffee while Doris worked feverously to get everything done on time. She was putting the last pan of biscuits in the oven when Javanna walked in.

"Good, you're here," Doris said. "I need to get started on the sausage gravy, but I want you to check on the potatoes. When they are almost fried, mix up two dozen eggs and then put the eggs on top of the potatoes."

Javanna looked at Doris with a questioning look on her face. "On top of the potatoes?"

"Yes, potatoes and eggs. Don't cook them too fast, but make sure you get the eggs scrambled around and through the potatoes."

"All right, if you say so," Javanna said, "but it seems to me like you'd make fried potatoes, and then you'd make scrambled eggs."

"Tell me, Missy, who's been doin' the cookin' around here the longest?"

"Yes, ma'am," Javanna said as she poured the eggs over the potatoes that were in two huge skillets.

"The first two pans of biscuits should be done, so take 'em out and then you go eat with the others," Doris said when the rest of the men came in. "I know you're going out with 'em today, and I don't want Mr. Dale blaming me if you're not ready to go when he is."

Javanna sat between Luke and Dale, as Doris began putting the food on the long table. Everyone was talking and joking as they passed the food.

"Boy, you better get you some more of them biscuits 'n gravy, you don't have near enough on your plate," Blake Coleman teased Carter Lynch, who was the youngest of them.

"Yeah," Ray Jaworski said. "You're liable to grab one of those heifers by the tail, and she'll drag you half way to North Dakota."

The others laughed at Carter, who took it in good spirits.

Javanna was amazed at how much food this crew could eat, and she was surprised at how good the potatoes and eggs were. When everyone was close to finishing, Dale stood up.

"Men," he started, then he looked at Javanna and smiled, "and lady," he added, "we've got a lot of work to do today. Some of these cows are going to be hard to find, some of them are going to be on the wrong side of the fence, and some of them are just going to be plain ornery."

"You'll be spottin' 'em for us though, won't you, Mr. Bryant?" David Wurtz asked. Wurtz was one of the Hutterites who Luke had brought over earlier.

"I'll be in the air by the time all of you are where you're supposed to be. Russell Turns Plenty will be in charge on the ground. If anybody needs help, he'll be on the four-wheeler to try to get to you, but all of you make sure you have your radios. I want you Hoots to pair up with my guys so nobody's ever out of communication.

"Javanna, I want you to stay close to Luke. You two go up to Wardlow, and Matt, I want you and Sage to be near the headgate at Sawyer. Make sure you keep an accurate count of how many cows come through. Does anybody have any questions?" When no one said anything, Dale continued, "When we get up higher, we're going to run into snow, and there may be patches of ice underneath. You men on the four-wheelers—watch where you're going. I don't want to find somebody sliding down the mountain, so all I'm asking is that everybody stay safe."

"Before anybody leaves, grab one of the orange vests," Russell said. "That way Dale will have an easier time keeping up with you."

Luke and Javanna walked out to find that someone had already saddled Pepper and Salt for them. Most of the cowboys were to be trucked to a spot about fifteen or twenty miles away where the horses had already been staged. In addition, several of the four-wheelers were on a trailer and they, too, would be taken to higher country.

Javanna was wearing her shearling jacket and for now it felt much too warm, but as Dale had said, when they got up in the high country, there would be snow. Unbuttoning her coat, she buckled her chaps around her waist, and then she was trying to close the zippers that ran down the back of her legs.

"You need some help, little lady?" Luke said in his best John Wayne accent.

"I sure could use a mite," Javanna said. "I was just a fixin' to zip that there leg up, but I kan't find the zipper."

Within a minute, Luke had both legs zipped. "There you go, little lady."

Javanna laughed. "If we're going to keep this up all day, it's going to be a long day."

"It's going to be a long day anyway," Luke said tossing the orange vest to Javanna. He circled his hand around his head. "Let's head 'em up, move 'em out."

After about a thirty minute ride, they reached McKenzie Coulee where they spotted about two dozen heifers grazing leisurely, unaware of what was in store for them. Luke circled the cows and began driving them toward one of the smaller fields that would be a temporary holding pen. Javanna moved alongside the cows yelling while Luke whistled to keep them moving and soon they had the cows safely in the fenced area.

"Now that was easy," Luke said. "Who said this was going to be a long day?"

Just then they heard the squawk of the radio.

"This is Navarro. I'm at Wardlow Ridge, and

I've got about a hundred head up here. If anybody's close by, I could use some help."

"Where on Wardlow are you, Alejandro?" Luke asked.

"I'm near the tanks, you can't miss me."

"We've got about twenty head in front of us, we'll be bringing them with us," Luke said.

The twenty cows responded easily so Luke and Javanna joined Alejandro within fifteen minutes.

For the next couple of hours Luke, Javanna, and Alejandro worked the cows, pushing them toward the alfalfa field where Luke and Javanna had left their others. This bunch was relatively easy to work as well, because by now most of the run had been taken out of them. Javanna counted them at the gate, and including the twenty she and Luke had already put in this field, the count came to one hundred forty-eight head.

"Who's close to Lodge Pole Creek?" Dale's voice cracked over the radio.

"This is Luke, Dad. I'm not too far away."

"Do you see me?" Dale asked.

"Yes, sir, I see you."

"All right, I'm going to wag my wings when I'm right over the cows I see. I'll make a ninety degree pass as well, so you can pin-point them."

According to Dale's fix, these cows were farther up the side of the mountain and definitely in the trees. When Luke got to the place he thought his father had pin-pointed, he moved into the pine trees. From what he could guess, he estimated there would be about forty head spread out among the trees.

This gather wasn't going to be as easy as the other two had been. One of the problems was the cows were considerably lower to the ground than either Luke or Javanna, and that enabled the cows to dart easily under low branches of the trees.

Javanna was glad she had her chaps on as her horse was taking her through the trees with branches whipping her at will. They would think they had the cows headed in the right direction, when one would dart back into the trees and then two or three more would follow. For the next couple of hours Luke and Javanna worked the cows down the mountain and out of the trees. Finally, they were able to join them with the others that were in the alfalfa field.

"Luke, where are you?" This was Russell on the radio.

"Just below McKenzie Coulee," Luke said.

"Meet us over by the tanks on the Sawyer Road. We'll put the horses in the trailer and haul them down."

"That sounds like a plan," Luke said as he clicked the radio. "What do you think, Pete, is this the way you remembered it?" He rode Pepper up close to Salt and Javanna.

"This is the first time I've been this far up the mountain," she said. "I said I didn't want to be the gate guard, but maybe that job wasn't so bad."

"Are you tired?"

"Let's just say I want you to wake me up when the truck gets us home."

When they got the horses out of the trailer, Luke loosened both cinches and then took off the tack. Javanna walked the horses up and down the alley while Luke put the tack away. After the horses were in their stalls, Luke got oats while Javanna filled up their water buckets.

"Hey, you two, Mom's got supper ready," Josh said as he stuck his head in the stable. "Hurry up."

"Tell her we'll be there in just a minute," Luke said.

"Are you as hungry as I am?" Javanna asked as the two started walking toward the Big House.

"Protein bars don't quite do it for me," Luke said. "I hope whatever she's cooked, there's a lot of it."

When Luke opened the door, Riley, who had been with Martha all day, yelped and jumped around in excitement when she saw Javanna.

"Did you think I forgot you, Baby Dog?"

Riley rewarded Javanna with lots and lots of kisses.

Martha had indeed fixed a huge supper. She had meat loaf, mashed potatoes, green beans, carrots, and hot rolls. And, as a reward for the hard day's work, she had made a cherry pie. The conversation at the table centered around the work that had been done in bringing in the cattle.

"And to think," Luke said, "we have at least another five, maybe even six more days of this."

Javanna groaned as she lowered her head to her hands.

"Dale, do you think you need Javanna?" Martha asked. "That's a lot of work and she's the only woman out there."

"What do you think, Javanna, do you want to do it, or not?" Dale asked.

"I signed up for this, and I'm not quitting now," she said.

"That's my girl," Luke said. "She's the best partner a man could ever need."

"Oh? Tell me, Luke, are you trying to tell us something?" Josh questioned.

Luke looked at Javanna and smiled, but had no further comment.

Javanna was thankful that Martha had sent Epson salts home with her, as she lay soaking in the steaming water in her bathtub. Her back hurt, her arms hurt, her legs hurt, and her derriere definitely hurt after spending the whole day on a horse. Martha had given her the perfect out to say she didn't want to go tomorrow, but she had told Dale she wasn't a quitter. And when Luke had said she was the best partner a man could ever need, nothing would stop her from climbing on a horse for another day. Then when Josh had teased Luke by asking if he had something to tell them, Javanna was pleased with Luke's reaction.

As she lay back sinking farther into the tub, her eyes closed. Did she want to read more into the comment that Luke had made or was it a throwaway exchange between brothers? However it was intended, she would be a part of the gather for as long as it took to bring every cow down from the high country.

When the cows were all in their assigned pastures, the activity of the ranch increased. The buyers came with their big eighteen-wheeler trucks to look over every steer Dale was offering for sale. Then each one had to be weighed and recorded and loaded on the cattle haulers. The cut-backs and the heifers that were not bred would be taken to Billings to the cattle auctions, and the ranching cycle began for another year. Everything was geared to the spring calving that would start near the end of February.

Everyone around the ranch was busy and Javanna tried to stay out of the way. Most of the time, she was in town helping Vincent. After she and Luke had had their date in Bozeman, Javanna had convinced Vincent that he should add microgreens to his line of produce.

The biggest obstacle was to try to explain to him what microgreens were.

"You mean people are going to be eating little bitty Brussels sprouts?"

"No, no, you eat them before they get to that stage."

"Then it's like bean sprouts."

"No, no."

"Then it's a garnish."

Finally, Javanna had gone to the Feed and Seed store and bought some organic vegetable seeds. She used some of the take-out trays from the restaurant and planted some radishes, lettuce, spinach, and basil in organic soil. Within two weeks the microgreens were ready to harvest, and after tasting them, Vincent was convinced he might be able to sell them.

After taking Riley up to the Big House to spend the day with Martha, the two women were drinking coffee. Javanna's cell phone sounded the Sherwood

Forrest signal that denoted a text message. Glancing down, she saw that it was from Melissa Caldwell.

Will U meet me at Grace 2 pm today?

For a second, Javanna was confused by the message, and then she realized Melissa meant Grace Gospel Church.

"That's strange," Javanna said, "Melissa wants to meet me at church today."

"Oh, dear, I have to go into Bozeman to pick up some new glasses, so I'll need my Jeep. You go find Russell and he'll give you the keys to one of the trucks, and Doris can look after Riley," Martha said. "You know, everybody has fallen in love with that dog."

"Everybody out here," Javanna said as she rolled her eyes, "but there are still those in town who would just as soon not have her around."

After leaving Riley with Doris, Javanna went to the machine shop to see if she could find Russell. When she walked in, the hood was up on one of the trucks and Russell and Luke were under the hood.

"Hi, guys," Javanna called out. "What's up?"

"A fuel pump—that's what's up," Luke said as he wiped his arm across his forehead. "It's been a long time since I've had to even think about doing something like this."

"But it's good for you," Russell said. "You never know when one of your fancy cars might break down on the side of the road."

"I hate to disappoint you, but my 'fancy car' is a four-year-old Mazda SUV," Luke said.

"Well, if you have a truck to spare," Javanna said,

"Martha is going to Bozeman today and I need a vehicle. What do you have available?"

"Definitely not this one," Russell said. "My helper here isn't worth much. If you had to depend on him, you wouldn't drive this truck for a week."

"What about Manly Truck?" Luke invited.

"Seriously? Manly Truck is still around here?"

"It was up at the Sawyer place all summer, but Matt drove it home the other night, and it's running fine. Unless you're planning on going someplace, where you need to be extra elegant," Luke teased.

"Depends on whether or not you consider church elegant. I'm going to meet someone there."

"You're going to church?" Luke asked, surprised by the comment.

"Yes, but I don't understand why I would meet someone there on a Thursday afternoon."

"Maybe you'll be meeting God."

Javanna smiled. "You do keep trying, don't you?"

Javanna was distracted as she went about her morning routine. She and Vincent were turning the pit he had built to house chickens in the winter into a growing area for the microgreens. Vincent was still skeptical about a market, because so far, except for Abby's Place, no one was using them.

Today they were constructing a makeshift solar system that would funnel warm air into the existing chicken house.

"Isn't a chicken a bird?" Javanna asked.

"Of course it is," Vincent said.

"Then how come chickens have to be protected in the winter?"

"You grew up in Montana. You tell me why we have to get some warm air into this hen house."

"All right," she said.

What they were constructing was quite ingenuous. Vincent had built a rather large box-like extension onto the chicken house. Then he covered it with Plexiglas that he put on a slant to catch the sun's rays during the day. To complete the project, Vincent had bought about a hundred children's balls, that he painted black and then injected with water. During the day, the water warmed up and during the night the heat was funneled into the chicken house.

At precisely two o'clock, Javanna pulled into the parking lot of Grace Gospel Church where several cars were parked, but she didn't see Melissa.

She stepped down from Manly Truck, zipped her jacket closed, then hurried through the chilly air to the church. The Reverend Owen Walker was waiting for her in the vestibule.

"Good afternoon, Javanna," the pastor greeted, "I'm glad you came."

"Reverend Walker, do you know what this is about?"

"Yes I do, but let's wait and let Melissa tell you."

By invitation, Reverend Walker led Javanna through the church and into the pastor's office. Melissa, who had been sitting there waiting on her, got up, and with a smile embraced Javanna.

"Javanna, thank you for coming."

"Would you like a cup of coffee?" Reverend Walker asked.

"Yes, thank you," Javanna said, noticing that Melissa already had a cup.

"I know you are wondering what this is all about," Melissa said. "Ever since you stopped by to see me at work, I've been trying to think of some way you and my parents can get beyond whatever it is between you. Especially if you are going to stay here in town."

"And if everyone is going to attend Grace Gospel," Reverend Walker added, "the church is not only a place of worship—it is a community of friends and family, and when a part of my flock is hurting, the whole church is hurting."

"What we're asking is, if you would consider meeting with my parents?"

"Of course I would," Javanna said. "Until Dane died, I always thought I had a good relationship with Barney and June. I know I didn't talk to June that often, but when we did, it was very cordial. Never did we have an argument, and the biggest disagreement we ever had was whether to have cornbread dressing or bread stuffing at Thanksgiving."

"And who won?" Reverend Walker asked.

Javanna frowned. "What do you mean?"

"Cornbread or bread? What did you have? I'd be on the cornbread side."

Javanna laughed. "Since June did the cooking, we did have cornbread dressing."

"You know what upset them—it's the cremation," Melissa said.

"But you told me yourself, that you knew that was what Dane wanted."

"Yes, and I think I have convinced Mom and Dad of that."

"Then what is it? What do they want?"

"Barney and June are devout Christians, and as Christians, Barney especially, is concerned that Dane never had a Christian burial. No prayers were ever said, no thanks were ever given for the life of their son," Reverend Walker said. "In their minds, burial is a Christian act, as it is in the minds of many Christians."

"Are you telling me they want a funeral? Now?" Javanna asked.

Melissa nodded her head.

"As Dane's wife, you have the final authority—whether or not we proceed with this burial," Reverend Walker said.

Javanna took a deep breath. "If that's what they want, then..." She shrugged her shoulders.

"I believe Barney and June will be pleased with your decision. Now, is there any way you can have his ashes sent from Chicago?"

"That's not necessary," Javanna said.

Reverend Walker and Melissa exchanged glances.

"You must understand. Even though Dane was cremated, those ashes are his earthly remains, and if we have a funeral, we would need to inter those ashes."

"His ashes are here."

"In White Sulphur Springs? You brought them with you on the plane?" Melissa asked.

Javanna's lips trembled as she fought to hold back tears. "The last two years have been hard, very hard. I blame myself for not..."

Reverend Walker reached for Javanna's hand. "Dane's death was tragic, but it was not your fault.

Ask and God will forgive. That is His promise."

"Keeping his ashes brought me some comfort, because it's almost as if he's still with me."

"He is still with you, Javanna," Reverend Walker said.

"I know the Christian concept of survival of the soul, and how that soul is still with loved ones," Javanna said. She shook her head. "But I'm afraid I no longer believe in God, and certainly not a benevolent God."

"Do you hold dear the memory of Dane?" Walker asked.

"Of course I do."

Walker smiled. "Then whether you believe, or whether you don't believe, that memory of him shall forever be kept green, and it is that memory that will give you solace and comfort. You don't have to have the physical connection with his ashes to preserve that memory."

Javanna thought about what the pastor had said. She thought that having Dane's ashes with her enabled her to speak to him. But Reverend Walker was right; she didn't really need his ashes for that. And if by giving up his ashes, she could effect a reconciliation with the Caldwells, then she was willing to do it.

"Barney and June are waiting in the adult Sunday school room. If you're ready to see them, I'll go get them."

After the pastor left, Javanna and Melissa were alone in the church office.

"Melissa, you said something when I stopped by

your office that's been bothering me ever since."

"Is it that I said Dane wanted a divorce?"

"Yes, I loved Dane, and I'm sure he loved me just as much. I don't understand how he could have said that he wanted a divorce."

"He wanted a divorce because he did love you. He thought he was a burden to you, that you deserved to have a husband that could be a real husband, that you deserved to have a child that he could never give you," Melissa explained.

"How could he have thought that? When you do something out of love, it isn't a burden."

Most of the members of Grace Gospel Church were present for Dane Caldwell's funeral service. Javanna sat in the first row with Barney, June, Melissa and Dane's younger brother, Wade. The Petersons sat behind her and the Bryants were behind them.

Brooke provided the music for the service and the sweetness of her voice touched Javanna's heart.

When she finished, Reverend Walker stepped up to the podium.

"Brothers and sisters, we are here to celebrate the life of Dane Caldwell, and before I start my remarks, I would like to read the poem said to be given to us by the poet, Mary Frye. I said 'given to us' because that is what she did. She gave it to the world, never having copyrighted it, so that her words may comfort us all:

Do not stand at my grave and weep
I am not there. I do not sleep.
I am a thousand winds that blow.
I am the diamond glints on snow.
I am the sunlight on ripened grain.
I am the gentle autumn's rain.
When you awaken in the morning's hush,
I am the swift uplifting rush
Of quiet birds in circled flight.
I am the soft stars that shine at night.
Do not stand at my grave and cry:
I am not there. I did not die.

When the minister preached his message, Javanna continued to contemplate the words of the poem. Do not stand at my grave and weep. I am not there. I did not die.

She knew that was the central core of the entire Christian faith. This day she wanted to believe that.

Chapter Thirteen

With Dane's funeral behind her, Javanna felt like a heavy burden had been lifted off her shoulders. After the burial, the church had hosted a reception in the fellowship hall, and for the first time, she had felt like she belonged. June and Barney were pleasant, but there had not been the opportunity to say anything substantive. Javanna had enjoyed talking to Wade whom she hadn't seen for years. He was ten years younger than she, and he was now a cattle buyer in Fort Worth. She had been amused when she saw Melissa and Josh Bryant engaged in what looked like a serious conversation.

There had been several flurries of snow since Javanna had been back and on one occasion, there had been enough to cover the ground, but that had soon melted. Today the quarter-sized flakes were coming down hard and it promised to be a significant accumulation. She was as excited as she had been as a kid, and she pulled a chair up to her window and watched as the scene in front of her was transformed into a wonderland.

While she was watching, she saw Russell out with the snowplow, clearing the runway and the lane out to the gravel road. While Javanna was enjoying all of this, she knew for the ranch hands, it just added more work.

As had been predicted, the snow was heavy bringing at least eight inches. When Javanna took Riley out for her last time, she bounded happily from one spot to another, as the moon was reflecting off the snow. Javanna had missed this and she was glad to be home.

The next morning, Javanna was awakened to the sound of bawling cattle. Nothing slowed the demands of a cattle ranch.

Russell had been out all night, and the road to the county highway was clear enough for her to get into town, and after visiting with Martha as had become her morning routine, she went to get Manly Truck.

"I thought you might be going into town today," Luke said when she went to pick up the key from the key board. "I filled the tank up and put a few rocks in the bed so you'll have more traction. I don't think you'll need tire chains but I put them in the cab just in case."

"Well that was nice of you," Javanna said. "I don't want to be calling you when I slide off in the ditch."

"You know I'd come rescue you no matter where you are," Luke said as he made a sweeping gesture, "but seriously, if it starts snowing like it was yesterday, don't try to come home. I'll take care of Riley if you can't make it. In fact, call me and tell me what you plan to do."

"All right."

When Javanna pulled into Abby's Place, there wasn't a car in the parking lot. When she went in, her mother and Brooke were eating breakfast together.

"We didn't think you'd get in today," Helen said. "I don't expect we'll have much business."

"Probably not, but this day will give you a chance to take a breather."

"I don't think so. It's too close to Thanksgiving and I've got a lot of orders that I should be working on," Helen said. "You know Howard and Paul give every one of their regular customers a basket at Christmas. That's fifty-five loaves of pumpkin bread, cranberry bread, banana bread, and lemon poppy seed bread. Thank goodness, Vince put a huge freezer in the bake shop."

"Then I'll help you bake today," Javanna said.

"And so will I," Brooke said. "I don't think we can mess up quick breads."

"Unless we let them burn," Javanna said. "By the way, Martha told me to ask if all of you would come out to Crooked Creek for Thanksgiving. Even Abby and Paul and the kids."

"Well, Abby and Paul won't come. They always spend Thanksgiving with Howard and Jolene, and I don't know if we could get away either."

"Why not, Mom?"

"We have a business to run."

"And how many customers do you expect to

come in for Thanksgiving? People spend time with their families that day and I want you to come out to Crooked Creek. Remember when we all ate at the Big House when Daddy was alive? He and Dale would always argue about the right way to carve a turkey."

"They did have their own ideas about things," Helen said. "It's a wonder Dale Bryant didn't fire your father every other month."

"And yet they were the best of friends. Can I tell Martha you will come?"

"I suppose we could close the restaurant."

"Of course you can," Brooke said.

"But you'll have to ask Vincent if he wants to go out to the ranch," Helen said.

"I can do that," Javanna said. "Now where are the loaf pans?"

It was snowing hard as Javanna drove back to the ranch. She had left earlier than she normally would have, but she wanted to get back before the road was drifted with snow.

Javanna had enjoyed the time in town and she was glad her mother had agreed to come out to Crooked Creek for Thanksgiving. Brooke had agreed to bring her guitar, and Javanna was looking forward to the day. Several loaves of overbrowned pumpkin bread were on the seat beside her.

When she got home, she made a cup of instant coffee and sliced off a piece of the bread.

"I don't know why Mom wouldn't keep these. They still taste good." Javanna slathered some butter on the slice and put it in the microwave.

While she was eating, there was a knock at the door. When she opened the door, Luke was standing there dressed in Gore-Tex pants and jacket. He was carrying a garbage bag.

"I see you're home early," he said as he stepped inside.

"Yeah, I didn't want somebody to come pull me out of the ditch," Javanna said. "Would you like to share some burned pumpkin bread?"

"Did you make it?"

"What do you think?"

Luke laughed. "How would you like to go for a ride this afternoon? I'm hiding out before Russell assigns me more jugs to clean out."

"This is sort of early to be worrying about cleaning pens for baby calves, isn't it?"

"Of course it is, but on a day like this, he can't find anything else for us to do. Now, do you want to go with me or not?"

"I don't have anything to wear that's warm enough," Javanna said.

"That's what I thought you'd say," Luke said. "Mom said to go raid Sam's room. When he was married to Francine, they used to go out a lot, and I found all her old gear." He handed the bag to Javanna. "I think these things will fit you."

Javanna took the bag. "If we're going to be gone awhile, will you take Riley out while I get dressed?"

"Sure." Luke cut himself a piece of the pumpkin bread as he grabbed Riley's leash.

When Javanna opened the bag, she found insulated bib pants, a jacket, socks, boots, a Gore-Tex balaclava, gloves, and goggles. He had thought of everything. She dressed quickly, and when she went back into the great room, Riley began barking at Javanna.

"Hey, it's me little girl," Javanna said as she knelt down beside her dog. "You're going to have to stay here by yourself for awhile."

Luke was sitting at the table and had eaten one of the mini-loaves of bread Javanna had brought home. "Good, I'm glad you could wear everything. The snowmobiles are in the shed."

In a lean-to shed attached to the hangar, Javanna saw a half-dozen snowmobiles, and she was reminded that just as the airplanes had a purpose on a ranch, the snowmobiles were work vehicles.

Luke grabbed a helmet out of a storage closet and tossed it to her.

"It's been a long time since I've ridden one of these," Javanna said as she put on her helmet. "Which ones are we taking?"

"You take the Ski-Doo and I'll take the Polaris," Luke said as he put an insulated bag into the storage behind the seat. "Do you remember how to start?"

"I think so."

"It's easy, you put it in neutral, turn the key to on, close the choke, and push the starter."

"I've got it," Javanna said as her machine started immediately.

"Try and keep up with me," Luke said as he moved out of the shed. "I don't want to have to come back looking for you."

Javanna laughed. "This from someone who rides a snowmobile all the time down in New Orleans."

"Let's go," Luke said as he opened the throttle. His machine leapt forward, and she had to react quickly to keep him from riding away from her.

It had been five years since Javanna was last on a snowmobile, but she felt very familiar and very comfortable with it. It was fun, racing through the snow so fast that she felt as if she would take wings and fly.

When they came down out of the foothills, they stopped near the creek, and Luke turned off the engine and climb down from the machine.

"I remember this place," Javanna said. "This is where Daddy would get our Christmas tree every year."

"It's still the place to get Christmas trees," Luke said as he put his helmet and goggles on the handle-bars. "That's why we're here now."

"We're going to drag a Christmas tree back with us?" Javanna asked, surprised by Luke's comment.

"No, we aren't going to cut them now." He held out a handful of red surveyor's ribbons. "We're going to mark them for when we do come and get them."

"How many do we need?"

"Well, let's see. One for the Big House, one for you, one for Russell, one for the bunkhouse dining room, and one for Jeff Graves to take to his house. And of course, we'll find the biggest one for the church."

"That's a lot of Christmas trees," Javanna agreed as she replaced her helmet with a sock hat.

"Well, we have plenty to spare. What do you say we start looking for them?"

For the next half hour or so they wandered through the trees, examining the pines and reject-ing more than they selected. Finally, they stood together looking at their choices. They had chosen six, but only four of the red markers were visible from where they stood. Two of them were away from the creek. The one they had chosen for the church was the biggest, and it was the closest because they wanted it where it would be the easiest to get to.

"How about some hot chocolate?" Luke invited, taking the insulated bag out of the storage compartment.

"I wondered what you had in your pack," Javanna said. "I can't think of anything that would taste any better, right now—unless it would be burned pumpkin bread."

Javanna sat down on the seat of the Ski-Doo, while Luke took out the thermos and two insulated cups. She moved over to make room for him to sit beside her.

"Look what else I brought." He withdrew a Ziploc bag of miniature marshmallows.

"You thought of everything," Javanna said.

"Of course, I did. Only the very uncouth person would attempt to drink hot chocolate without marshmallows."

Dropping a handful into each cup, Luke poured the hot chocolate from the thermos. It was still hot enough that a little curl of steam came from each cup.

"You might think I'm crazy," Luke said, "but I really missed snow while I was in New Orleans."

"I never had to want for snow in Chicago, but, I did miss this," she said, taking in the vista with a wave of her arm. "The openness, the isolation...no, I wouldn't call it isolation, I would call it personal space. You just don't have that in the city."

"I guess I can relate to the lack of personal space," Luke said. "New Orleans isn't as big as Chicago, but it's certainly large enough to make you feel closed in."

"Uhmm, you make good hot chocolate," Javanna said as she took a sip.

"Yes, well, first I had to select the cocoa beans, then crush them, then..."

Javanna interrupted him with her laughter. "You had a can of cocoa?"

"Worse than that. What you're drinking is a package of Nestlé's."

"Well, I'm sure you did a good job tearing open the package," Javanna teased.

"Hey, that takes more skill than you might imagine."

The two were quiet for a few moments, then Luke interrupted the silence. "Are you going back, Javanna?"

"What?"

"To Chicago, are you going back?"

"I...I don't know. I do love my job."

"Have you ever zoomed with any of your clients?"

"Of course, I do that all the time."

"How far away do you get before Zoom loses its signal?"

"Well, you can zoom from anywhere, there is no...I see what you're saying. You're telling me I could work from here."

"Well, couldn't you?"

Javanna shook her head. "Not really. I do zoom a lot, but it's necessary for me to have direct contact with my clients. I have to see their restaurants in person before I can work up a campaign that's unique to each business, and with some clients, I see them about every week." She smiled as she thought of Giorgio Moretti.

"In a way I guess I'm sort of in the same position. I'm in New Orleans because of the state's tax policy for film makers. On the other hand, I'm writing well here, better than I have in a long time."

Javanna smiled. "A butterfly flutters by."

"What?"

"It's a poem you wrote for me when I was twelve years old. Don't you remember?"

Luke laughed. "A butterfly flutters by. I think I actually do remember that. There was a time when I thought I was going to be a poet."

"I thought it was the most romantic thing that ever happened to me."

"Don't tell me you still have that poem."

"No, it's long gone, but I still remember it."

"I don't recall it as being all that romantic. Besides I was only fifteen, what did I know about romance?"

"You don't understand. It wasn't necessarily romantic because of what you wrote; it was romantic because you gave it to me."

"I'd like to think that now I'm a lot more romantic than that," Luke said, looking at her with an expression indicating that this wasn't some teasing remark.

"You've kissed me," Javanna said in a quiet, expectant voice. "It really doesn't get much more romantic than that."

Luke looked at Javanna and he knew that she wanted to be kissed. And what's more, he knew that he wanted to kiss her.

They were sitting side by side on the seat, and putting their cups on the snow he put his arms around her and pulled her to him.

No words were needed as their lips met.

Returning from their ride, the snowmobiles were put away. Making certain that they weren't being observed, they kissed again.

Luke held her for a moment longer, then with obvious effort pulled away from her.

"I, uh, had better find Russell and report in. I'm pretty sure he's found something for me to do."

"Luke?" Javanna called as Luke started to walk away. He stopped and turned back toward her.

"I enjoyed our snowmobile ride."

Luke smiled. "Yeah, I did too. We'll have to do it again."

Javanna wanted to talk to someone, a relative, or a girl friend that she could relate to. But there was no one. Abby was too involved with her own life, Brooke was too young, and this wasn't a conversation she wanted to have with her mother.

There was only one person she could talk to, and as soon as she got back into her house, she called him.

"Hey, girl," Jay answered, "how are things going out there in Big Sky Country?"

"Jay?" Javanna started, but then stopped, because she decided it wasn't appropriate to have this conversation just yet. So she was silent for a long moment.

"Javanna?" Jay replied, a worried expression in his voice. "Javanna, is everything all right?"

"Yes, everything is fine. I just wanted to see how you were doing."

"I'm doin' fine, the riots have stopped happening down town, and everything is trying to get back to normal. I've even used some of your gift certificates," Jay said. "I do miss you, though."

For the next hour Javanna and Jay talked about everything that was happening in their lives. Jay hadn't sold much of his furniture, Javanna told about convincing Vincent to branch out into microgreens, Jay said he was now going into the office a couple of days a week, Javanna told about bringing the cows down from the high country.

When she hung up, she felt rejuvenated, but there was something missing. She hadn't told Jay that she was in love.

Chapter Fourteen

Javanna remembered that as a child her family had always celebrated Thanksgiving with the Bryant family. As the daughter of the ranch foreman, she was in and out of the Bryant house so often that for a long time she thought she was a part of the family.

Javanna had been watching for the gray Highlander that Vincent drove, and when she saw it turn into the lane, she hurried to meet them in front of the garage at the Big House.

"I'm glad we're doing this," Helen said. "It seems like old times. Javanna, help me carry these pumpkin pies, and Vincent, will you get the cranberry salad."

When they walked into the Big House, the nostalgic smells of the traditional food were inviting. Helen and Javanna took the pies to the kitchen, and Vincent set his cranberry salad on the counter.

Martha and Helen embraced. "Why haven't we done this every year?" Martha asked. "Russell and Doris always go to be with their families and of course all the hands are off, too."

"I'm glad you asked us," Helen said. "Now, how can I help you?"

"Check the potatoes and see if they're done. Then you can mash them," Martha said.

"What about me?" Javanna asked.

"Just go on in with the boys," Martha said. "Somebody needs to keep them from telling such tall tales."

Javanna went into the Great Room where the fireplaces located at each end of the large room were both blazing. Dale was sitting in his recliner and Vincent took the wingback chair while Luke, Josh and Matt were on the sofas. Josh stood up and moved leaving the spot next to Luke for Javanna. Brooke set her guitar down and sat on the hearth by the fireplace.

Outside the large bank of windows, they could see snow on the ground, and in the distance, the Castle Mountains.

"What about the other boys?" Vincent asked. "Are they coming in?"

Dale chuckled. "The only one that could possibly come would be Noah. He's in Bozeman but he took our grandson to Washington D.C. for Thanksgiving."

"Why would anybody want to go there?" Brooke asked.

"You don't know my son or his wife. They both are trying to save the world from itself. He's an environmental analyst and she's a lobbyist for some environmentalist group. They both take their work pretty seriously."

"Too serious, if you ask me," Matt said. "He could probably find so many things we're doin' wrong out here, that he could shut us down."

"He's not that bad," Dale said. "Anyway, he and Ty have gone to Washington to spend Thanksgiving with Patricia.

"And Gabe—we thought he would be here, but they moved the PRCA championship to Texas, this year and he decided to stay in the South rather than risk getting up here and not being able to get out."

"Why Texas? Isn't it usually in Las Vegas?" Javanna asked.

"It's the same reason you and Luke are here. The virus shut it down. And then Sam couldn't get away for Thanksgiving, but he promises he'll be here for Christmas."

"He's not still flying helicopters in Afghanistan is he?" Vincent asked.

"No, he came back last year and now he's in Alabama at Ft. Rucker. We're really looking forward to seeing him, because this will be the first Christmas he has been able to spend with us in five or six years. Actually, if all goes the way it's supposed to, this Christmas will be the first time all the boys have been home for Christmas together in a long, long time."

"I know that will make Martha happy," Vincent said. "You must be very proud of Sam. Serving his country like he is."

"I am proud of his service, but then I'm proud of all my sons."

"Come on, Pop, are you trying to tell us you're proud of Matt?" Josh teased. "Who could be proud of someone like him?"

"Oh, I don't know," Matt said. "Maybe someone who got kicked in the head and had to be carried back to the house, then put in a truck and taken to the clinic."

"The doc said all that happened was that I got knocked out. You could have left me there and I would have been all right."

"I should have," Matt said.

"I swear you two have been at each other for more 'n twenty years," Dale said, but the laughter between the two boys indicated that it was all in fun.

The inevitable questions were asked of Luke and Javanna. "Are you going back, and if so, how long are you going to stay here."

Both Luke and Javanna answered with non-committal responses.

Martha and Helen came into the great room then.

"Everything's ready except for the rolls, and they'll be out within fifteen minutes," Martha said.

"Just long enough for Brooke to sing something for us," Javanna said, smiling at her younger sister.

"Yes, please do," Martha said.

Brooke picked up her guitar, and after doing a beautiful instrumental introduction, began to sing, her voice pure and sweet.

"We gather together to ask the Lord's blessing; He chastens and hastens his will to make known; the wicked oppressing...

"I don't know if it is appropriate to applaud a hymn," Luke said when she was finished, "but I'm going to clap."

"You know what, I think Brooke's song counts as a blessing for our food," Dale said. "Let's eat."

The Thanksgiving meal was baked turkey,

cornbread dressing, shoepeg corn with cream cheese and jalapeno peppers, broccoli and cheese casserole, mashed potatoes with gravy, cranberry salad, baked rolls, and pumpkin pie.

"Every year I see all this food on the table, and I think there's no way we will eat it all, but somehow it always gets eaten," Martha said.

"Well, Mom, don't forget, we have Josh," Matt teased.

Conversation continued around the table, though it was subdued by the act of eating.

"Mom, you know what I've missed most about your Thanksgiving dinners?" Luke said.

"The turkey?" Martha asked.

"No, you can get turkey anywhere. What I've missed most is the corn. Oh, and I remember Helen's pumpkin pie. It's better than any pumpkin pie I've ever tasted."

"I'll bet that corn is good," Josh said, "but we'll never know, though, because you ate all of it."

"Says Josh as he has half his plate covered with it," Luke replied with a little laugh.

That night as Javanna collapsed into bed, she replayed the events of the day. This was the most pleasant Thanksgiving she had had in years. Thanksgiving had never been anything special with her and Dane. Generally they went to one of the restaurants that Javanna represented, doing so on the gift certificates the restaurants had given her.

As she thought back on them now, those Thanksgiving meals, grabbed on the run without any ceremony, or even significance, seemed shallow, and a little sad compared to what she had experienced today. And a huge part of it, she realized, was that she had celebrated it with Luke.

Javanna smiled in the darkness as she came to a decision. She was not going back to Chicago. She was going to stay here with him.

A week later, Luke brought Doc and Tinker into the barn, and then he asked Russell to help him get the big Clydesdales into their harnesses. Because there were so many different components, it took at least forty-five minutes to get everything in place. The bridle and bit were the easy part, but then there was the collar, the hames, the traces, the martingales and at least a dozen more straps, bands, and pads that had to be put in place and adjusted.

"Do you think all this is worth the trouble?" Russell asked as he hitched the horses to the sleigh.

"Sure it is," Luke said as he put on the neck strap with the sleigh bells. "We did this every year when we were kids."

"How many trees are you going to get?" Russell asked.

"Six."

"Then we'd better put the sledge on, too," Russell said as he got into the sleigh to move the horses. "You'd better get up here. Even though Doc and Tinker have done this for years, you'd better let me show you how to handle the reins."

When Luke felt comfortable driving the team, he pulled up in front of Javanna's cabin. Hearing the sleigh bells, she opened the door and Riley ran out barking at the big horses.

"Are you ready to go chop down some Christmas trees?" Luke asked with a big smile on his face.

"I'm ready to go with you, but I'm not sure about the chopping part," Javanna said as she gathered Riley up in her arms.

"We'll leave the chopping to Paul Bunyan. We've got a power saw."

"Then you can definitely count me in." Javanna said. "Just let me get my gear on."

Javanna put on the same things she had worn on their snowmobile trip, and when she stepped outside, she saw Luke and the sleigh coming down the airstrip. Josh and Matt were with him, and when they stopped, Josh jumped down and got in the back.

"You didn't have to do that. I could've gotten in the back."

"I don't think so," Matt replied. "Our big brother said that if we didn't let you sit up there with him, he'd beat us up."

"Well, now, we certainly wouldn't want that to happen, would we?" Javanna said with a little laugh as she climbed into the sleigh.

"Get over here close to me," Luke said as he shared his lap robe with her.

"Is this the same lap robe we used as kids?" Javanna asked as she pulled the fur robe over her legs.

"It is," Luke said. "Dad always said Grandpa Zeke trapped the beavers himself."

"Well, it's perfect for a sleigh ride," Javanna said as she snuggled next to Luke.

"Too bad he didn't trap enough for a second one," Josh said.

Luke snapped the reins, and the horses stepped out. There was a jingle of bells as the team pulled down the lane heading for the creek.

"Sleigh bells ring, are you listening," Matt sang from the back seat.

The others joined in, and they sang until they reached the limit of their known lyrics, but then they started over again.

Luke stopped the sleigh when they reached Crooked Creek, and tying off the team, the four of them got out and Matt picked up the chainsaws.

"There are six trees, and four of us to cut them down," Luke said, "so you two get three and we'll get three."

It took very little time for the five smaller trees to be cut, as all were about seven feet tall. They were dragged back to the sledge.

"All right, Javanna, it's your turn." Luke held out the chainsaw. Javanna knew which one was left for her—it was the twelve-foot tree that was designated for the church.

Javanna stepped up to the tree and looked at it. It seemed huge, and cutting it down would be almost like a lumberjack felling a tree in the forest.

"Would you like me to start the saw?" Luke asked.

"No, I can do it. But do me a favor."

"What?"

Javanna gave him her phone. "You're the big-time movie producer, I want you to video me cutting down this tree. I want to send it to Jay and to Devin."

Luke took the phone from her. "Quiet on the set!" he shouted. "Slate, action."

Javanna jerked on the starting cord and the saw roared into life. Then she put the chain saw to the trunk and notched the tree being mindful of where she wanted the tree to fall. Then holding the saw at the proper angle, she began. The saw roared and the chips flew until Josh called out, "Timber!"

It fell perfectly, without breaking any of the limbs. Luke moved toward the tree to get a close-up of Javanna with the tree behind her, then he stopped filming. "That's a wrap," he said, handing the phone back to Javanna.

The tree was so big, it took all three of the Bryants to drag it to the sledge. They wrestled with it to get it on the sledge, then carefully put the other five trees along side it.

On the way back, Javanna typed in Jay's phone number, then sent the video to him as a message. She did the same thing for Devin, and a few minutes later, before they were back to the Big House, her phone gave the Sherwood Forest horn notification that she was getting an incoming message from Jay.

That looks like fun. U didn't say u had taken a job as a lumberjack or would that be lumber jill? U sure u don't want to come back home? U won't have to work so hard.

A few minutes later she got one from Devin.

Enjoyed the video. Your friends at CDMI miss you.

When Martha saw the tree for the church, she thought it was too big, but Luke convinced her it would be just fine. They had to call for more help to get it loaded, but when it was on the truck, it was so big that some of it protruded over the back of the tailgate.

"Oh, yes," Reverend Walker said, enthusiastically when Luke and Javanna pulled up in front of the church. "The children are certainly going to enjoy decorating it, this Sunday."

"Do you need help getting it into the church?" Luke asked.

"No, no, you've done enough getting it here. Several of the women are coming tonight to hang the greens, and I'll ask them to bring their husbands. We'll get it up."

Leaving the church, Luke and Javanna stopped by Abby's Place where they had a cup of coffee and a piece of lemon meringue pie. Abby was there as well having just come back from the doctor in Bozeman.

"I think you and Paul ought to get a room in town," Helen said. "You shouldn't be driving back and forth like this."

"Mom, first of all, the baby isn't due until the middle of January," Abby said, "and if you think my kids would let me stay in Bozeman over Christmas, you're crazy."

"None the less, you know that Caroline came early," Helen said.

"And Gavin was three weeks late."

"The important thing is, how are you feeling?" Javanna asked.

"Big, fat, clumsy—like any other eight-month pregnant woman," Abby said. "Brooke, is there another piece of pie?"

Brooke got up and went to the pie case. She brought back a piece of chocolate pie.

"There isn't any more lemon?" Abby asked as she took a bite of the chocolate.

Helen looked at Javanna and shook her head. "What are we going to do with your sister?"

"Give her chocolate pie," Luke said.

They talked for a while longer, the visit ending with Javanna showing the video of her cutting down the tree.

"It's been a busy day," Luke said as they were driving back.

"But it's been a fun day."

Luke reached over to take Javanna's hand. "It's too bad we have a heater."

"Why do you say that?"

"Because if we didn't have a heater you could slide over here and sit beside me."

Javanna did just that as they continued back to the ranch.

Chapter Fifteen

That Sunday, Javanna went to church with the Bryant family, just as she had every Sunday since she had left Chicago. Coming to church provided her an opportunity to visit with everyone, including some of the people she had gone to school with. And though she enjoyed it, she couldn't help but feel like a hypocrite for making a purely social event out of what should have been a spiritual one.

"I want you to take particular notice of this big Christmas tree," Reverend Walker said. "We have the children to thank for putting on the many, many lights and the beautiful ornaments that adorn the tree. But the tree itself was provided by Crooked Creek Ranch. I understand there was a sleigh ride involved in getting the tree. Is that right, Luke?"

"Yes, sir," Luke said.

"And I understand that it was Javanna who cut it down," Reverend Walker continued.

Javanna smiled.

"Maybe Brooke gave you some pointers on how to use the chainsaw—you know she attended the

Red Ants Pants workshop learning how to do just that. But I digress—thank you Luke and Javanna for bringing us one of the most beautiful trees Grace Gospel has had in a long time.

"But we have more Christmas cheer in store," Reverend Walker continued. "On Christmas Eve, we will be presented with a wonderful program that the children are preparing, thanks to Melissa Caldwell."

"Josh Bryant is helping too," Melissa called from her pew, to the suppressed laughter of many in the congregation.

"Yes, and Josh as well," Reverend Walker added. "If you get the opportunity, thank all these young people for their dedication to this church. And now, if you would as we get more Christmas spirit, turn to page 264 in your hymnal, and we will sing, Joy to the World."

When the music was concluded, Reverend Walker stepped up to the podium to deliver his message.

"In the time of Christmas, we must ask ourselves, how many celebrate Christmas as a season, but not as a blessed event? How many have become comfortable with the idea of Christmas, but not with the birth of our Savior? Many pray by rote, giving the blessing at the dinner table, saying the Lord's Prayer aloud in church, but feel no personal connection with God.

"Someday you may call out to God in anguish, or fear, or need. Will He be there for you? The answer is yes, if you believe. Believe in the Lord our God, and He will be there for you."

"Are we going to Abby's place for lunch?" Luke asked when they got out of church.

"We might not be able to find a table," Matt said. "Everyone goes either there or the Branding Iron after church."

"I can't go anyway," Josh said.

"Why not?"

"I'll be picking up pizzas for Melissa to serve to the kids today. We're going to be in the fellowship hall for our first meeting to put together the Christmas program."

"Oh yes, Melissa told us that," Luke said.

"Melissa told everyone that," Matt added with a little laugh. "But still there are five of us; we might not find a table."

"Don't worry about that," Javanna said. "There's always one kept for family. It's the one in the back right corner."

"What if the family is there now?" Luke asked.

"Paul and Abby hardly ever come there on Sunday, Mom and Brooke will be working. The only one that might be there is Vincent, but he's probably sorting the produce in his store."

"I think we're going to pass on lunch today," Dale said. "Russell went down to Billings to pick up Cedar for Christmas, and I hate to be away when he's not there."

"Well, we'll miss you," Javanna said.

Matt was right in his declaration that the restaurant would be full, because every table but one was full, and that one empty table verified the veracity of Javanna's observation.

"Hello, Katie. Are mom and Brooke in the kitchen?" Javanna asked as the waitress approached their table.

"Your mother is."

"What's special today?" Matt asked. "I mean, besides the best-looking waitress in town."

Katie blushed a little before she responded. "The special for today is lasagna, garlic toast, and salad with," she looked down at her notes, "we've added something new. It's called microgreens."

"Microgreens?" Javanna asked.

"Yes, ma'am they are part of the salad. They are very nutritious, and besides that, they are good."

"Katie, you're a good waitress. Vincent must be pleased with you."

Katie smiled when Luke complimented her.

"What do you have to drink?" Matt asked.

"Soft drinks, unsweetened tea or lemonade."

"The tea?" Luke asked, polling the other two. They agreed.

"We'll have the lasagna, and the tea," Luke said, ordering for all.

Katie brought the tea, salad, and bread to the table first, then after clearing the salad plates, she brought their lunch.

After Javanna was finished, Luke and Matt each ordered a piece of cheesecake for dessert, while she stepped back into the kitchen to see her mother. Besides Helen and Bessie, there was a new cook in the kitchen.

"Katie told me you and the Bryant boys were here." Helen said as she put a ham sandwich together.

Javanna chuckled. "I'm not sure how they would

react to being called boys."

"Humph, I remember when every one of them was born, I even changed their diapers."

This time Javanna laughed out loud. "I'm sure they wouldn't want to talk about that. Where's Brooke?"

"She's still at church with Melissa. She's going to perform for the Christmas Eve program." Helen grabbed the next ticket and began dishing up a bowl of dumplings.

"If Brooke is going to be in it, it's bound to be good," Javanna said. "I know you're busy and the 'boys' as you called them are ready to go, so I'll see you in the morning."

"Bye, darlin'," Helen said, as she filled a bowl with soup.

Javanna climbed into the front seat of the truck as they left the restaurant. Luke and Matt were talking about how busy Abby's Place had been, and about how the Christmas tree at church was the prettiest they could remember. They were joking about Josh working so closely with Melissa on the Christmas program and they liked the Christmas carols that had been sung.

There was not one word spoken about the sermon Reverend Walker had given. Not one word.

Javanna was thinking about it, though. Since Dane had died, she had given up any pretense of religion in general. So why did this message resonate with her?

"Javanna?"

Javanna had been so deep in thought that she hadn't heard Luke's question.

"I'm sorry, what did you say?"

Luke chuckled. "I don't know what you were thinking about, but you were way zoned out there. I asked if you were going to trim your tree this afternoon."

"Oh, I have it put up, but I haven't bought any decorations or lights or anything. Mom said the Feed and Seed has a few lights, but I keep forgetting to go by and get some, and by this time they're probably out. I'd planned to run over to Helena and go to Walmart, but I haven't taken the time."

"Don't worry about it," Luke said. "I'll bring everything you need. If you want to we can trim the tree together."

"You have everything?"

"Yeah, you have to remember, this is the Bryant family—a family with six kids."

"Then that would be wonderful," Javanna said with a happy smile. "I think it'll be fun."

"All right. It'll probably be sometime around six before I get there."

"Ha, six o'clock," Matt said. "Did you catch that? He's going to get there right at supper time. You think that's a coincidence?"

"Well if he's supplying all the lights and ornaments, and if he's going to help me trim the tree, the least I can do is get a pizza out of the freezer."

"Wow, did you hear that big brother? She's going all out for you. Why, I'll bet she'll have to open the box all by herself," Matt said.

Luke laughed, and even Javanna joined into the frivolity.

"You've got to help me," Josh said as he stepped into the office where Luke was at the computer.

"What do you need?" Luke asked.

"I need you to write something for this Christmas program. Melissa asked me to come up with an idea, and I don't have anything in mind. I thought since you write all the time, you could help me out. I don't want to look like a fool in front of Melissa."

Luke chuckled. "You don't want to look like a fool in front of Melissa huh? I would think you wouldn't want to look like a fool in front of the whole church, why Melissa in particular?"

"Quit raggin' me, Luke, are you going to help me, or what?"

"All right, what do you need?"

"We need you to write a play for the kids."

"That's simple, just do the Christmas Story."

"That's what you say, but I don't have any idea where to start."

"Start with Luke," Luke said with an amused grin.

"What do you mean, start with Luke? That's what I'm doing."

Luke laughed out loud. "No, not with me. I'm talking about the book of Luke, in the Bible. That has the Christmas story."

"Yeah, I know that, but, would you write it out for the kids?"

"How many kids?"

"What difference does it make how many kids?"

"If I'm going to do this, I'll need to have a part for every kid."

"Okay, but I'm not sure, I didn't count them."

"Call Melissa and ask her. I'm sure she'll know."

"Yeah, good idea," Josh said, taking out his phone.

Luke smiled when he saw that Josh had Melissa's number in his favorite file.

"Melissa, Josh. How many kids do you think there will be for our play?

"Why? Because we'll need to have a part for all of them. We can't have a few of them just standing around sucking on their thumb.

"What do you mean none of them would be sucking on their thumb? Matt sucked on his thumb 'til he was sixteen." Josh laughed.

"Ten? Okay, I'll get to work then. I'm going to Luke.

"No, not my brother. You know, Luke in the Bible.

"All right, I'll have something as quick as I can get it together.

"Good, talk to you later."

"There'll be ten kids," Josh said after he ended the call.

"So Matt sucked his thumb until he was sixteen, did he? I wonder if he remembers that."

"Come on, Luke, there's no need in getting Matt all upset. I was just joking with Melissa."

"All right, I won't tell him, but now you'll owe me for helping you out with Melissa, and for not telling Matt what you said."

"What do you mean, helping me out with Melissa? It's the church you'll be helping."

"Uh, huh. When do you need the script?"

"We're going to start rehearsal next Sunday but I'll need it before then. I'll have to take it in and let Melissa see it first."

"I'll see what I can do. Now, I have a tree and a pizza to take care of."

That evening, in preparation for Luke's coming to help trim the tree, Javanna took the pizza from the freezer and pulled the tab on the box. She chuckled as she thought of Matt's comment, then set the oven temperature to four hundred.

Twenty-five minutes later, the little timer bell told her the pizza was ready. She had just taken it out, when she heard singing on the front porch.

"We wish you a Merry Christmas, we wish you a Merry Christmas..."

When Javanna opened the door, she saw a smiling Luke, burdened with boxes.

"May I come in?"

"Certainly, here, let me help you." Javanna reached up to take the top box.

"Oh, yeah, sure, you would take the little one," Luke teased. "Do I smell pizza?"

"You do. And I have cold root beer."

"You really know how to treat a man," Luke said.

"The pizza's out so we can eat now, and then trim the tree," Javanna said.

After the pizza was eaten that evening, Luke and Javanna decorated the tree. It took a long time to put on the lights, because Luke insisted upon wrapping every branch. When they were finished there were at least eight or nine hundred white lights.

Then they opened the box of ornaments. Most of them were homemade.

"Oh, Luke, these are adorable. Where did they come from?"

"This is the Luke box. When we were growing up, every year, Mom would have us make an ornament, and then on Christmas morning, there would be an ornament beside our plate at breakfast."

Javanna picked up one that had a picture of Luke glued to a Styrofoam apple divider.

"This is cute," Javanna said as she put it on the tree. "How old were you?"

"I think I was about eight. We did those in Mrs. Cunningham's class in school. Wasn't she your teacher, too?"

"She was, but I don't remember ever doing this."

Javanna enjoyed looking at each ornament, and was impressed that Luke could remember where and when he had gotten most of them. When they were finished, Javanna stepped back and admired the tree.

"This is the most beautiful tree I think I've ever seen."

"Too bad we can't enter it in some contest," Luke said.

"That wouldn't be fair," Javanna said.

"Why not?"

"Because no tree could possibly compete with this one. Look at it."

Luke studied the tree, then nodded. "I think you're right."

Chapter Sixteen

For most of the following week, Luke was kept busy with his father and the others in gathering the steers that were to be sold. A cattle buyer came in and chose the animals he wanted from among those herded into the corrals behind the scales. When nine hundred steers were weighed and loaded onto waiting cattle haulers, the eighteen wheelers pulled out leaving only those relatively few animals that had been weeded out. These remaining animals were known as cutbacks and Dale and Ray Jaworski would drive them to Billings to the auction yards.

"How did we do?" Matt asked Dale when the last truck had left the compound.

"I'm pleased," Dale said. "I had to haggle a little, but we're getting $1.37, and that's more than I expected."

"Wow, I think it was a good year," Josh said. "Makes all the hard work worth it."

"I want to remind you of this when I ask you to fix fence," Dale said. "Now all of you work on getting the cut-backs in the corrals, and Matt, you take Jeff and Ray and round up the dry heifers. And Josh, you make sure the Peterbilt is gassed and ready to roll first thing Monday morning. Check the tires and change out any that need it."

"Hey, what's Luke going to be doing?" Matt asked.

"He's going to be sitting at the computer working on the budget for next year," Dale said. "Come on, Luke, I want to get you started on the books."

When Dale and Luke walked away Matt and Josh were standing beside the corral.

"How come it is, Luke can walk in here not more than two months ago, and Dad turns everything over to him?" Matt asked.

"Because he's the oldest," Josh said. "Maybe Dad thinks if he sees what goes on, he'll want to stay and give up the movie business altogether."

"Do you think he'll go back to New Orleans?"

"I don't know. He acts like he's pretty happy here," Josh said.

"I think he's happy because Javanna's here. What's going to happen when she goes back to Chicago?"

Josh shrugged his shoulders. "We'll just have to wait and see."

Javanna drove Manly Truck into town every day that week. She took Manly Truck because she knew no one else would be using it. She kept herself busy working with Vincent, enlarging the trays of microgreens, as well as planting more vegetables to be ready later in the winter.

She was also helping in the bake shop or the

restaurant or wherever she was needed. Whenever she could, she visited with Abby, always making sure she entertained Gavin as much as possible. And she spent time with Brooke. Brooke had come around to being tolerant of Riley, and that was good.

Luke had been working on the children's Christmas program and he had most of it finished.

"I'm going to need a couple of adults to play Joseph and Mary."

"Nobody's going to want to do that. Just pick out two of the tallest kids and that'll do," Josh said.

"It will be better if we have two adults. What about you and Melissa?"

"I don't think so."

"All right, then, I guess I'm not going to finish the script."

"Luke, you have to. Melissa thinks I'm doing it, and if I tell her I can't finish it, what will she think?"

"That's not my problem." Luke stood up from the computer.

"Wait, wait—Melissa and I will be Joseph and Mary if you have to have adults in the play."

"Thanks," Luke said. "When you think about it, Joseph and Mary are fairly important to the story."

"Are we going to have to learn a lot of lines?"

"The way I'll write it, you won't have any lines at all."

"That's good. Maybe we can find someone else to be Joseph and Mary because Melissa and I will be busy making sure the kids are doing what they're supposed to be doing," Josh said. "What have you written so far?"

"The shepherds in the field," Luke said. "That will take care of four of the kids."

"Four?"

"Three shepherds and one angel."

"Can it be a girl angel? Lila Baker is really smart and she wants to be in the play. I need a good role for her."

"I don't know why the angel couldn't be a girl," Luke said. "The Bible doesn't say, 'and a male angel of the Lord appeared'. It just says angel."

"Good, good, that will work out well."

Luke's phone rang and when he looked at the caller i.d., he saw the name Sherman Morris. He hadn't heard anything from his business manager for a couple of weeks.

"Hello, Sherman, what's up?"

"Just calling with some good news for a change. Hallmark called to see if you have a Christmas script you could let go of. They're going into production for 2022 and since they want to film in Canada, they don't have all the COVID protocols that we have to follow."

Luke laughed. "Funny you should want a Christmas script—I'm working on one right now."

"Great," Sherman said. "How soon do you think you'll be finished with it?"

"This isn't one for Hallmark. It's for the Christmas program at church. My brother and his girlfriend are in charge of it, and they've roped me in to writing it for them."

"Do they know how valuable your time is? Stop playing around and get a script as fast as you can. I know this wouldn't be a LTN production, but it would bring in some much needed cash. Did you hear me say—much needed cash?"

"I know. I've asked you to do a lot down there. How's everybody holding up?"

"I'm down to just Maya and me on the payroll. I hated to do it, but if you plan on coming back, we need a roof over our heads more than we need a set designer or a movie editor."

"I trust your judgment, Sherman."

"I want to know, other than your kids' play, are you getting any writing done?"

"As a matter of fact, I am. It's called In God's Hands, and I feel really good about it."

"Good. But back to the Hallmark deal. Could you get a script ready in the next couple of weeks?"

"Sherman—have you forgotten, it's almost Christmas now."

"You can get in the mood, then. By the way, do you know Christmas Past is going to be on TV Sunday night?"

"No, I didn't know. I'll have to watch it," Luke said.

"I'm serious, Luke, come up with a good quick Christmas script. Not too complicated—just simple to film."

"I'll do my best."

"All right, and if I don't talk to you again before Christmas, good luck on your kids' program and Merry Christmas."

"Thanks, Sherman, and Merry Christmas to you, too."

After he ended the call with Sherman, he turned to Josh.

"Sherman said to tell you, you're getting a bargain on this script," Luke said.

"What do you mean saying 'Josh and his girlfriend'," Josh asked.

"It seems to me like that's what Melissa is," Luke said. "You're spending an awful lot of time with her."

"Is that the definition of a girlfriend? That you spend a lot of time with a woman?"

"It could be," Luke said.

"Well then Javanna is your girlfriend."

"It could be." Luke pulled out his phone and sent Javanna a text.

Would you like to watch a movie with me Sunday?

He got an immediate answer.

Sure, where?
Your living room.
My living room?
I'll pick up burgers and fries from the Montana Road House. I'll be there at six.
Looking forward to it.

"What was all that about?" Brooke asked when Javanna quit texting.

"I've got a date with Luke Sunday night," Javanna answered.

"Where's he taking you? To Helena? He flew you to Bozeman once before, didn't he?"

"Yes, but this is going to be more local."

"How local?"

"My living room," Javanna said. "We're going to have dinner and watch a movie."

Brooke laughed. "That's pretty local all right."

That evening Javanna's phone rang and as she picked up, she saw that it was a call from Devin Myers.

"Hi, Devin, what's up?"

"Good things are happening, that's what's up," Devin said.

"I always like to hear good things."

"I'm counting on that. Have you had enough of the fresh air out there?"

"Why are you asking?"

"Because I need you back in Chicago," Devin said. "I'm offering you your old job back."

Javanna took in a quick breath of excitement. "My old job?"

Devin chuckled. "Yes, your old job. You remember, the one where you got restaurants to give us obscene amounts of money to handle their advertising campaigns?"

"But I don't understand. Why would they want to advertise if they are closed?"

"Ah, but that's just the thing. The Governor has allowed restaurants to have more in-house seating, and most of your old clients are coming back," Devin said. "They're clamoring for campaigns to say that they're open again and you're the best one to put those together."

"What about the riots?"

Devin laughed. "Protesters don't like cold weather, so in Chicago at least, they're over."

"And the restaurants that were vandalized are open, too?"

"For the most part, yes. Now, how about it? When do you think you can come back?"

Javanna had put fifteen years into her career, and before the pandemic hit, she was at the top of her game. She had been crushed by the events that had taken all that away from her, but now, Devin had just told her she could have it all back.

This was just what Javanna wanted to hear. Or at least it was a few weeks ago. Now, she wasn't so sure.

"Javanna? Javanna, are you there?"

"What? Oh, yes, I'm here."

"You went so long without talking, that I thought we had been cut off. How soon do you think before you can get here?"

"I don't know," Javanna said. "I'd really like to wait until after Christmas. Is that okay?"

"I suppose that would be all right, but you know how this business is—we have to get a campaign in the works or else these accounts are going to go someplace else."

"I know," Javanna said. "I'll let you know as soon as I can."

"Javanna, I can't impress upon you enough—you coming back will have a big impact on whether or not CDMI survives."

When she ended the call, Javanna was torn. She could hear the anxiety in Devin's voice, but she wasn't ready to go back to Chicago yet. First of all, where would she live? And secondly, what about Luke?

Yes, what about Luke?

In her heart, she knew that she loved Luke, and she felt like he cared for her. When they were together, their actions showed that they enjoyed one another's company, but beyond a kiss or two, they had never expressed those feelings to one another. When he came over for their movie date, she would tell him Devin had called and see how he reacted. If he showed encouragement for her to go back to Chicago, she would know that his feelings for her weren't as strong as her feelings for him.

Sunday night, Luke showed up at Javanna's door with a sack of take-out from the Montana House in White Sulphur Springs.

"This smells so good," Javanna said as she unwrapped the hamburgers and put them on plates. "Since I eat at Abby's Place so much, I don't think I've had a good hamburger since I left Chicago."

"What about the cheese poppers?" Luke said as he put one in his mouth. He divided the French fries and took out packages of ketchup.

"They're not an item usually found on the menus I work with, but I love them."

They sat at the table and Javanna thought it felt so right. This was the table where she and her family had had their meals together, and she could envision Luke and her sitting at this very table. Maybe they would have a child or two.

Stop, Javanna! Stop.

"Are you ready for this movie tonight?" Luke asked. "They tell me it's the best Christmas movie ever."

Javanna smiled. "I love It's a Wonderful Life."

"Ouch! You know how to hurt a guy's feelings," Luke said. "We're watching Christmas Past."

"Christmas Past? That's one of your movies isn't it?"

Luke smiled. "I guess you just redeemed your-self. You know Christmas Past is mine."

"Of course I do. I've seen it twice before. Should I make us some popcorn?" Javanna asked.

"Who can watch a movie without popcorn?"

"Then popcorn it is."

Chapter Seventeen

Javanna and Luke sat next to each other on the sofa, sharing popcorn from the same bowl as they watched Christmas Past. As did all of Luke's movies, it had a message of hope, redemption, and commitment to God.

Javanna watched the movie with mixed emotions. It was easy to get into the story and she strongly related to the Madison Carmichael character. But she couldn't get beyond knowing that the actress who portrayed Madison was Tia Brown, Luke's ex-wife.

Maybe watching this movie hadn't been such a good idea. Javanna was beginning to grow a little uncomfortable. Was Luke watching the movie or was he watching Tia?

"How did you like it?" Luke asked when the movie was over.

"Tia is a wonderful actress, and I never realized just how beautiful she is," Javanna said.

"She may be one of the most beautiful women I've ever known, but the funny thing is, it hasn't affected her."

"What do you mean, it hasn't affected her?" Javanna asked.

"When you're around her, she doesn't seem to know how beautiful she really is. And that unawareness, that total lack of self-importance, is what makes her easy to work with, from the director to the smallest bit-role actor in the production."

"You miss her, don't you?"

Luke didn't get a chance to answer, because his phone rang at that very moment. He took it from his pocket and looked to see who was calling.

"Well, speak of the devil," he said cryptically. "Hi, Tia."

Tia? He was getting a call from Tia? Javanna felt a sudden sense of emptiness, as if she had had the breath knocked out of her.

"Yes, I was watching the movie with a friend of mine. You know this is the third year they've shown it."

A friend? Luke referred to her as a friend?

"Yes, I agree it may be the best script I've ever written, but it wasn't necessarily your best performance, even though you did dominate the screen."

Luke laughed.

"What? Now wait a minute, you said you'd never hold that against me."

Javanna studied Luke's face. The smile left his face, and he took on a more serious expression.

"I'm in Montana."

Another pause.

"What are you doing in New Orleans?"

Javanna couldn't hear Tia's voice.

"Of course you can stay in our house. Get the key from Sherman."

Javanna tried to read Luke's face, but she couldn't.

"Just a minute, Tia." Luke turned to Javanna and took the phone down. "I'd better be going back to the house. Thanks for the popcorn and thanks for watching the movie with me."

"You're welcome," she said, quietly. It was the only thing she could think of to say.

"All right, I'm back," Luke said as he was walking out the door getting into his coat. Javanna heard no more of his conversation after that.

The TV was still on, and someone was sitting in front of an inviting fire in a fireplace, sharing some platitude with the audience, but Javanna had no idea what he was saying.

Riley came over and lay down by her feet. Javanna picked her up. When she lifted the little dog up to her face, Riley started giving her kisses as she pulled Riley to her breast. She had no idea, until that moment that she was crying.

"I love you, Riley. And I know you love me." She buried her face in Riley's coat. "You're all I need," Javanna said.

Luke, could not believe what Tia was saying.

"I want you to come back to New Orleans, Luke. You asked why I am in New Orleans, I came for you. I made a mistake when I left. I made a huge mistake, and I want you back."

"Tia, you can't just drop out of someone's life, then drop back in like all you had done was go to the store or something. I don't think you know how much you hurt me when you did that."

"Do you think I wasn't hurting?" Tia replied. "Yes, I know it was my fault, I know I'm the one who left, but my hurt was all the more because I knew I was at fault. I want you to come back, Luke. You can't just turn your back on what we had, can you?"

Luke remained silent.

"Luke, you can't tell me that in the last two years you've never thought about getting back together. You know we were good together. And we both know LTN hasn't been the same since I left."

"I don't disagree with you, but there's an elephant in the room. It's a little thing called The Long Journey."

Tia was the one to stay quiet this time. Finally she spoke.

"Luke, are you a Christian?"

"Yes," Luke said.

"If I understand anything about Christianity, I know that forgiveness is one of the main tenants. Is that not right?"

"Yes."

"Then it is your Christian duty to forgive me," Tia said.

"Another tenet of the Christian faith is the sanctity of marriage," Luke said. "I believe that has been severed in our case. I promised to love, honor, and cherish until death do us part, and you chose to throw that away."

"It says in the Bible, that the greatest of these is love, and I know I love you and I want you to come back to me. I know we can work these things out."

Luke took a deep breath. "That's just it. I don't want to work things out. I'm not in love with you, Tia."

"Oh, Luke, you can't mean that. Think of the franchise. If you don't love me, at least think of LTN. I know you love your company."

"It's not the same thing."

"All right, but we'll talk again," Tia said.

"We will but it will be as friends—not as husband and wife."

"I guess I respect you for telling me the truth. Good night, and I do love you."

"Good night," Luke said, punching out of the call.

Luke had reached the house by the time he finished his call, and now he walked over to the sofa in front of the fireplace. He had laid a fire a few days ago, but he had not lit it. Now seemed a good time to do that.

It took a few minutes for the fire to catch, then when it was going well, he sat on the sofa and stared at the flames. They had sort of a mesmerizing effect on him, allowing his mind to rearrange all the thoughts that were tumbling around in his brain right now.

"Luke?"

Martha had come down the stairs and was standing back in the shadows, illuminated only by the flickering flames.

"Hi, Mom."

"What are you doing, sitting down here in the dark?"

"It's not dark. I've got the fire," he said, indicating it with a wave of his hand.

Martha sat beside him on the sofa. "Your dad and I watched the movie again. It's such a great movie."

"Thanks, Mom." Luke continued to stare at the fire. A gas bubble trapped in one of the logs, ignited with a pop, and sent out a little spray of sparks.

"What's wrong, Luke?"

Luke continued to stare at the fire.

"I thought you were going to watch the movie with Javanna tonight."

"I did."

"But, you're back so early. Did something happen?"

"No," Luke said. "Nothing like that."

"Then what's wrong?"

"Tia called. She called right after the movie ended."

"She had watched the movie?"

"Yes."

There was another pop from the fireplace.

"Tia's in New Orleans and she wants me back. She wants to get remarried."

"Oh, my," Martha said.

"Yes, oh my."

"What did you tell her?"

"I told her that's not what I wanted."

"And what did she say?"

"She said she loved me."

Martha didn't say anything, allowing the question to remain unasked.

"She said we should get back together for the good of LTN. Can you believe that? She thinks my business would take precedence over my happiness.

"And then when I brought up her role in The Long Journey, she said that as a Christian it is my duty to forgive her. And Mom, I can forgive her as a person, but I can't forgive her as my wife. Does that make me less of a Christian?"

"Do you love Tia?"

"No."

"Then I think God understands," Martha said. "What did Javanna say?"

"She knows Tia called, but I left before the call was over."

"So she doesn't know what Tia wanted?"

Luke shook his head.

"You know that girl loves you, don't you, Luke?"

"She's never said as much."

"How do you feel about her? Do you love Javanna?"

"I don't know what I think. I've made one big mistake, and I don't want to make another one." He took a deep breath before he continued. "I need to find myself first, before I can give myself to her. Trust me, Mom, I just don't think she would want me unless I can be one hundred percent sure this is what should be."

"In a relationship, remember it's not just about you. Don't be afraid to talk this out with Javanna. If you lose her, I think you'll regret it the rest of your life."

Chapter Eighteen

"Luke, Luke, are you awake?" Dale asked.

Luke opened his eyes to see his father standing over his bed. "What time is it?"

"It's four o'clock."

Luke sat up quickly. "Dad, has something happened?" he asked in a concerned voice.

"I need you to go with me to Billings this morning. Ray's so sick he can't get out of bed."

"To Billings? To take the steers? You know I haven't driven an eighteen-wheeler since I left here twenty years ago."

"It's like riding a bicycle, it'll all come back to you. Besides, the Peterbilt has automatic transmission, so you won't have to worry about shifting gears."

"Do we need to load the cattle hauler?"

"No, Russell's doing that now," Dale said. "Come on upstairs, Mom's got breakfast ready. I want to be at the auction yard no later than eight o'clock."

"I'll be right there," Luke promised.

Luke dressed quickly, then hurried upstairs to the aroma of coffee and bacon.

"Mom, you didn't have to get up so early, we could have gotten something in Harlowton."

"And cost us an extra half-hour?" Dale said. "Don't you worry any about your mom getting up early. She's been doing it for the forty-five years we've been married."

"Well, not every morning, thank goodness," Martha said as she lifted the pancakes off the griddle. "Have you given anymore thought to your problem?"

"Do you mean Tia?"

"No, I mean Javanna," Martha said. "And you listen to me, Luke Bryant. You've got to get that worked out."

"Yes, ma'am."

When Javanna woke up, she had no idea that Luke and his father had left the compound with a load of auction cattle, three hours earlier. Javanna lay in bed for several minutes, thinking about last night. Why did Tia call? And why did Luke feel he had to leave to talk to her?

She had overheard enough of the call to know that Tia was back in New Orleans. Did she want Luke back, but more importantly, is that what he wanted?

She and Luke had never talked about Tia and the divorce. She had told him everything about Dane—maybe it was time to have another real conversation.

Riley had been sitting on the bed staring at Javanna, and now she barked, just a little yip, actually, to let Javanna know she wanted to go outside.

"All right, Little One, just let me get dressed," Javanna said.

When Javanna came back into the cabin, she made herself a cup of coffee, then went into the living room to sit on the sofa. The same sofa she and Luke had been sitting on last night. Why didn't Luke come back after Tia's call? Why hasn't he stopped by this morning, or called, or at least texted?

She got an idea. She would invite him to have breakfast with her. Then, over breakfast, they could discuss Tia and his reaction to her call.

Had she so badly misread all of his signals? She was sure that he loved her, even though he had never said the words.

She chuckled. Well, they were even. She had never told him that she loved him, either.

She took out her phone and began to text.

Luke, I think it is time for me to tell you that I love you

No, that's not something you say in a text. That's something you say in person.

She cleared that message and tapped in another.

I haven't eaten yet. Come join me for breakfast if you can.

Dale was dozing and Luke was driving the eighteen-wheeler when he heard the text signal on the phone. He read the message and saw that it was from Javanna and he smiled—maybe the telephone call from Tia hadn't been such a big problem after all. Now, he wished he hadn't taken this trip with his father. He knew he had to say something to Javanna, but he was driving, so he managed to type in one word.

Can't

"Can't? That's all you have to say to me? That you can't?" Javanna said aloud.

"This is ridiculous, Riley. I can't sit around here moping all day."

It was then that Javanna decided to go for a ride, so bundling up against the cold one more time, she went out to the corral, saddled Salt, then started out at a trot. She wasn't sure where she was going, but she needed to get away this morning.

She heard a coyote howling, and perhaps it was that, the howl of the coyote, that caused her to head to Dallas Bluff. The bluff was named after her father, because this was where it had happened.

Dallas Reed and several other cowboys had been going after coyotes, because the coyotes had been killing new-born calves. Dallas had heard the bark of some pups, and climbing up to the ridge, he had discovered a den in some rocks. He went back to the truck to get a shovel and a pickaxe from Russell, then returned to destroy the den. He dismounted and dropped the reins to hold the horse in place, but as he approached the den, he dropped the shovel and when he did, a coyote came darting out. That startled the horse and he began twisting around and kicking. Dallas couldn't get out of the way, and the frightened horse kicked him several times in his side, his chest, and his head.

The horse started running, and as it ran, rider-less, by Russell's truck, Russell began honking his horn. When the other cowboys came to see what was wrong, Russell told them Dallas's horse had galloped by with its saddle empty, and everyone began looking for Dallas.

One of the younger hands found him, conscious and crawling on all fours. Dallas told them what had happened.

Russell and the others were able to get Dallas to the truck and then back to the house. When Dale saw the severity of his injuries, he put him and Helen in the plane and flew them to Bozeman where a waiting ambulance took him to the hospital.

Javanna was fifteen at the time, and she was in school when Martha Bryant came to get her to tell her about the accident. Both she and Abby stayed at the Big House that night waiting for word from their mother, and the next morning Martha drove them to Bozeman. When they got there, Dallas was still alive and Abby and Javanna got to see him. By noon, he was dead.

At first, Javanna wouldn't even come to Dallas Bluff but gradually she came to see it as a memorial to her father, and now she appreciated that the site was named for him. Getting off Salt, she sat on the rock that would have been where the coyote den had been so long ago. Except for the buffalo jump, Javanna thought this was one of the prettiest spots on Crooked Creek Ranch.

Crooked Creek Ranch. She had no rightful claim to this land, but she thought of it as her home. The Bryants were as much a part of her family as was her own mother and sisters. It had never occurred to her that at some point in the future, she might actually be a part of the Bryant heritage. But as her feelings for Luke had deepened, she had begun to think of herself as being one of the Bryants.

But with one phone call, that thought had been erased. And now she could add one word that further told her where she stood. Can't.

Javanna rode Salt back at a trot, then unsaddled him and turned him loose in the pasture behind the corral. She glanced over toward the airstrip and saw Luke's Cessna 210 was still here. If his plan was to go back to New Orleans and Tia, he hadn't left yet. She wondered if she should find him and talk to him.

No. Not now.

Can't.

That one dismissive word was all that was needed for her to know where he stood. She wouldn't try to find him.

Luke was sitting in the bleachers of the sale barn, but his mind wasn't on the cattle being auctioned. It was on Javanna. His mother was right—he should have gone back last night to explain the phone call. What must she have thought?

He feared, as he lay in bed until late last night, that he might have ruined things between them beyond repair.

But she had sent him a text message, inviting him to breakfast, and he knew she wouldn't have done that if the rupture between them had been too deep. Luke's relationship with Javanna, since both had returned, had been...he strained for the word. Complex. Yes, that would explain it. It was a complex situation.

He thought back to when he had first seen Javanna going into church. It had been like seeing an old friend who had been a major part of his youth. At that time what he had felt for her could best be described as a platonic love. But over the last couple of months his feelings had become less and less platonic.

Did he love her?

The question was what is love? If it meant wanting to be with someone all the time, then yes he loved her. If it meant wanting her to be happy, then yes he loved her. If it meant he felt he couldn't live without her, then yes he loved her. And if it was the way she made him feel when he kissed her, then yes he loved her.

He took his phone from his pocket, intending to send a text to tell her how he really felt about her. No, not a text, he would call her.

No, he wouldn't call her. Something like this had to be delivered in person.

Luke made up his mind. He was going to go see Javanna as soon as he got back to the ranch. He would apologize for how he had acted last night and he would explain what Tia had wanted. And then he would tell her he loved her.

Luke smiled at the thought. He could uncomplex this relationship just real quick.

Javanna had given Luke a deadline to contact her before noon. Of course, Luke didn't know that he was on a deadline, and that was as it should be. She didn't want his response to be of some artificial construct. She wanted it to be genuine, and she wanted it to be because Luke was in love with her.

But when Luke had not contacted her by noon, she called Devin.

"How soon do you want me?" she asked when Devin answered.

"I thought you said you wanted to wait until after Christmas," Devin said.

"I've changed my mind. I think I've had enough of family."

"Javanna, I want you to come back, but I don't want you back if you're coming because you're in a huff about something,"

Javanna laughed. "If you're saying you don't want me, I'm going to call Jay and tell him I want to work in his office."

"Now, let's not be ridiculous," Devin said. "You know I want you back, the sooner the better."

"I have a favor to ask. I know it will be Christmas, but could I stay with you and Beverly until I get my own place?"

"Of course you can. Edwin's still in the guest

room, but we can put you on the sleeper sofa in the basement."

"Thanks, Devin, I'll be there tomorrow. I'll call you from O'Hare when I arrive."

Ending the call with Devin, she called United Airlines in Bozeman and booked a flight leaving Bozeman tomorrow at 12:35, and arriving in Chicago at 4:30. That worked out just right. She would have Martha take her to town and then have Vincent take her to the airport.

She was in the middle of packing when the phone rang. It was her mother.

"Hi, Mom."

"Abby's contractions have started," Helen said. "Paul's taking her to Deaconess Hospital in Bozeman, and I'm going, too."

"Oh, Mom, is there anything I can do?"

"No, honey, we've got everything under control. They're not strong enough, nor close enough together to cause us any worry, but you know how Paul is. After how quick Gavin came, he wants to be there in plenty of time."

"What about the kids? Who's taking care of them?"

"The girls are going to be with Jolene, and Brooke is looking after Gavin. If you want to stop by and help out, she could probably use a rest."

"Vincent isn't going with you, is he?"

"No, he'll be here."

"Good. Maybe he and I could come to Bozeman in the morning."

"You don't have to do that, because if this baby comes as quick as Gavin did, she'll have him tonight."

"Well, whatever. Tell Abby I'll keep her in my prayers."

Keep her in my prayers? Javanna thought after she hung up. She knew that was the right thing to say, people said that all the time. But what if you say it, and you don't really mean it? Not that she wouldn't keep Abby in her prayers—if she believed in the power of prayer.

This was working out well. Jeff Graves, one of the ranch hands, was married and lived in town, so she could ride into town with him tonight. She would tell Martha that Abby was having her baby. That would explain her absence. She wouldn't mention going back to Chicago until after she got there tomorrow. She felt guilty about how she was treating Martha, but doing it this way would save any uncomfortable confrontation.

Javanna returned to her packing. She could stay with Devin and Beverly, there had been no problem in scheduling her flight, her transportation to Bozeman would be easily arranged, and she wouldn't have to face Luke.

So why was she crying?

Chapter Nineteen

"That's wonderful news about the baby," Martha said. "Take Manly Truck and keep it as long as you need it."

"I don't think I'll need it. I've talked to Jeff and he said I could ride into town with him," Javanna said. "And then tomorrow, Vincent can take me into Bozeman. He'll want to pick up Mom of course, and he'll want to see Abby and the baby if it's here by then."

"Stay as long as you need to. I'll take good care of Riley while you're gone."

"Thanks, but I think I'm going to take her with me."

A strange expression crossed Martha's face. "All right, you let me know when the baby is born."

"I will."

Javanna started to leave, then she turned back toward the woman who had been such a part of her life for so long. She gave her an affectionate hug as tears gathered in her eyes.

"Oh, dear," Martha said when she saw that Javanna was upset. "No matter what you do, we love you. And as a mother, I can tell you he loves you, too."

"I wish I could believe that."

Jeff Graves helped Javanna load her bags into his truck and then they pulled out onto the Crooked Creek Road. A knot formed in her throat as she looked around trying to memorize every detail of the ranch. This place had played such a part of her life, and now it could be the last time she would ever see it.

Javanna was glad when Jeff started talking, telling her about his wife and his two children. She kept asking questions in an effort to keep him talking until he dropped her off at Vincent's place.

"Thanks, Jeff," Javanna said as he set her bags by the door.

"No problem," Jeff said. "Now you and Mr. Peterson be careful driving into Bozeman tomorrow. The weather report says we could be in for some snow tonight."

"That's good. That'll be more snow for Christmas."

"Yes, ma'am. I'll be takin' my kids over to the sleddin' hill."

"That sounds like a lot of fun, and if I don't see you, Merry Christmas."

"Same to you." Jeff touched his hat and got in the truck and drove away.

"Forty-three thousand, seven hundred and fifty dollars," Dale said. "This was a good trip."

Luke and Dale were having lunch at Hitt's the Place, a restaurant near the sale barn, and one that catered specifically to people doing business at the Billings Cattle Auction.

"Yes, it was," Luke agreed. "Even if you did wake me in the middle of the night."

"I know you got used to sleeping until mid-day down there in New Orleans, but up here time doesn't mean anything. When you've got work to do, you do it, no matter what time it is."

"Speaking of time, we should get back home just in time for me to get cleaned up and take Javanna to town to have supper."

"Why do that? Why not just invite her to eat with us?" Dale asked. "You know it wouldn't be any trouble for your mom to put on an extra plate."

"No, after what happened last night, and the way I handled it, I need some time alone with her to make up for it."

During the drive to Billings, Luke had shared with Dale the story of Tia calling just after he and Javanna had finished watching the movie. He told also how he had walked away from Javanna during the call, and hadn't returned.

"Mom will understand if I miss supper," Luke said. "She's the one that pointed out the error of my ways."

Dale chuckled. "Well, you'd best listen to your mama, boy. She's got more common sense than anyone I've ever known."

It was a little after seven when the big Peterbilt truck, the cattle hauler now empty and with Luke driving, arrived back at Crooked Creek Ranch.

Luke parked the truck in its usual place, and was met by Josh and Matt.

"Well, I see you made it," Josh said. "How much did you get at the auction?"

"We never got to the auction," Luke teased. "About half-way there, we hit a bump, and all the cows got loose."

"Yeah, that would be about like you," Matt said.

"A dollar-thirty," Dale said.

"Wow, that's pretty good. We were looking at a dollar-twenty-five," Matt said.

Luke saw Manly Truck, so he knew that Javanna was home. He thought he would stop by to invite her out for supper now, before she started cooking for herself.

She wasn't there, so Luke thought perhaps she was visiting with his mother.

"No, honey, she went into town with Jeff," Martha said.

"How come she didn't take Manly Truck?"

Martha took a deep breath. In her heart, she knew what Javanna was going to do, but she felt it wasn't her place to interfere. "Abby is having her baby. Vincent is taking Javanna into Bozeman tomorrow."

When Vincent and Javanna got ready to leave the next morning it was snowing, just as Jeff had predicted the night before.

"The snow will slow us down a bit," Vincent

said, as he put Riley's kennel in the back seat, "but we should be there no later than eight o'clock."

"Good, that'll give me time to visit with Abby, and still get to the airport in time for my flight."

"What will you do with Riley while you're visiting with Abby?"

"She'll be all right waiting in the car for me."

"I wish you would postpone going to Chicago, at least until after Christmas. Christmas is only three days away."

"I know, but I need to get back."

"Well, what can I say? Your mom and I have certainly enjoyed the time you've been here. And I sort of got the impression that Luke was enjoying it too."

"Well, yes, and I've enjoyed my time in White Sulphur Springs, but I imagine it will be a long time before I get back. Devin said I'm going to be really busy at CDMI, because all my old accounts want a new campaign starting the first of the year. By going before Christmas, I'll be able to get an apartment set up and be ready to go."

"The snow's getting worse," Vincent said. "We may have to turn around."

"No, don't do that, I'll miss my plane," Javanna pleaded. "We'll get there in plenty of time even if we have to drive really slow."

"All right, we'll keep going. But the truth is, Javanna, I doubt that anything will be flying in this kind of weather."

The snow was falling in such big flakes that you couldn't see beyond the hood of the car.

"Javanna we're going to have to..."

Chapter Twenty

It was quiet, very quiet as Javanna stared out the window at the heaviest snowfall she had ever seen. They weren't moving, but Javanna didn't remember them stopping. She was very confused. Something must have happened. Then she saw the deflated crash bag hanging down from the dashboard. What had happened?

She heard Riley barking.

"Vincent, have we been in an accident?"

Vincent didn't respond, and looking over toward him, she saw that he was slumped forward against the steering wheel.

"Oh, my God, Vincent, are you...?"

Javanna stared at him. She felt now, exactly as she had felt when she discovered Dane on the back porch.

"Oh, Lord, please let Vincent be alive. Please, God, don't let me go through this again. I beg of you, Lord, let Vincent be alive."

"Uhh," Vincent said.

"Oh, thank you, God. Thank you," Javanna prayed.

"Vincent? Vincent, please say something."

Vincent was unresponsive to her calling out to him, or even to her probes, though she knew he was alive.

Riley barked again. She looked behind her and saw that Riley's kennel was hanging upside down between the seats.

"Riley, it's all right," she said as she righted his kennel. "I'm calling for help."

Riley grew quiet.

With shaking hands, Javanna called 911.

"This is 911, what is your emergency?" a professional sounding woman's voice asked.

"I've been in a car accident. Please send someone, my stepfather has been badly hurt."

"Is he bleeding?"

"I don't know."

"Ma'am check to see if he's bleeding. If he is, stop the bleeding any way you can."

Javanna checked Vincent as best she could.

"No, he isn't bleeding, but he's unconscious."

"What is your location?"

"We're on highway 89 about ten miles south of White Sulphur Springs."

"What type vehicle are you in?"

"We're in a gray Toyota Highlander."

"The response team from White Sulphur Springs is currently on a transfer to Helena. Your response will come from Bozeman."

"Oh, please, tell them to hurry."

"They'll be there as fast as they can, ma'am, but with the weather conditions I can't say when that will be."

"I understand."

After Javanna ended the call, she tried again to get some response from Vincent, but she got nothing.

"You know I'd come rescue you, no matter where you are."

Those words, spoken by Luke, came back to her as strongly as if he were here, speaking them.

"Luke, yes!" Javanna said aloud.

She found Luke's name in "favorites" and put her finger on it.

"Oh, please Lord, let him answer this phone," she prayed.

"Javanna, is the baby here?" Luke answered.

"No. Luke, we've had a wreck. Vincent is unconscious. I called 911, but they said they would have to come from Bozeman, and in this snow, and as far away as that is, I'm scared."

"Where are you?"

"We're on 89, about ten miles south."

"I'll be there as fast as I can," Luke said.

"Oh, Luke, it's snowing so hard. Please be careful."

"I'll be as careful as I can."

"I'll be praying for you, sweetheart."

"I'm on my way, keep the prayers coming."

Luke was in the horse barn and he left it, running through the snow to the house.

"Mom!" he called out. "I'm taking the Cherokee."

Martha had been in the kitchen and hearing Luke's call, she hurried out to him.

"Oh, Luke, not in this weather. It's snowing so hard you can barely see."

"I've got to go, Mom. Javanna's been in a wreck and she called me. I can't leave her out there; I have to go to her."

"What about 911?" Martha asked.

"They're coming from Bozeman. In this weather it could take them three hours to get there. I'm taking your Jeep, it's four-wheel drive, and I'll need that."

"Wait, I just made a pot of coffee. Take a thermos with you. If they're trapped in a cold car, they might need some coffee. And let me grab some blankets," she added.

"Thanks, Mom."

Two minutes later, Luke was backing out of the garage. He called Javanna.

"Luke?" she answered.

"I'm leaving right now and I'm in Mom's four-wheel drive. I'll be there in half-an-hour."

"Please call again when you can."

"I'll call every ten minutes," Luke promised.

"Oh, thank you, Lord, thank you," Javanna said after she ended the call. It wasn't until then that she realized, as if for the first time, that she had been praying. Now, she prayed again.

"Lord, I have been a lost soul. I have turned my back on You, and belittled those who have prayed, and even though I've been going to church, I've closed my mind to the worship services."

Then, she remembered something Reverend Walker had said in one of his sermons.

"Someday you may call out to God in anguish, or fear, or need. Will He be there for you? The answer is yes, if you believe. Believe in the Lord our God, and He will be there for you."

"Lord, I have cried out to you in fear and need, and you have been there for me. Please now, be here for Vincent."

The phone rang, and it was Luke.

"It's hard going but I've made the turn onto 89. I'll call again when the road splits."

"Thank you, Luke, thank you. I'm praying to keep you safe."

"If ever I've been in need of prayer, it is now, so keep praying."

Luke punched out of the call, then offered his own prayer. "Lord, be with Vincent and Javanna. Let her be strong, and please keep me safe so that I can get to her."

Then, almost as if it were a miracle, the snow stopped. The roads were still covered with snow, about six inches, he figured, but now, at least he could see.

When Luke reached the turn in the road where twelve and eighty-nine separated, he called Javanna again.

"I'm at the road split, and it's stopped snowing," he said.

"I know it has," Javanna said. "I prayed for the snow to stop, and it has."

"I expect you're getting cold, aren't you?"

"Yes, I am."

"I'm bringing blankets and hot coffee."

"Luke, you're an angel."

Just as Javanna ended the call, Riley barked again. "Don't worry, Riley, Luke will be here soon and..." Javanna stopped in mid-sentence, because she saw, for the first time, the truck that had broadsided them. It had been obscured by the falling snow, but now that the snow had stopped, she could see it. However, the hood of the truck was bent into a tent shape, preventing her from seeing if anyone was inside the truck.

She heard Vincent moan.

"Vincent, are you all right? Can you hear me?"

She got no response from him.

Javanna's phone rang.

"Luke, where are you?" Javanna asked.

"I'll be there in about five more minutes. How's Vincent?"

"He's alive, but he's still unconscious."

"Hold his hand," Luke said.

"What?"

"Hold his hand. If he has any awareness at all, that will let him know that he isn't alone."

"All right."

"I'll be there soon," Luke promised.

Javanna picked up Vincent's right hand and wrapped both her hands around it.

"Vincent, I don't know if you can hear me, but you know that I love you. Please don't die. Luke will be here soon and then everything will be all right."

Vincent made no audible response, but she believed he moved his hand.

"Oh Lord, be with Vincent, keep him alive until the ambulance gets here. And keep the ambulance driver and Luke safe on this road."

Javanna continued to pray, holding Vincent's hand, willing him, almost, to respond. Then she heard a honking sound, and when she looked around, she saw Luke's Jeep.

"Vincent, Luke is here!" Javanna said excitedly.

Luke saw Vincent's Highlander, and the truck that hit him. This was at the junction of 89 and 294. Apparently, the driver of the truck was blinded by the snow, and he had come out of 294 and broadsided Vincent.

Luke parked behind, then got out of the car and carrying several blankets and a thermos of coffee, started up to the Highlander.

Even before he got there, the door opened and Javanna ran back to him. "Oh, you're here, you're here," she said relieved. She threw her arms around his neck, hugging him awkwardly because his hands were full.

"Here," she said when she dropped her arms. "I'll carry the coffee."

"How's Vincent?"

"I don't know, he hasn't spoken yet. But I held his hand like you said, and I think I felt it move."

"What about the driver of the truck that hit you?"

She shook her head. "I haven't checked. I didn't want to leave Vincent."

"I'll go see," Luke said taking one of the blankets. "You put one of these around Vincent."

As Javanna hurried back to the car, Luke stepped around to look into the pickup truck that had hit them.

Luke wiped the snow away from the window,

and he saw the man's face. His eyes were open, but Luke saw that they were seeing nothing. He was sure that the driver was dead, and when he opened the door his suspicion was confirmed.

When Luke got back to the car, he saw Javanna had wrapped one of the blankets around Vincent.

"How's the other driver?" Javanna asked.

"He's dead."

"Oh, his poor family."

"Get back here with me," Luke said. "We've only one blanket, but if we're close together, we'll stay warmer." He opened the door and Javanna got in, then he slid in beside her. She took Riley out of her kennel and put the dog on her lap. "Poor baby. Riley was so scared."

The dog reached up and began kissing Javanna.

"Here, don't I get any kisses?" Luke asked.

"From Riley or from me?" Javanna asked.

"I was talking about you," Luke said, leaning toward her. The kiss was deep and meaningful.

"I'm so glad you're here. I was so scared, but now I know everything will be all right."

Luke gave Javanna another kiss, this one was a comforting kiss.

"Shall we drink some of Mom's coffee?"

"Yes."

For the next several minutes they sat together under the blanket with Riley nestled there with them.

Javanna's telephone rang interrupting her thoughts.

"Hello?"

"This is the emergency medical team. Can you pinpoint where you are, now that the snow has let up?"

"Luke, the EMT's want to know where we are? What do I tell them?"

Luke took the phone. "We're at 89 and 294. A truck pulled out and broadsided the vehicle."

"We should be there within the next fifteen minutes. Is the patient mobile?"

"No, he's alive, but he hasn't regained consciousness."

"Do you know the status of the other vehicle?"

"From what I can tell, I believe the only occupant is dead."

"All right, thank you."

"No, thank you," Luke said as he ended the call. "He says they'll be here in fifteen minutes."

"Do you think Vincent is going to be all right?"

"Let's hope so."

They had just finished their coffee when they saw the flashing red and amber lights, the first traffic they had seen attempting to go in either direction. When the ambulance arrived, Luke saw that there were two vehicles, the ambulance, and a highway patrol car, and both Luke and Javanna got out of the car. Two men came from the ambulance with a gurney, and the highway patrolman was right behind them.

While the EMT men got Vincent out of the car, the highway patrolman checked the other vehicle and then spoke to Luke and Javanna.

"Were either of you in the car?"

"I was," Javanna said.

After getting their names and the insurance information, he continued to question Javanna.

"Do you have any injuries?"

"A few bruises I suppose, but nothing that I know of."

"Ma'am, can you tell us what happened?" the highway patrolman asked as he continued to make notes.

Javanna said that she had no memory of the actual accident, but had surmised that the truck, its driver apparently blinded by the extremely heavy snowfall, had come off highway 294.

"And you, sir, did you just come up on the accident?"

"No, sir, Javanna called me and I came from Crooked Creek Ranch. I brought blankets and coffee."

"You said you saw the driver of the other vehicle. Did you recognize him?"

"I did not," Luke said.

"A fatal accident is bad at any time, but this close to Christmas only makes it worse," the patrolman said. "Telling a family is the worst part of my job."

"I don't envy you," Luke said.

They watched as Vincent was carried to the ambulance.

"Officer, will you need us anymore?" Luke asked. "We'd like to follow the ambulance to the hospital."

"Go ahead. Get anything of value out of your vehicle, and I'll take care of getting the road cleared," the patrolman said.

"We're from White Sulphur Springs," Javanna said. "If possible, could the Highlander be taken there? In fact, could it be towed to the lot behind Abby's Place? That's a restaurant on 89 that's on this side of town."

The patrolman smiled. "I know the place well. Some of the best food in Meagher County."

Luke transferred the luggage from Vincent's

car to the Jeep, while Javanna carried Riley. They watched as the ambulance turned around and then Luke maneuvered the Jeep around the wreck thankful for four-wheel drive.

For the first few miles, neither Luke nor Javanna spoke, keeping their eyes on the ambulance in front of them.

"Forty-five miles an hour," Luke said. "That's pretty good, given the road conditions."

"It seems too fast."

"Javanna, I have to know. Why did you have all your luggage with you? Mom said you were going to see Abby in the hospital."

"I have a flight to Chicago at 12:35," she said, as she looked at her watch. "I may have to rebook."

Luke jerked his head around. "What? You can't be serious! Why would you do that, especially now?"

"I suppose I'll wait until I see how Vincent is," Javanna said.

"Were you just going to leave—not tell anybody—not tell me?"

Javanna stared straight ahead.

"Is this all about my call from Tia?"

"What do you think? We'd had a fun time together, watching a great movie, and then poof! You get a call, you walk out, you don't come back, you don't say anything, and when I send you a text inviting you to come for breakfast, your answer is can't. Now why do you think I want to leave?"

Luke clinched his teeth before he answered, and then he took a deep breath. "About the can't. Ray Jaworski was supposed to go with Dad to take a load of steers to the auction, but he was sick, so Dad asked me to go with him. When your text came in, Dad was sleeping and I was driving an eighteen-wheeler truck, that I didn't feel that comfortable driving. I couldn't text any more, and I sure couldn't pull off the road and let you know what I was doing."

"All right, that's a good explanation. Now what about the call from Tia?"

"As you probably heard, Tia is in New Orleans. She called to say she made a mistake and she wants me back."

When Luke said those words, it was as if he had hit Javanna in the stomach. This was exactly what she had feared. She waited until he was ready to continue.

"I said that I couldn't forget that by her undressing in The Long Journey, that it undermined every picture we had ever made."

"And what did she say about that?"

"She said that if I was a Christian, I was supposed to forgive her."

"Do you?"

"Do I what?"

"Do you forgive her?"

"I suppose I do in my head, but I can never forgive her in my heart. I told her I could be her friend, but I could never be her husband." Luke hesitated. "I should have told her I love someone else."

It was Javanna who turned her head away from

watching the ambulance in front of them.

"Do you really mean that?"

"I do, Javanna. When I think about it, I think I have loved you since we were kids, but these last few months have been the happiest days of my life. I want to hear it from you. Do you love me?"

"Oh, Luke, I can't begin to tell you how much I love you!"

Chapter Twenty-One

When they reached the hospital, they made Riley a bed out of the blankets and left her in the car. Then Luke headed for the emergency room to be there when Vincent was admitted, and Javanna went to find Abby and her mother.

Javanna found the maternity floor, and before entering Abby's room she stopped and sent Devin a text.

Change of plans. In accident. Vincent in hospital. I am good. Will talk to you when I get a chance.

When Javanna walked in, she found both Abby and her mother asleep. Helen opened her eyes and seeing Javanna, she put her finger to her mouth indicating that she shouldn't talk.

When the two of them stepped out into the hallway, Helen spoke.

"Where's Vincent? You shouldn't have left him by himself. You know he'll never find his way around this hospital," Helen said.

"Mom, he's in the emergency room. Luke is with him."

"Oh my God, what happened?" Helen put her hand to her mouth.

"We were hit broadside just south of White Sulphur Springs. He is unconscious, but he's alive."

"Thank God for that," Helen said. "I have to find him."

"I'll go with you, but where is Paul?"

"He went down to the cafeteria to get a bite to eat. The baby—Reed Peterson Baker, was born this morning and Abby just got back into her room. While you are here, let's walk by the nursery."

As the nursery was just around the corner from Abby's room, they stopped in front of the window and saw eight little bundles lying in bassinets. There was only one with a blue cap on.

"That's him," Helen said. "Vincent will be so proud that he is named Peterson." She turned and headed for the elevator.

When they got to the emergency room, they found Luke in the room by himself.

"Where's Vincent?" Javanna asked.

"They took him to get a CT scan," Luke said. "He's not awake yet, but they are checking to see if he has a skull fracture or any bleeding in the brain."

Helen put her hands over her face. "No, no, no— not another husband gone."

Javanna put her arm around her mother. "You have to believe he's going to pull through this. As Luke said, he's in the Lord's hands now."

"I'll stay here and wait. You two go find Abby or Paul and tell them what has happened."

"Are you sure you don't want me to stay with you?" Javanna asked.

"No, I think I'd rather be alone for a minute."

"All right."

They found Paul in the cafeteria, and grabbing a bowl of soup and some crackers, they joined him at his table. Javanna told him about the accident, and he left to go back to Abby.

As Luke and Javanna were leaving the cafeteria, they saw a sign pointing to a chapel.

"Would you mind if we stepped inside?" Javanna asked.

Luke smiled as he put his hand on her waist. "I think that's a great idea."

When they walked into the chapel, Javanna felt an overwhelming sense of peace, as if she knew that everything would be all right. There was a massive piece of stained-glass artwork that portrayed the mountains and a waterfall that had so many different shades of blue that it almost made you feel you were actually sitting beside it. Trees and flowers and rocks were all around the water.

Javanna took Luke's hand as they found a seat and sat down. Tears were streaming down her face, and Luke cradled her in his arms.

After a few minutes, Luke and Javanna went upstairs to the maternity floor. When they walked in, Abby had just finished feeding Reed and he was in her arms. His eyes were open and Javanna went to sit on the bed beside them.

"He's so tiny," Javanna said as she reached out to take his hand in hers.

"Would you like to hold him?" Abby asked.

"I don't know. Except for when Brooke was born, I've never held a newborn."

"Then it's high time you did." Abby lifted Reed over to her.

At first, Javanna was uncomfortable, but when the little guy began squirming, she looked at Luke and he was beaming.

"A baby looks good in your arms," he said as he moved over to sit on the bed as well.

"Do you want to hold him?"

It was then that the door opened and Helen came into the room with a big smile.

"He's regained consciousness," she said. "The CT scan says there's no skull fracture or bleeding in the brain. The doctor says he has a concussion and they want to keep him overnight for observation, but if all goes well, he'll get to go home tomorrow."

"That's wonderful news," Javanna said. She handed the baby back to Abby. "So many things to be thankful for this Christmas."

The following day, Luke flew to Bozeman to meet his brother, Sam. Luke was waiting in the lobby when he saw a tall man in an army uniform coming through the gate. He smiled and stood to meet him.

The two men shook hands. "Man, it's good to see you. You don't look a day over fifty," Sam said as he looked over the gray hair that was showing in Luke's dark hair.

"Sometimes I feel like I'm fifty," Luke said. "A lot of water's gone under the bridge since I last saw you."

"For both of us. Are you going back to New Orleans?"

"I suppose I'll go eventually, but right now I don't know when that will be."

"Since I'm at Fort Rucker, maybe when you get back, I can take a long weekend and come see you."

"That would be good," Luke said. "What's this?" Luke pointed to the rank insignia on his shirt. "Is this new?"

"I got my promotion right after I got back from Afghanistan."

"A Chief Warrant Officer 3?"

"That's right, I've kept my nose clean," Sam said with a smile. "So how are Mom and Dad doing?"

"Mom still rules the roost, and Dad still thinks that he does," Luke said with a chuckle. "Let's get your bag; I've got my plane outside."

When they got out to the tarmac, they walked over to Luke's Cessna 210.

"Wow, I'll be coming home in style."

"Ha, wait until you see Gabe. He came in driving a brand-new F-450 diesel that was pulling a horse trailer with living quarters in front."

"Whew! That had to cost a pretty penny," Sam said.

Luke was cleared for takeoff and they rose into the air.

"It sounds like he did really well this year, even though the coronavirus shut down some of the major circuit rodeos. They even moved the championship to Texas this year."

"What about the barrel racer? Did he say anything about her?"

"You know about Dusty?"

"Yeah, Gabe and I talk every now and then."

"Well, Miss Valentine is with him."

"Uh, oh. How are Mom and Dad dealing with that?"

"When they got home, Gabe had planned on them staying in the horse trailer, but Dad put his foot down. He said it wasn't fair to Mom—that she'd been so looking forward to having all her boys home for Christmas, and he wanted everybody in their old rooms."

"Then, will she be in the guest room?" Sam asked.

"No, that's Ty's room," Luke said. "She's staying down at Javanna's cabin."

"Javanna? You mean Javanna Reed?"

"Yes, well it's Javanna Caldwell now, but Dane died a couple of years ago, so she's back at the ranch."

"Ah, is she as pretty as she ever was?"

"She is."

"Good, maybe I'll ask her out, while I'm here."

"I don't think that would be such a good idea."

"Do I detect a little jealously in my big brother?"

Luke changed the subject, calling Sam's attention to the site of one of the forest fires that had ravaged the area.

"I suppose Noah's all over that," Sam said. "He'll find some way to claim it was caused by global warming. Are he and Ty at the house already?"

"Noah said they'd drive over tomorrow. Patricia's here from Washington and she'll be with them."

"And are we excited about that?"

"Well, we're looking forward to seeing Ty."

Javanna was in town. Jolene Baker had brought the girls back home, and Brooke had called to see if she could come help entertain Gavin.

"What do you think this one is going to do with a baby brother?" Javanna asked as she stopped the two-year old from climbing onto the kitchen counter.

"I want a cookie," Gavin said. "I want a Santa Claus."

"Why didn't you ask?" Javanna said as she got a cookie out of the cookie jar and gave it to him.

"You shouldn't give in to him," Brooke said.

"Why not?" She picked up the child and began dancing around with him.

"You need a baby of your own," Brooke said. "You spoil Gavin."

"In order to have a baby, I need a husband first," Javanna said as she put Gavin on the floor.

"Are you trying to tell me something? You and Luke seem to really get along well."

Javanna thought of the conversation she and Luke had had in the car yesterday on the way to Bozeman.

She smiled. "We do get along well."

"It's mama and daddy!" Lila called out excitedly. "Mama and daddy are here!"

"They aren't the only ones here," Brooke said as all of them scrambled to get to the door. "Your new little brother is with them, too."

"What did you say his name is?" the five-year old asked.

"His name is Reed," Javanna said. "That used to be your mama's name before she married your daddy."

"I think it's a funny name," Caroline said as she moved back and sat on the sofa.

Javanna sat down beside Caroline. "Look at how much fun you have with Gavin. When Reed gets a little older, you're going to have just as much fun with him."

"Gavin's mean." She folded her arms and pouched out her lips.

"Mama, I'm so glad you're home," Lila said as she threw her arms around Abby.

Gavin was climbing into the car as Paul was taking out the car seat. Gavin still had a part of the cookie Javanna had given him and he tried to give it to the baby.

"No, no," Paul said as Abby rescued Gavin.

"Did Mom and Pop come home with you?" Brooke asked.

"Yes. We dropped them off at your place as we came by," Paul said.

"Does Pop seem like he's all right?"

"He'll probably have a headache for a few days, but other than that and being tired, he is in good shape," Abby said.

"Then I think I'll go on home," Brooke said.

Abby hugged Brooke. "I can't thank you enough for staying here."

After Brooke left, Javanna stayed for a while longer. She took Gavin outside and pulled him around the neighborhood on a sled. Abby had good kids, and she did enjoy being with them.

Brooke had told her she needed a baby of her own. In the early years when she and Dane were married, they had both been too involved with their careers and after the accident, although it would have been possible to conceive Dane's child, they had never discussed having children.

But now she was thirty-seven years old. Was she too old to have a child?

"Javanna! Stop thinking like this," she said aloud as she took Gavin back to the house.

"I want another cookie," Gavin said.

"You'll have to ask your mama this time."

Abby had already put the baby in his crib, and she was involved in a conversation with the girls as they told her everything they had done while she was gone.

Javanna waved and then went out to start Manly Truck. She stopped by the annex to see Vincent and then she headed out to the ranch.

"Noah said Patricia would be with him and Ty when they come over tomorrow," Martha said. "I sure wish Francine could have come with Sam."

"Mom, Sam and Francine are divorced," Matt said.

"I know they are, but I've always liked Francine, and I've always had the thought in the back of my head that they might get back together."

"We don't need one more. We're going to have a house full for Christmas dinner, as it is," Dale said.

"Dad, when you had all of us, you already had a house full," Matt said with a little chuckle.

"Yes, and now I only have one grandchild," Martha said.

"You know Tia didn't want any babies. It might have made her gain two pounds," Josh said as he cut off a piece of fruitcake. "And even if she did have a kid, she probably wouldn't ever let him come to Montana. Oooh, it stinks. Those cows are too noisy. How do you stand to live so far away from any civilized people?"

"Boys, that's enough," Martha said. "Every one of you gets to choose his own wife, and none of us has anything to say about it. Do you understand?"

Even though Josh was twenty-eight years old, and Matt was twenty-seven, they both lowered their heads, just as if they were kids again.

"What about you, Josh, are you going to marry Melissa?" Dale asked.

"Dad!" Josh said.

"Well, you are spending a lot of time with her. I'm just askin'."

"I'm helping her with a Christmas program—that's all there is to it," Josh said.

"Uh huh, you hear that, Mama, he's helping her with the Christmas program," Dale said.

Martha shook her head. "You're as bad as the whole lot of 'em."

Javanna got home later in the afternoon, and when she parked Manly Truck, she saw the pickup truck with the horse trailer, so she ran up to the Big House.

"Javanna," Gabe said as he grabbed her and held her in a bear hug. "How's my old riding partner?"

"I doubt I could beat you now," Javanna teased.

"Ha! What makes you think you ever could beat me?"

"Oh, I don't know, maybe it was all the times we raced and I won."

"That wasn't fair. Your dad always picked the fastest horse for you, and anyway, I was always heavier than you," Gabe said as he released her.

"Javanna, I have to ask," Martha said, "how is Vincent?"

"I just left the annex. He's home and he seems to be okay."

"That's a miracle, and it's a miracle that you're all right, too," Dale said, "and we're glad to have you back home."

Javanna's face flushed as she thought of how she had left without telling anyone what she had planned to do. She was embarrassed and she should be.

"I saw Luke's airplane is gone." For an instant she had a moment of panic—what if Luke had pulled a stunt like she had tried to pull?

"He went to pick up Sam," Dale said. "I have the radio on his frequency and a few minutes ago I heard him ask for take-off clearance at the Bozeman airport."

"I'm sure they'll be here any minute," Martha said. "By the way, I think I should tell you something. No, Gabe should tell you," she added. "Gabe?"

"Tell her what?" Gabe asked.

"About her house guest."

"Oh, yeah. Javanna, I hope you don't mind, but Dusty will be staying with you while she's here."

"Dusty?" Javanna raised her eyebrows.

"Yeah, she's my girlfriend," Gabe said. "When we left Arlington after the championships, we took one of her horses out to a barrel rider friend of hers in Wilcox, Arizona, so I think she's taking a nap, now."

"Then maybe I should go down and meet her. What did you say her name is?"

"Dusty Valentine," Gabe said. "That's the name she uses for rodeos."

The obvious next question was "then what's her real name", but nobody asked it, so Javanna assumed everyone knew the answer.

"I'll go on down and introduce myself, then," Javanna said.

When Javanna went into her house a few minutes later, she found a woman lying on the sofa with Riley curled up behind her legs. Riley barked when he saw Javanna and jumped down, waking Dusty as he did.

"Hi, you must be Dusty," Javanna said as she went over to sit in one of her chairs.

"And you must be Javanna. I've heard a lot of stories about you."

"Knowing Gabe, I know they can't all be true," Javanna said.

"He said you were the closest thing to a sister he ever had."

"That's probably true. Of all the Bryant boys, because we were the same age, Gabe and I were the closest. I'm so proud of what he has accomplished."

"He's good. He enters a lot of jackpot roping events, and this year at the Bob Feist, he lost the championship by only seven hundredths of a second. Now that's close," Dusty said.

"I used to know a lot about the rodeo circuit when I lived here, but I don't know what you mean by Bob Feist," Javanna said.

"It's probably one of the most prestigious team roping venues in the country, and this year, everybody was very happy to go to Guthrie to participate. The Lazy E Arena opened, when a lot of others stayed closed due to the coronavirus."

"I didn't think of that," Javanna said, "but this pandemic hit just about every profession there is—unless you run a grocery store or something else that really is essential."

"I hope you don't mind my staying here," Dusty said. "Gabe said we'd stay in the quarters in the horse trailer, but I guess his dad said no."

Javanna smiled. "Of course, it's all right. Martha has been so excited that all her boys are going to be together. I think she has baked every day since Thanksgiving."

Dusty put her head down. "I wish I hadn't come. I don't want to be the cause of ruining her Christmas."

"Don't think that way. Martha Bryant is the kindest, most tolerant woman you could ever meet."

"Is she tolerant of a man and a woman who live together when they aren't married?"

"I won't sugar coat it," Javanna said. "I'm sure she doesn't like it, but she loves her son. And if he cares for you, then she will care for you."

"Oh, Javanna, I hope you're right. When I thought I was going to have to stay up at the 'Big House' as everyone calls it, I was scared to death."

"Being around the Bryants could be intimidating I guess, but I grew up in this very house, at least until I was fifteen when my father died. Never once did it ever occur to me that they were above me."

"I would have loved to have been raised in a

place like this," Dusty said as she looked around the cabin.

"Where did you grow up?"

"I don't know what you mean by grow up. If you mean when did I have to start taking care of myself, it would have been when I was about fourteen." Dusty stopped talking and then she continued. "My name isn't Dusty Valentine. That's a name I thought sounded like a rodeo barrel rider." She laughed. "Can't you just hear an announcer saying 'and now in the chutes, Rachel Philbrick'. It doesn't sound like much of a winner.

"I never knew my father, and I'm not sure my mother knew who my father was either. She worked in one bar after another, and we moved at least every two years. I don't really know how many towns we lived in, but I say I'm from Abilene, Texas, because I think that was where I was born." She shrugged her shoulders. "You didn't know what you were getting into when you asked your question, did you?"

"Dusty, or would you rather I call you Rachel?" Javanna said.

"Dusty. If you called me Rachel, I wouldn't know who you're talking to."

"Well, Dusty, I think it's wonderful that you're with Gabe. He's a good man, and whatever you had to endure growing up, he will never hurt you. This family will accept you for who you are." Javanna moved over to sit on the sofa beside Dusty. The two women hugged each other.

"Thank you, Javanna. I can see how Gabe could think of you as his sister. If what Gabe and I have ever becomes something more, I want to think of you as my sister, too."

"I'd be honored to have you as my sister," Javanna said.

They heard an airplane then.

"Oh, that airplane sounded like it's right over the house," Dusty said.

Javanna smiled. "I'm sure it is. That means Luke is back with Sam. Come on, let's go up to the Big House. The fun is about to begin."

"And there were in the same country shepherds abiding in the field, keeping watch over their flock by night. And, lo, the angel of the Lord came upon them, and the glory of the Lord shone round about them: and they were so afraid." Reverend Walker's son, Ezra, was the narrator for the Christmas play that the children would present on Christmas Eve.

"Ezra, that's sore afraid," Melissa corrected

"Sore afraid? Are you sure? I've never heard of anybody saying they were sore afraid, so I changed it."

"Just read it the way it's written," Josh said. "Shepherds and Angel, you're on next."

"What was that?" one of the shepherds asked.

"I don't know but I am sore afraid."

"That's 'so' afraid, Kenny," Melissa said.

"You just told Ezra it was sore afraid."

"That's in the narrative, but in the dialogue, the word is so," Melissa insisted.

"Angel," Josh said.

Lila Baker, stepped up onto a step stool. She held her arms straight out by her side.

"Oh, look, it is an angel," one of the shepherds said. "Isn't she beautiful?"

"Why is she here? I'm still afraid," Kenny said.

"Fear not: for, behold, I bring you good tidings of great joy, which shall be to all people," Lila said. "For unto you is born this day in the city of David a Savior, which is Christ the Lord. And this shall be a sign unto you; Ye shall find the babe wrapped in swaddling clothes, lying in a manger."

"What's a swaddling?" Neil asked.

"It means they just wrapped bands of cloth around the baby Jesus," Josh explained.

"Why heck, that's not clothes at all."

"Just say your lines," Josh said. "People, people, people, we've been working on this for sixteen days, and tomorrow night is when we do it. Shall we just call it off, or do you think we can get this right?"

"We can do it, Mr. Bryant," Lila said. "I promise you we can do it."

"All right. Let's start from here."

Chapter Twenty-Two

"Grandma, Grandma!" Ty shouted, rushing into the house.

"Oh my, I think you've grown three inches since I saw you last," Martha said, opening her arms to give him a big hug.

"Noah, Patricia, I'm so glad you could come," Martha said as they came through the door.

"Where is everyone?" Noah asked.

"Well, Luke, Josh and Matt are in town, getting the church ready for the Christmas Eve program tonight. Gabe and Dusty are exercising a couple of his horses, and I think Sam took out on a snowmobile ride about an hour ago. Javanna is with her sister, Brooke."

"Javanna? You mean Javanna Reed?" Noah asked. "What's she doing here?"

"She's been here since the beginning of October," Martha said. "She was an account executive for an advertising agency in Chicago, but she had the misfortune to have upscale restaurants as her main clients. You can just imagine what happened to them when the pandemic hit."

"But what's she doing out here? At the ranch?"

"She's here because I asked her to come," Martha said, offering no further explanation. "And, Patricia, how nice it is to see you." She did not attempt to give her daughter-in-law a hug, because long ago, Martha decided Patricia was uncomfortable doing that.

"I thought for a while I wouldn't make it," Patricia said. "So many flights out of D.C. were cancelled."

"Well I'm glad you got out of the swamp," Dale said. "I suppose you've got a lot of cases going."

"Yes, it's extremely hectic right now," Patricia replied. "I have three lawsuits that will be going before the Fourth District Court after the first of the year, but the biggest one might be of some interest to you here in Meagher County."

"Why would you say that?" Dale asked.

"Because it deals with copper mine waste disposal, and that one might go all the way to the supreme court."

"Which copper mine is being sued?" Dale asked.

"The particular copper mine in question is in Arizona, Maricopa Copper, but it's an all-inclusive suit so the results will affect every copper mine in America."

"And that would include the mine that is in the works over by Smith River. Will it be affected by your lawsuit?"

"Grandpa, did you know I played little league football this year?"

"Did you, now?"

"Yep, I was a quarterback on the National Lock team," Ty said.

"I wish I could have seen you," Dale said as he looked pointedly at Noah. "How did your team do?"

"We won six and we lost two."

"That's pretty good, you'll have Montana State scouting you, pretty soon."

"I'll be even better next year," Ty insisted.

"Well, you'll be a year older, and if your dad gets out there and throws the ball with you, you'll be better for sure."

Luke, Josh, Matt, and Melissa were at Grace Gospel Church, getting all ready for the evening's performance. The children had completed what Melissa had called their final rehearsal the evening before, and everyone seemed excited that it was almost Christmas Eve.

The area behind the altar rail had been converted into a stage. To the left was the rock the angel would stand on. It was made from two step stools, draped with gray sheets. The steps were to the rear so the angel could easily mount the 'rock'. To the extreme right rear of the stage, Matt had built a stable, the floor of the stable covered with straw.

The four of them worked the whole morning and, when they had the area beyond the railing decked with all the props and equipment they thought they would need for the program, Luke, Josh, Melissa and Matt went to Abby's Place.

"This is going to be the best Christmas Eve program ever done in White Sulphur Springs," Josh said with confidence.

"Hello, Katie," Matt said. "How's the prettiest waitress in town?"

"Katie, Javanna and Brooke were supposed to meet us here at noon. They aren't in the back, are they?" Luke asked.

"No sir, I haven't seen them all day."

"Have you told anyone?" Brooke asked Javanna.

"No."

"Not even Luke?"

"No, I haven't told him. I want to surprise him," Javanna said.

"We're going to surprise everyone," Brooke said.

"It's about noon, I told Luke we'd meet him over at the restaurant.".

"Noon? No wonder I'm getting hungry. Let's go eat."

The two walked from the annex, over to the restaurant. When they stepped inside, Luke stood and smiled at Javanna as he waved from the family table in the back corner.

"Go ahead and kiss her, Luke. We'll close our eyes," Josh said, jokingly when Javanna got to the table.

"No need for you to close your eyes," Luke said, as he gave Javanna a quick kiss on the lips.

When the meal was over, Javanna and the Bryants left Brook and Melissa sitting at the table.

"We'll see you tonight," Josh said. "If you think of anything we've forgotten, you call me, Melissa. I'll come right back."

"I can't think of anything else. Just don't be late," Melissa said.

"How did everything go?" Javanna asked, as they pulled out onto the highway.

"It went great," Josh said. "Thanks to Melissa and me, there are going to be a lot of proud mamas and papas here tonight."

"Yeah, well, it's because I did such a good job building the set," Matt said.

"Which I designed," Luke added with a smile.

"Why don't you just admit it, all three of you have been wonderful," Javanna said with a chuckle. "Have you always been like this?"

"Have all three of us always been wonderful?" Josh asked. "Yeah, I'd pretty much say so."

Josh's comment brought laughter from all of them.

"Javanna, why don't you leave Manly Truck here, and ride back to the Big House with us?" Luke suggested.

"All right," Javanna agreed.

"I wonder if Noah is here yet," Luke said as they turned toward Crooked Creek Ranch.

"It'll be good to see Noah and Ty again. Ty's a good kid," Josh said.

"I wonder if Patricia came," Matt said.

"Your mom's pretty sure she's going to be here," Javanna said.

"I don't care much for her," Matt said.

"She's Noah's wife, Matt. It doesn't make any difference how you feel about her," Luke said.

"That's Noah's car," Josh said, pointing to the

Range Rover parked in the driveway of the Big House.

"That's Patricia's car," Matt said. "She just let's Noah drive it."

"Are you coming in?" Luke asked Javanna when they were out of the truck.

"I think I'll wait a little while," Javanna said. "Do you think you could come over to my place at about two o'clock this afternoon?"

"I can come over right now, if you want me to. It could get nasty in there when these two go after their sister-in-law," Luke said as he hit Matt on the shoulder.

"No, you need to stay and defend poor Patricia," Javanna said. "I want you to come at two o'clock. I have something I want you to see."

"Now you have my curiosity up," Luke said. "I'll see you at two."

Luke went into the Big House with his brothers, where he greeted Noah and Patricia, and true to the Bryant upbringing, all three were very friendly and polite toward both of them.

"Where's Ty?" Luke asked.

"Oh, he and Sam are down at the airstrip," Noah said. He chuckled. "I think Sam is teaching him how to fly."

Luke checked his watch. It was one-thirty, and he wanted to make sure he was at Javanna's at two o'clock. He left the house and walked out to the airstrip. Sam was standing under the wing of the Cessna 150, and Ty was sitting in the pilot's seat with his hands on the wheel.

"No, for heaven's sake, never pull the wheel that far back. You'll stall out."

"Looks like you've got your work cut out for you, Little Brother, if you're going to teach that one to fly."

"Uncle Luke, look. Uncle Sam is teaching me to fly. He said you taught him when he was sixteen."

"The army taught him to fly, I just gave him a little stick time."

"What does that mean?"

"It means I took him up and let him control the plane."

"Uncle Sam, can we do that? Will you take me up and let me do that?" Ty asked excitedly.

"Sure, if your mom and dad say it's okay, I'll take you up," Sam said.

"I'm going to go ask them!" Ty said excitedly, as he jumped down and started running back toward the Big House.

"It looks like we may have another aviator in the family," Luke said with a smile as they watched Ty head toward the house.

"He's certainly been eager," Sam said. "How did things go with the rehearsal? Are we going to have a dynamite production?"

"Well, I don't expect any Tony nominations, but I think the parents will be pleased."

"Josh said he talked you into writing it, so I know it'll be good."

Luke chuckled. "I didn't write it. Luke did. That is, St. Luke. And I'm certainly no saint."

"Ha, no you aren't. And if you're ever put up for sainthood, I plan to testify. I've got a few of your little sins I could throw in as a witness."

"You don't really want to start trading sins, do you?" Luke replied. "Because I could drop some of yours in as well."

"Ouch," Sam said, making an exaggerated grimace.

"I meant to ask you do you hear anything from Francine?" Luke asked, changing the subject.

"Oh yeah, she's in Newport News, still teaching school. But you'll never guess what else she's doing. She's become an author."

"Really?"

"She's had a couple of books published, and I guess she's dynamite with internet promotion. I think she's doing well enough that she might be quitting her day job before long."

"Well, good for Francine. Did you tell Mom?"

"No, I didn't tell Mom. If I told her I'm even talking to Francine, she'd have us back together."

"I always did think Francine was Mom's favorite daughter-in-law," Luke said. "She was really upset when you two were divorced."

"I guess I was too," Sam said as he looked toward the mountains. "But I don't blame Francine for leaving me. I was in a bad way when I came back from my last tour, and I think I must have been impossible to live with."

"Do you think it was PTSD?"

"Are you kidding—I know it was, but I'm getting better. It's probably been over a year since I had my last flashback," Sam said. "How about you and Tia? Any chance of the two of you ever getting back together?"

"Not a chance," Luke said.

Sam smiled. "Mom filled me in. She said you and

Javanna have been hitting it off pretty well."

"I love her, Sam."

"Then hang on to her," Sam said, reaching out to put his hand on Luke's shoulder. "You've known Javanna for her whole life, and she's as fine a person as I've ever known."

"I can't say that I disagree with you," Luke said as he looked at his watch. "Oh, it's almost two o'clock. Javanna wanted me to come by her house at precisely two o'clock, though I have no idea why."

"Well, you've got ten minutes to find out," Sam said.

"It's five 'til two," Luke said with a smile as he opened the door of the cabin. "Am I too early?"

"No, you're just in time. I have a Zoom call set up with Devin."

"Devin? Look here, Javanna, you aren't going to...?"

Javanna interrupted him with a smile and a raised hand. "You just sit by and observe the conversation."

Javanna turned on her computer, brought up the Zoom app, then invited Devin to join.

A moment later, Devin's face popped up on the screen.

"Hello, Javanna, everyone's been so worried about you. Are you all right?"

"I'm doing fine."

"Great, that's good to hear. So, when are you coming back to work?"

"That all depends," Javanna said.

"What do you mean?"

"It depends on whether or not you will let me work using Zoom."

"Oh, I don't know."

"Devin, you know for six months before this all hit, I was doing business with Kurt Hoffman and Jason Peters, and it was all by Zoom. And I don't think it would be that hard to convince some of my other clients to work that way. It would save their time and mine," Javanna said. "I have no doubt that I could set up an account list that would be as productive as what we were doing before."

"I don't know, you're in Montana."

"Yes, and you're in Chicago. But you can see me just as well from here, as you could if I was across the street from you."

Devin chuckled. "Yes, I guess that's true."

"What I'm asking you is if you will agree to allow me to do all my work by internet, then I'll work with you. If I need to have any personal contact, Carrie can handle it."

"All right, you've convinced me. We can at least give it a try," Devin said. "Do you want me to speak with Carrie, or do you want to?"

"I want to talk to her first, so she'll understand what we expect from her, and then I'll have her talk to you."

"Good, that sounds like a plan."

"She's going to have a lot more responsibility now, so I think a ten percent raise might be in order."

"Done."

"Then we'll get this started right after the first of the year," Javanna said. "And tell Beverly I miss her."

"She misses you, too. Merry Christmas."

"And Merry Christmas to you, and, Devin, thank you for being the best boss I've ever worked for."

Devin laughed. "I believe I'm the only boss you've ever worked for. I'm going to miss having you in the office."

After the Zoom meeting ended, Javanna looked over at Luke. "I thought you might like to see that."

"It's the best Christmas present ever," Luke said as he pulled Javanna to her feet and gave her a long and endearing kiss.

When Luke and Javanna got back to the Big House, everyone was abuzz about Sam taking Ty up in the plane.

"I don't know why you gave him permission," Patricia said. "What if he gets hurt?"

Noah lowered his head as his jaw clinched. "Ty will enjoy it, and you know Sam won't let anything happen. For goodness sakes, Patricia, the man has flown in combat."

"You always undermine me," Patricia said. "You let him play football when I said no."

"And he enjoyed that, too. When you're not around, I get to make the decisions."

"Humph," Patricia said as she stalked over to the stairs and went up to their bedroom.

Noah looked over at his mother, a faint smile on his face that showed a touch of sadness. "Sorry."

Martha moved over to Noah and gave him a hug. "I love you, Noah, and I love my grandson."

"Thanks, Mom, I'd better go upstairs."

After Noah, left the great room, there was a period of silence, where no one wanted to speak first. Finally, it was Josh who spoke up.

"I'm going to have to go to the church early tonight to make certain everything's ready for the big show."

"Sure, sure," Matt said as he snickered. "We all know what's going on. I don't suppose Melissa is going to be there early, too, is she?"

Josh just smiled. "Mom, don't let these guys make you late. You don't want to miss a minute of this grand production."

"Don't worry, we'll be there on time, or at least your father and I will be there. I can't speak for anyone else."

When the congregants entered Grace Gospel Church that evening, it was very dimly lit by candles on the windowsills, augmented by the strings of battery-powered Christmas lights that were under the pews. The raised front portion of the church had been turned into a stage and it was almost dark. There were three children, dressed in shepherd's robes, sitting around what appeared to be a campfire which had been artfully created by an orange light under a pyramid of sticks. Two live sheep were standing by.

Covering the ceiling was a frame with black cloth stapled onto it. Scores of holes had been punched through it, and again, it was back lighted with Christmas lights giving the illusion of stars.

When the congregation was seated, a spotlight, borrowed from the producers of the Red Ants Pants Festival, fell upon two beautiful young women, Brooke Peterson and Javanna Caldwell.

"Javanna?" Gabe asked quietly.

"I don't know what this is all about," Luke said shaking his head.

June Caldwell was at the piano, and she began to play the opening notes of a familiar Christmas carol.

O Holy Night!
The stars are brightly shining.
It is the night of the dear Savior's birth.

Brooke carried the lead and Javanna added perfect harmony. When they were finished, there was a spontaneous outburst of applause.

After their song, Brooke joined the choir, while Javanna slipped down into the congregation and sat beside Luke. He put his arm around her and drew her to him.

"Why didn't you say anything? You two are really good together," Luke said.

"We wanted it to be a surprise."

The piano began the opening notes of Hark the Herald Angels Sing and the choir began to sing. As they did so, Joseph and Mary processed up through the center aisle. There were audible oohs and ahs when people recognized Paul and Abby Baker as they portrayed Joseph and Mary. They moved to the corner where Matt had built the stable. The manger was in place and Joseph and Mary took their positions beside it, dimly illuminated by an unseen, orange light.

During the singing of the hymn, Lila had taken advantage of the darkness and was standing on the rock, though at the moment, not visible to anyone.

Ezra Walker began his narration, and at the appropriate time the same spotlight that had shone on Brooke and Javanna, now found Lila. She was dressed in a long gauzy white dress and angel wings were attached to her back. They were covered with sequins so that she sparkled as she delivered her announcement to the poor shepherds in the field.

When the shepherds approached the stable to pay homage, Abby reached down into the manger, then lifted the baby Jesus.

"Oh, how sweet! That's baby Reed," someone said, trying to speak quietly, but heard by everyone. "He's only three days old!"

After the shepherds left, other 'citizens of Bethlehem' walked by the little stable to pay their homage.

The stage went dark, as the choir sang We Three Kings. Three boys, each dressed in costume and holding a gift, processed down the center aisle.

As they climbed upon the stage, a bright light appeared through the cloth ceiling, portraying the star that had guided the wise men.

After the wise men delivered their gifts the stage gradually darkened, and as it did so, the choir and the congregation sang Silent Night. When the song was ended, footlights behind the altar came on and all the children plus Abby, Paul and baby Reed, came forward to take a bow.

The congregation, to a person, stood and began clapping. Baby Reed continued to sleep.

Chapter Twenty-Three

Following the Christmas Eve service, a caravan of four vehicles made its way up to the Crooked Creek Ranch. Dale and Martha had Sam and Matt with them, Dusty and Gabe rode with Luke and Javanna, Noah, Patricia, and Ty were in their vehicle, and Josh was riding with Melissa in her car. When they pulled up, the lights that outlined the house were on and the big Christmas tree could be seen through the front bank of windows.

"This is by far the most memorable Christmas Eve I've ever had," Dusty said. "I shouldn't say this, but it's the first time I ever went to church on Christmas Eve."

"It was meaningful to me, too," Javanna said. "It's been several years since I went to a Christmas Eve service."

"It doesn't matter how many years it's been since you went to a Christmas service, you made up for it tonight," Gabe said. "The duet you sang with Brooke was beautiful."

"Yes," Luke said. "I didn't know you could sing like that."

"That's a lie, Luke Bryant—you knew I could sing."

Luke looked at her with an odd expression on his face.

"You even wrote a song for me. Don't you remember—Giovanna's Pizzeria?"

Luke laughed uproariously. "Of course, I did. How could I forget?"

"I remember that," Gabe said, and then to Dusty he added. "Luke wrote a play in high school that won some prize and that got him the scholarship that turned him into a big shot film producer. His whole career started in WSS high school. Everybody thought Javanna was the star, but it was really me."

"You? I don't remember you being in the play," Luke said.

"There you go—you're getting old, Big Brother. Who sat at the table and ate the pizza Javanna served? Me, that's who. You can't have a pizzeria if you don't have customers so that makes me the star."

When they got out of the truck, the four of them were all laughing and Ty ran over to join them. He took Gabe's hand and they walked up the steps together and followed the others inside.

"Hey, Ty, what are you doing holding on to your Uncle Gabe? I thought I was your favorite uncle," Sam said.

"I don't have a favorite," Ty said. "I love you all."

"Now that boy has a future in politics," Dale said as he sat down in his big chair as Ty burrowed in beside him. "Matt, get the fire going."

Before long the fire was blazing and everyone began singing Christmas songs, including some of the secular ones. Everyone was amazed at how many of the words Ty knew—many more than the adults.

Josh and Melissa had not come in with everyone else, and they now stepped inside.

"Hey, Josh, where ya been?" Sam asked.

"I was just showing Melissa your outfit. She thinks a family could set up house in that thing, if he had a mind to."

Gabe reached over and took Dusty's hand. He smiled. "I'll have to think on that."

"If you ask me, I don't think it would take much thought," Dale said.

"Girls, I could use some help over here," Martha said. "Patricia, will you fill the glasses? Javanna, you bring the bowls over here, and Dusty, you put cookies on this tray. Melissa, you put the stollen bread in the microwave and watch it so the icing doesn't melt."

"It sounds like Mom's got a whole new crew to boss," Sam said.

"I heard that, Sam," Martha said. "And you know one of my best hands is missing."

"You brought that on yourself," Luke said as he went into the kitchen. "Do you want me to help Javanna carry the soup bowls to the table?"

"If you spill one drop of oyster stew on my table cloth, I'll have your hide," Martha said. "And Matt, you get the candles lit."

"Yes, ma'am."

When everyone came to the table, there were

thirteen. Ty was at the head of the table with Dale, and before they sat down, Dale asked that they all hold hands. Tears were building in his eyes, and with a choked voice, he said the blessing.

By the time the family had finished their meal it was close to eleven o'clock.

"Ty, do you think you can stay up a little longer and open your presents?" Dale asked.

Ty had a huge grin.

"I take it that's a yes."

As everyone was moving toward the tree, Melissa went into the kitchen where Martha was filling another tray of cookies.

"Mrs. Bryant, I can't tell you how much I've enjoyed this evening. Thank you for letting me be a part of it."

Martha hugged her. "And we enjoyed having you. I'm so glad you asked Josh to help you with the program. What the two of you did was fantastic."

"There were a lot of people who made it what it was," Melissa said.

"And one more thing—all my girls call me Martha."

Melissa beamed at being called one of Martha's girls.

"I have a feeling we might see a lot more of you around here."

"That could be," Melissa said as Josh brought her coat.

When the presents were all opened and the wrapping paper recycled, everyone began saying their goodnights.

"Now don't get too comfortable," Dale said. "It's going to be a short night for you people. You know we give all the hands the day off for Christmas, but the animals don't stop needing to be tended. Just to make Sam feel at home, I'm going to blow reveille at six o'clock, and I expect every one of you to fall out."

Ty groaned.

"I mean it—now don't let me down."

Luke walked Javanna back to her cabin and when they got there Riley was waiting patiently.

"Poor little girl," Luke said. "Everybody's forgotten you." He put her leash on her and he and Javanna took her for her last walk.

"Javanna, is it awful for me to be thankful for the COVID?"

"Luke, you can't mean that."

"Oh, but I do," Luke said. "If it hadn't been for that, I'd be in New Orleans and you'd be in Chicago. And I would never know how much I could love—I mean really love—someone." He took her in his arms and they kissed until Riley barked.

Javanna laughed. "I guess she's telling us we're going to be up in six hours."

"You won't hear reveille. You can sleep in if you want to."

"Absolutely not!" Javanna said.

"All right, see you in the morning." Luke took

Javanna in his arms and kissed her.

Gabe and Dusty were coming up to the cabin.

"Well, now, is that the price to get in to this place?" Gabe asked as he turned to Dusty. "I guess we have to pay the toll."

After Luke and Gabe left, Javanna asked Dusty if she would like a cup of hot chocolate.

"It won't be something Martha would serve, but it'll be hot," Javanna said as she got two packets out of the box. Putting two cups of water in the microwave, she turned to Dusty while they waited. "The Bryant family is pretty amazing, isn't it?"

"I've never experienced anything like this. Everyone seems to genuinely like one another, except maybe..."

"I know who you're going to say," Javanna interrupted as she took the hot water out of the microwave. "Now that the rodeo circuit is over what will you do?"

Dusty laughed as she took a swallow of her drink. "The rodeo circuit is never over. Since we're here, Gabe has us entered in the Montana Pro Rodeo in Great Falls, and that's the first or second week in January I think."

"Really. That's less than a hundred miles from here," Javanna said. "Guess who will be in the audience?"

"That would be nice to have family come see us. I know Gabe's parents used to catch as many as they could, but they haven't come for a while." Dusty hesitated. "I don't know if it's because of me or not."

"I think you can rest assured; you aren't the reason. As hard as it is to believe, when you see how much work they do, Dale is sixty-seven years old and Martha is sixty-five, and speaking of rest, we'd better get some."

"Thank you again for letting me stay here," Dusty said.

"You're welcome but now we do have to say goodnight."

The next morning at six o'clock on the dot, the Alexa hub blared out reveille at the highest volume.

Matt was the first one down the stairs.

"We're coming—nobody could sleep through that," Matt said. He saw that his mother was already in the kitchen, dressed and pulling biscuits out of the oven.

"When did he wake you up, Mom? You couldn't wait for reveille?"

"You might know what's coming, because you and Josh do this every day, but the others are going to need a bite to get them through the morning," Martha said. She handed Matt a biscuit and he put a piece of fried ham on it.

All the others stumbled into the kitchen, grabbing a cup of coffee and two or three biscuits apiece.

"Where's Dad?" Luke asked.

"He's out getting the trucks started. Russell always does that, and Dad was afraid one of you would take off without checking the hydraulic fluid."

"Did he go to sleep at all?" Sam asked.

"He did, but he's so pleased all of you are here, it

took a while for him to get to sleep."

"Patricia's not going with us," Noah said. "I left her in bed."

"She's probably tired. All the activity, and then her internal clock is set on D.C. time," Martha said. "I'll take care of her."

"Let's get this show on the road, before Dad comes up here to get us in gear," Josh said.

Both Luke and Gabe grabbed a couple of biscuits apiece and headed for Javanna's cabin.

When they got there, Javanna and Dusty were standing outside waiting for them.

"You're late," Javanna said.

"And here I brought you breakfast," Luke said handing her the biscuits.

"Thanks. I suppose Martha was up to fix these."

"Of course, what else has she got to do on Christmas Day?"

"Where are we headed?" Dusty asked.

"I'm sure they're all at the stackyard."

The stackyard was an area where row upon row of huge bales of hay were stored behind high fences. The fences were there to keep elk and deer or even the occasional moose from getting a free lunch. Each round bale weighed at least eight-hundred pounds.

"And here comes the last of my help," Dale said as he climbed down over the brush guard in the front of the truck. He had been scraping the windows.

"Who wants to be the driver?"

"Josh and I should drive," Matt said. "We'd be hunting around all day just to find the right pastures with these guys out looking for them."

Josh brought up a truck pulling a gooseneck

trailer behind it. Then Matt maneuvered a Bobcat with a front loader and a hay bale spear into position. He lifted each bale and placed it on the trailer, and when there were seven bales, stacked two high, that truck was ready. Then the second outfit was brought up and the same procedure was followed again.

"All right, Luke, you and Javanna go with Matt, and Sam and Noah go with Josh," Dale said. "Gabe, you and Dusty go to the horse barn and put out oats and hay and make sure the horses have water and, Ty, you stay with me. We need to go chop ice in the creek."

When Matt pulled out, the sun was just breaking over the mountains that were silhouetted against the gray sky. The snow-covered pastures looked even whiter as they moved along the fence line trying to avoid the biggest snow drifts. When he came to a gate, Luke jumped out and opened it. Almost immediately they found themselves in the middle of a mass of cattle, all sending little clouds of condensation into the air, and letting it be known that they were ready for their breakfast.

When they reached a relatively level spot, Matt stopped.

"Javanna, do you think you can drive this thing?" he asked.

"It depends on what you want me to do."

"Make a big circle, and try to stay on the flat land. Luke, you and I will get on the load. The first bale is the hardest, but if we work together, we can do it," Matt said. "If we don't, one of us is going to be in a terrible hurt, and I mean that literally, so don't try to move it until we're both ready."

"Got it," Luke said as he got out of the truck, barely suppressing a smile. This was his youngest brother, and he had sounded just like their father as he barked out orders.

Chapter Twenty-Four

Martha was in the kitchen with Christmas music playing on the radio. She knew it would take about three hours before all the morning tasks were completed, and she went about preparing for the Christmas brunch.

She took out her list of what she had planned for the meal.

Glazed ham was out of the oven and resting.

Cinnamon rolls were rising.

Apple coffee cake was done.

Egg casserole was ready to go in the oven.

French toast was soaking.

Fruit was sliced and in the refrigerator.

Martha decided she had a moment to herself. Pouring a cup of coffee, she moved to the breakfast nook where she and Dale ate when they were alone. The window overlooked the horse pasture and she saw that Gabe and Dusty were exercising their horses. They were riding comfortably together and she could see that Gabe was laughing at something that had been said.

Dusty seemed like a very likable woman, and Martha was sorry she hadn't had any time to sit down to talk with her. Watching the two, she could tell that Gabe cared for Dusty. The living arrangement that the two shared was not what Martha would have preferred, but she was open-minded enough to know that not all people saw the world as she did.

She prayed daily for all her children and because of the profession Gabe had chosen, she prayed especially hard for him. So far in the many years he had been on the rodeo circuit, he had suffered a broken collarbone and a broken leg, twisted his ankle and strained his back once. Now she would add Dusty Valentine to her prayer list.

"Do you mind if I join you?"

Martha was startled. She had forgotten that Patricia had not gone out with the others.

"Please do. Get a cup of coffee."

Patricia pulled back the chair and sat down bringing her coffee with her.

"Did you sleep through the reveille this morning?"

"That was a most effective way of waking up the household," Patricia said.

"Well, I hated to do it, but Dale insisted. I'm so glad you and Noah are here. You have done a wonderful job raising Ty. I couldn't ask for a better grandson. He's polite, he's loving..."

"Noah and I are getting a divorce."

"Oh, dear," Martha said as she reached across the table and took her daughter-in-law's hand.

Patricia lowered her head.

Martha was at a loss as to what to say. She said a

silent prayer asking God to give her the wisdom to say the right thing.

"Is that what you want? Is that what you both want?"

"I—I don't know." Patricia's lower lip began to quiver. "I've made such a mess of things. What will this do to Ty?"

Martha rose from the table, and went to put some of the waiting dishes into the oven. Then she returned, bringing the coffeepot to refill the cups.

"I know it's not my place to say this, but may I offer a suggestion?" Martha paused, and when Patricia didn't respond, she continued her thought. "Do you think Noah could be happy in Washington?"

"Why do you ask?"

"Perhaps if the two of you could spend some time together, you might be able to work this out."

"Washington would not be a good place for Ty. He loves it here in Montana."

"Ty seems to love Crooked Creek, and we very much love Ty. Nothing would make Dale and me happier than to have him come and stay with us. If Noah would agree, that might be the answer."

Patricia smiled. "I knew you would be the only one I could talk to."

"That is the greatest compliment you could ever pay me, Patricia. Now why don't you run upstairs and get yourself put together before the others get back. They'll be dirty and hungry when they get here."

When Patricia stood, Martha hugged her. On an impulse, she kissed her.

Martha was putting the last pan of cinnamon rolls in the oven when the door opened and the whole crew came into the great room.

"I haven't worked that hard in fifteen years," Sam said. "By nightfall, I may not be able to move."

"Think about me," Noah said. "At least in the army you're active. I sit behind a desk all day."

"You're all so soft," Josh said. "This was a light day for Matt and me."

Javanna was listening to the complaints, and though she was hurting too, there was no way she was going to say anything. She knew that Luke had to be hurting as well, but he hadn't complained, either. She smiled. He had probably enjoyed the morning as much as she had.

"Everything will be ready within fifteen minutes," Martha said. "Get your hands washed or whatever you're going to do and get ready to eat."

The conversation around the dining room table was brisk as everyone joined in the discussion. They brought up many of the old stories of things that happened when the boys were young, and while Martha's heart was troubled, she enjoyed seeing her sons all together.

She was pleased to see Patricia sitting beside Noah, and at one time she had seen him reach over and take her hand. Patricia had not rebuffed the gesture. Martha closed her eyes for an instant. Please God, let there be hope.

When the brunch was over, the boys cleaned up the kitchen for their mother, and then everyone disappeared. The late night on Christmas Eve and the early morning reveille necessitated an afternoon nap.

Luke walked Javanna back to the cabin.

"Are you tired?"

"Yes, but it's a good tired," Javanna said. "Are you going to take a nap like everybody else?"

"I don't think so. I'm too excited. How would you like to go for a snowmobile ride again?"

"I'd like that," Javanna said. "Give me a minute to get cleaned up and put my gear on."

"Put your gear on, but don't take the time for a shower. You're fine just the way you are." He kissed her on the nose.

"All right, if you can put up with me," Javanna said. "I'll be ready in ten minutes."

"I'll be here."

Luke hurried back to his room and pulled on his Gore-Tex pants and coat—then put on his Pac boots. He went to the shed by the hangar and checked the gas in the Polaris. Then grabbing two helmets, he sped over to Javanna's cabin.

"Only one snowmobile today?"

"That's right."

"You don't want me to beat you again," Javanna said as she put on her helmet. "Am I driving, or are you?"

"I'll drive out—you can drive back if you want,"

Luke said as he moved up a bit to make room for Javanna behind him.

She climbed onto the seat and wrapped her arms around him.

"I'm ready, cowboy."

Luke revved the engine and they were off.

For the next hour or so Luke and Javanna explored many corners of Crooked Creek Ranch. They stopped to watch six elk led by two big bulls clear the fence in order to munch on some of the remaining hay that had been put out earlier and they saw an eagle soaring overhead.

Finally, they reached the pishkun and Luke stopped the snowmobile.

"I do believe this is my favorite spot on the whole ranch," Javanna said as she got off. She walked up near the edge of the buffalo drop.

"It wouldn't scare you that you might be sleep-walking and fall off in the middle of the night?"

"I wouldn't be here in the middle of the night," Javanna said.

"You could be."

Luke opened his jacket and pulled out a folded piece of paper.

"Come sit beside me," he said as he swung his leg over the seat.

Javanna sat down and he opened the folded paper.

"I've been thinking—this is what I think a cabin built up here would look like—unless you want something different."

"What are you talking about?" She took the

piece of paper and saw a house plan that would fit this site perfectly. She looked at the paper and then back to Luke.

"I have something else I want to show you." Again, he reached inside his jacket and brought out a black velvet pouch. "This belonged to my grandmother, but I never knew her because she died just after Dad was born."

He withdrew a dainty ring that had a small diamond with two blue sapphires beside it.

"Oh, that's beautiful," Javanna said as she took off her mitten. "May I see it?"

"Sure," Luke said. He slipped it on her finger. "It fits perfectly."

"It really does, it's almost like it was made for me."

Luke smiled. "Maybe it was."

Javanna started to remove the ring and give it back to him.

"No, don't take it off. Javanna, you know that I love you, and I want you to be my wife. Will you marry me?"

"Yes, yes, yes!" Javanna threw her arms around his neck and had never been happier in her life. "I love you; I love your family; I love this ranch!"

"Then let's go back and tell everybody."

If you like this, check out Willow Falls by Ken Pratt

Welcome to Willow Falls. The town young Matthew Bannister ran away from fifteen years before. Now famed U.S. Deputy Marshal Matt Bannister is coming home to reconcile with his family. He prayed he wouldn't see his ex-best friend Tom Smith nor the only girl he ever loved, Tom's wife, Elizabeth. However, old feuds unsettled never die and spark a powder keg of action when the desperate Moskin Gang kidnap Elizabeth and leave a murderous trail behind them. In anguish, Tom, the Willow Falls sheriff, turns to his despised old-friend to help get the woman they both love back alive, if they can.

Sometimes God's greatest blessing is unanswered prayer.

AVAILABLE NOW

About Robert Vaughan

Robert Vaughan sold his first book when he was 19. That was 57 years and nearly 500 books ago. He wrote the novelization for the miniseries Andersonville. Vaughan wrote, produced, and appeared in the History Channel documentary Vietnam Homecoming.

His books have hit the NYT bestseller list seven times. He has won the Spur Award, the PORGIE Award (Best Paperback Original), the Western Fictioneers Lifetime Achievement Award, received the Read west President's Award for Excellence in Western Fiction, is a member of the American Writers Hall of Fame and is a Pulitzer Prize nominee.

Vaughan is also a retired army officer, helicopter pilot with three tours in Vietnam. And received the Distinguished Flying Cross, the Purple Heart, The Bronze Star with three oak leaf clusters, the Air Medal for valor with 35oak leaf clusters, the Army Commendation Medal, the Meritorious Service Medal, and the Vietnamese Cross of Gallantry.